D1554054

UNLIKELY FRIENDS

BY SAHAR ABDULAZIZ

UNLIKELY FRIENDS

Copyright © 2019 by Sahar Abdulaziz.
All rights reserved.
First Print Edition: February 2019

Limitless Publishing, LLC
Kailua, HI 96734
www.limitlesspublishing.com

Formatting: Limitless Publishing

ISBN-13: 978-1-64034-527-0
ISBN-10: 1-64034-527-2

Dedication

This book is dedicated to all the courageous, yet sometimes lost or wounded souls who have defied bitterness and hate to create an existence filled with happiness, friendship & trust

You fall. You rise,
you make mistakes, you live, you learn.
You're human, not perfect.
You've been hurt, but you are alive.
Think of what a precious privilege is it to be alive—
To breathe, to think, to enjoy,
and to chase the things you love.
Sometimes there is sadness in our journey,
but there is also lots of beauty.
We must keep putting one foot in front of the other
even when we hurt,
for we will never know what is waiting for us
just around the bend.

Unknown.

CHAPTER 1

Irwin

Irwin Abernathy, barely able to conceal the venom oozing out of every pore on his craggy old face, cringed at the slightly hungover, college-aged female with smeared day-old mascara caked beneath her drooping eyelids, making her look like a rabid raccoon.

"I think this belongs to you," he said, dangling with two fingers the powdery orange Cheeto he had found lodged between the pages of her returned library book.

"Huh? Ha! Right…" She reached over the reception desk to reclaim it, then popped it into her mouth.

"*Ohmygawd, ewww,*" Irwin gagged, struggling to control his retching reflex. He took three rapid panting breaths until the feeling subsided. "You have a late fee," he griped, his eyes watery but detached. "You owe a dollar-ten."

"Do I?" The young woman fumbled through her pockets, digging for change, but only managed to collect a combination of pennies, dimes, nickels, a single quarter, and one tortoiseshell button to dump onto the desk. "Hold up," she said, waving a crooked finger with a nail covered in chipped black polish in the air. "I have more; just give me one-hot-second."

Irwin glanced over the woman's shoulder at the long line forming behind her and ever so slightly bit his bottom lip. "No, take your time. Really," he said, eyes rolling to the ceiling. "I have all day."

If the young woman heard him, he couldn't say, and although irritated by her total lack of social decorum, Irwin couldn't help but be riveted, mesmerized by how easily she plunged her arm into her soft canvas bag, only to belt out a few colorful expletives when she pulled out everything but her wallet.

"Ma'am, if you could step to the side for a moment while I help the next person…"

"Damn it. I know it's in here somewhere," the woman mumbled, completely ignoring Irwin's request, depositing a pen without a cap, a twisted, smooshed granola bar, and a tampon, thankfully still in its original wrapper, onto the desk. "One more second, I swear." She shook her bag and stuck almost her entire face inside. "Come to mama," she said, voice muffled. Irwin's brow furrowed, but even he leaned closer in suspense.

"Ah-ha! Got it," she crowed triumphantly and gave a cute curtsey to the sarcastic slow clapping taking place behind her and a wide smile to Irwin, who could only stare back dumbfounded. Then she whipped a twenty-dollar bill from her purse and waved it in the air. "I'll need change."

Irwin's nostrils flared.

A twenty-dollar bill? What do I look like—a pole dancer?

Irwin plucked a single dime from the discarded change pile and slid the remainder of the money and junk back towards her. Then he plucked the twenty from between her two-finger grasp and held it up to the light, hoping against hope that it turned out to be a fake so he could have her arrested and dragged out of the library by her forelock, banished for life. But alas, the bill appeared legit.

"Here," he said, handing her the change. "And here's your receipt...or perhaps a future bookmark."

The young woman snorted at Irwin's wisecrack and flashed him an acerbic smile. "*Ciao*," she called over her shoulder, saluting him with the receipt as she pranced out of the building through the automatic doors, appearing not to have a care in the world. Irwin watched in total fascination as her hobo bag swayed in lockstep with her every swish and shimmy. Just one more colorful character to add to the book he never actually intended to write.

"Next," Irwin bellowed, glancing at the clock behind him and wishing he could be in his bed reading instead of here, waiting on Neanderthals and social misfits.

"Excuse me," interrupted a well-dressed man, pushing past the next person waiting on line. "Where's the restroom?" he asked Irwin as the young child whose hand he held tight—presumably his son—used his free small hand to squeeze his crotch through his pants, evidently to prevent an accident.

Irwin pointed. "Down the hall, to your right."

"Thanks," said the father, dragging his kid forward by the arm. When the kid glanced back and caught Irwin staring, the little monster returned the favor by sticking his tongue out.

"Next!"

Two adolescent boys reeking like unwashed armpits, their baby sister, and their mother barreled noisily forward. Irwin made a mental note to breathe through his mouth until they left...and possibly for a few minutes after.

"You three, put your books up here!" ordered their stressed mother, who then proceeded to dump her load with a loud thump on the desk, leaving them stacked high and precariously unbalanced.

Free of books, her boys moved to the side to wait, much to Irwin's olfactory relief, but the little girl had other plans and clutched her book tightly to her chest, refusing to acquiesce.

"Come on, Becky, give me your book," coaxed her mother, but the child, with a flair for the dramatic, could not be deterred and started to wail, easily hitting an operatic pitch.

As a matter of record, Irwin disliked children, specifically children who used loud noises to torture others. And although he appreciated this little runt's adoration for the written word, as a professed bibliophile himself, he did not welcome her predilection for being a screeching, bombastic shrew.

"Becky!" admonished the mother, attempting to tug the book free from the child's death-grip but having little success. "Give…me…the…book."

"No!" yelled the tenacious child, her brow stubbornly creased and lips in a tight pout.

"You better stop this right now! Give me the book."

"No!"

"Listen, just give me the book for two seconds. I'll give it right back to you as soon as the nice man scans it."

"NO!" screamed Becky, twisting her tiny body away from her mother, who strained to retain her grip.

"Enough," hollered Becky's mother, snatching the cover and pulling it toward her.

"Ma'am, don't pull on the cover. It might—" The cover tore in half. "—rip."

Pint-size Becky, her half of the cover still clenched in her tiny, grubby fingers, lost her balance and tumbled backward onto her bum.

"Oh no! I'm so sorry," screamed the mother, reaching down to help her child. "I'll pay for the book," she said to Irwin. "Now see what you've done!" she yelled at Becky, now sprawled out spread eagle on the floor, kicking and screaming. Meanwhile, her two malodourous brothers giggled off to the side, thoroughly enthralled by the spectacle.

"Grab your sister!" their mother snapped at the two hyenas. "I'm sorry," she said to Irwin. "I really am. I don't know what's gotten into her lately.

What do I owe you?"

Irwin, whose heart broke—not for the child, but for the damaged book—was half-tempted to call the lady a liar after witnessing this same bratty child on more than one occasion behave like the spoiled, unruly little tyrant she was. But unemployment held little attraction for the aging librarian, who was close to retirement, so he begrudgingly remained silent. He rung up the woman and wisely kept most of his more colorful snide observations to himself.

Choosing to become a librarian had been more of a calling than a career choice for Irwin, who proudly acknowledged a sizable familial lineage to a host of renowned readers and book hoarders. One of his great uncles, his grandmother's brother, had at one time owned his own publishing company. It had been a reasonably prosperous business until Uncle Mortimer, charged with extortion and racketeering, was sent to prison where he languished and died. Irwin's grandmother, Ethel Chamberlin Abernathy, never believed the stories surrounding her brother's guilt and proclaimed to anyone willing to listen that she had no doubt he had been framed. However, as much as Irwin adored his grandmother, the blind loyalty she held for her nefarious sibling was wasted, especially after Irwin conducted a Google search of his own. Not only did his uncle extort, gamble, and racketeer his way into vast amounts of wealth and prestige, but at the time of his masterminding, Mortimer had involved himself in some highly shady deals, some of which turned out fatal. Nevertheless, Irwin, unwilling to see her hurt, refused to reveal to his grandmother what he had discovered. Instead, he let her go on believing her imaginary accounts until the day she perished, steadfastly safeguarding the secrets of Ethel Chamberlin Abernathy—the one decent person in his miserable, wretched life who had not only raised and loved him but protected him from himself.

***

By early evening, Irwin felt ready to call it a day. That was until he spotted a young woman, probably no older than fifteen or sixteen, sitting alone on his favorite cushioned seat by the computer station. He noticed she wore reading glasses but no makeup. Each of her long fingers boasted a silver ring, and a stack of leather bands obscured her thin wrists, some laden with beads or charms. Irwin couldn't imagine how heavy they made her arms.

Long, dangling feather earrings hung from her ears while her chestnut brown hair, piled high upon her head, mimicked what the library's style magazines refer to as the "messy bun."

Messy was right.

Irwin was curious as to how the girl had sewn her unquestionably homemade jean skirt, with fitted bands of yellow calico fabric in the middle, which he thought complimented her white peasant blouse nicely. But it was the work boots that really set the stage for him, like something straight out of the 60s. A hippie-dippy special.

Unfazed, the girl glared back at him, making Irwin wince.

Busted!

She'd caught him prying. Embarrassed, Irwin looked away. As a consummate people-watcher, he abhorred being outed—and certainly not by a child.

Second time today. I must be getting rusty.

"Irwin," called Roger Ledbetter, one of the library staff and, in general, a human hemorrhoid. "Janice wants you to either cover for Regan in the children's room or go back to the circulation desk. She said it was your choice."

"I'd rather get a lobotomy than be stuck in the children's room," Irwin replied flatly, not joking.

"Front desk it is. Roger that."

Idiot.

By seven-forty-five, the library speakers began making announcements that the library would be closing in fifteen minutes.

Thank God.

Irwin was exhausted and ready to go home to a steaming bowl of soup, a couple of water crackers with slices of cheese, and a hot cup of tea, perhaps even a hot bath instead of his typical quick shower. And then off to bed. Glorious bed, where he could finally finish his new cozy murder mystery uninterrupted.

"I'm heading upstairs to make sure everyone's gone," called Janice Stroop, the head librarian and resident know-it-all. "Irwin, can you handle the adult section?"

Irwin, can you handle the adult section?

Irwin merely nodded.

Such an irritating woman.

He started from the back row, collecting

8

forgotten jackets and hats, returning books to their proper place, and pushing in chairs, all while mumbling, grumbling, and complaining in his head until he glanced up and noticed the young hippie girl grinning at him.

What's so funny? "We're closing in five minutes," he barked.

"I heard."

"That means you have to leave."

"Evidently."

"So? Hop to it. Shake a leg." Irwin snapped his fingers. "What are you waiting for? A personal invitation?"

"I'll leave," she said, "soon-ish," and went right back to reading her book.

The nerve.

Irwin continued his appointed rounds, but just a tad bit grumpier, knowing there was nothing he could do but wait the little waif out.

Ten minutes later, he returned, anxious to kick the insolent girl to the curb, but by the time he arrived, she was long gone, the book she had been reading left face down on the chair.

Everyone thinks I'm their maid.

He lifted the book and turned it over. "*All the Light We Cannot See* by Anthony Doerr."

Now, why would someone her age be reading this?

He was quite impressed by her selection: a *New York Times* bestseller about a French girl and a German boy whose paths collided during WWII and the occupation of France.

Maybe for school.

As he turned to walk away, a piece of paper fell out of the book and fluttered to the floor. Irwin picked it up.

It read: "See you tomorrow, Mr. Grumpy."

Why that little...

"Irwin, let's go already," yelled Janice, shaking her keychain in the air, ready to flip off the lights. "I want to lock up and get home sometime tonight."

Irwin slipped the note into his pocket and returned the book to the shelf.

"Tonight, Irwin," called Janice, tapping her foot by the front door.

Irwin sprinted to his locker, grabbed his coat, his hat and keys, and tripped on one of the book carts along the way, stubbing his toe.

Argh!

Irwin brushed past Janice, out the door, limping to his car.

"Good night, Irwin."

"Good night, Janice," he replied, but in his head—where he held most of his truest and most revealing conversations—he thought otherwise.

What's the chance I'll die in my sleep and never have to come back to this place again?

Janice locked the door. "See you tomorrow, bright and early."

God, if you're up there, feel free to kill me now.

CHAPTER 2

Irwin

After changing out of his work clothes and into comfortable pajamas and bathrobe, Irwin padded through the living room, past the den lined with overflowing bookshelves, and into his kitchen to put on the kettle. He tugged his bathrobe tighter, but it did little to avert the chill still lodged in his bones from working at the library's reception desk. Although patrons had to walk through two distinct sliding doors to enter the library, bursts of cold air still managed to breach the setup somehow and flow into the general front section. Irwin cranked up the heat in the old, three-story Victorian, dreading his next month's heating bill.

Famished but too exhausted to make up his mind about what to eat, Irwin yanked the refrigerator door open and stood in front of it, staring. Trusting that at any moment, something worth eating would materialize and tempt his discerning palette. Unfortunately, he hadn't gone food shopping in over two weeks, so only slim pickings were left. On the bottom shelf, Irwin slid a jar of black olives to one side and an unopened can of fruit and a bottle of maple syrup to the other. Nothing remotely appetizing. The second shelf boasted a quarter stick of unsalted butter, four eggs, a small container of questionable milk, and a horde of upmarket condiments. The side door held a wide assortment of goopy jars filled with sauces and dressings, many of which he swore at the time of purchase that he needed, despite more often than not letting them hit their expiration dates before actual use.

"A-ha! Now we're talking!" Behind an oversized jar of mayonnaise, Irwin discovered a plastic container filled with…well, he wasn't quite sure what it was filled with. He lifted the dish up to the light. Shook it. Turned it upside down and right-side up. Other than its deep orange-brown hue, he couldn't make out or remember what was inside, so he did the only thing left to do and popped the top. He took a deep whiff and…"Argh!" His head felt like it snapped in two. The most heinous—*the* most rancid, garlic-laden acidic stench, the likes of which no human had ever likely encountered—catapulted up his nostrils and assaulted his brain cells. Eyes burning, Irwin couldn't toss the fetid container away quick enough.

"Ewww, ick, disgusting," he gagged, jostling the dish like a hot potato. "Gross, gross, gross," he yelped at a fevered pitch, spinning in circles, keeping the container at arm's length, and breathing through his mouth in exaggerated gulps. Without his realizing it, the belt of his bathrobe had come undone from all his vaulting about, and now half of it trailed on the floor. As Irwin bounded towards the garbage, his foot landed on the tip of the belt, which in turn yanked him forward and sent him flying face first onto the floor, covered in toxic food waste.

"I hate my life."

Once he and the kitchen were both cleaned up, and even after his sense of smell finally returned, Irwin no longer felt inclined to do much of anything, so he settled for a simple meal of tea and dry crackers. Occasionally, his next-door neighbor and her feline sidekick would pop over for tea and a chat, but for the most part, Irwin preferred spending his evenings alone. He tried to keep busy. He found falling asleep too soon meant being jarred awake, vacillating between slumber and consciousness. Waking up feeling disorientated from thrashing and moaning or his need to kick off sweat-soaked sheets…the never-ending battle against the flood of recurring nightmares.

He sat down on a soft, comfortable chair, searching for something to read that would tire his eyes and help him drift off to sleep. After sifting through his growing To-Be-Read pile, Irwin eventually settled on a new book by a local indie author. But as soon as he began to read, his eyes wandered aimlessly about the page, incapable of staying fixed to the story. Sometimes skipping words or whole paragraphs.

That strange girl from the library and her puerile little note…

Mind racing and incapable of blocking out his annoyance, Irwin eventually gave up and slammed his book shut. "Gah. This is ridiculous," he grumbled, returning the book to the top of the heap.

Who does she think she's messing with?

Irwin usually went out of his way to discourage human interaction outside of work. As far as he was concerned, dealing with people only brought problems, and their problems inevitably caused him headaches—all of which he had enough of, *thanks anyway*. Instead, he used his self-imposed isolation as a ready excuse for his not participating in the world outside, preferring to exist between the pages of his books, exploring new worlds without the threat of heartache, loss, and personal catastrophe.

His stomach growled. Irwin contemplated having another cup of tea but decided against it. If his nightmares didn't jar him awake, his unruly bladder most assuredly would. Instead, he trekked through the dining room into his chilled office to retrieve his laptop and set himself up at the dining room table to open emails—mostly spam. Once finished, he lifted his finger to push the button to shut the computer down when his eyes fell on the folder labeled **"Gilly."**

He shouldn't, but he did.

Irwin clicked opened each photo, starting from the top.

Gilly's beautiful, smiling face filled the entire screen. Irwin leaned back, shrinking down into his seat, while a rush of memories flashed before him. His tired eyes greedily waltzed over the contours of her exquisite eyes, her cheeks, and her lips. His mind taunted him, demanding him to preserve every last detail they'd spent together.

14

He eventually reached the end, but there was still a video, recorded only a day before the accident. Irwin could never forget that day.

Gilly's soon-to-be ex-husband had finally agreed to the terms of the divorce. Her lawyer had phoned and left a message for Gilly to come to her office to finalize the paperwork.

Could we meet early next week?

It was the news they had been waiting and wishing for. Irwin and Gilly had been ecstatic and had chosen to celebrate their new lease on life with a leisurely stroll through the park. Away from prying and suspicious eyes where they could talk and plan their future unimpeded.

Irwin clicked start. The next round of torture began…the last full day spent together, happy beyond measure and madly in love.

The musical sound of Gilly's playful voice hung heavy in the air.

"And here we have the mighty oak tree," she announced, pretending to be Irwin's tour guide. Giving him a goofy, play-by-play account of their immediate surroundings in a most romantic and lighthearted manner. "The towering oak is a noble tree, favored for its strength and endurance," she exclaimed.

Irwin increased the volume.

"Because they are so sturdy and strong, they can live for hundreds of years." Gilly picked up a leaf and waved it under Irwin's nose. "Their leaves and bark protect the oak from insects and fungi, while their dense stems act as a perfect water storage system, especially during dry spells."

"A hearty tree indeed," Irwin said.

"You are correct. And over six hundred species."

Irwin watched himself pick an acorn off the ground and roll it around with his fingers. "These little buggers are all over my lawn. I got pelted with one the other day. Hurt like hell."

Gilly picked up an acorn and lobbed it at Irwin. "Don't knock it. Acorns are a rich food source for many animals."

Irwin ducked and tossed his acorn at Gilly's behind.

"Eeeek," Gilly giggled. "You missed me, you missed me."

Irwin laughed. "I didn't miss. You just didn't feel it with all that extra bark you got protecting your trunk," he teased.

Gilly stuck her tongue out at Irwin. "Very funny," she said and turned the camera on him. "Any other illuminating comments from the peanut gallery?"

Irwin pushed pause. A tear rolled down his craggy cheek. The video froze on him grinning and cheesing it up for the camera, smiling right along with Gilly, who had a way about her that made him drop all his pretense. He wiped his face and pushed start again.

"Excuse me, um, Miss…" His goofy, happy face filled the screen.

"Ranger," corrected Gilly. "I'm a Forest Ranger."

"Why, of course. Pardon. My mistake, Miss Forest Ranger. I do have a question."

"I'm listening."

"What would you call this?" Irwin held up a single, long blade of grass.

"Is this a trick question?"

"Not at all." Irwin twisted the blade into a circle. Then he reached out for Gilly's hand and slipped the knotted greenery onto her ring finger. "And now what would you call it, Miss Forest Ranger?"

Overcome, Gilly had let the phone camera slip, causing it to bounce. The photo frame moved in and out of focus, but there was no mistaking her answer.

"This, dear sir, is no simple blade of grass but a dream come true," she had whispered, her face pressed against his neck.

"I love you, Gilly Satterfield. Say you will be my wife."

The rest of the video's sound continued to fade in and out. And although their voices were muffled from the phone being pressed against the back of Irwin's coat, the camera somehow focused long enough on Gilly's face when her lips answered, "Yes. I will marry you."

How full of promise they both were that day, each immersed in the other. Idyllically unaware of what pain and treachery Life had waiting in store for them.

Irwin turned off the computer and brought his laptop back into the office. Then he walked around lowering the heat, shut off the downstairs lights, and lumbered up to bed, anticipating another round in the ring, him against his demons.

***

17

Over the coming week, Irwin kept a close, almost imperceptible eye on his teen antagonist from his post behind the library's reception desk. She had become bolder—a bit cheekier, which only served to fling open the door on his snarkier side.

"Excuse me, Mr. Grumpy, sir," said the teen person in possession of more silver rings than fingers. "Where might I find a book on suicide?"

"Why, bless your heart, aren't you just the sweetest little thing," Irwin replied with an awful, mock southern drawl. "Check over there," he said, jutting his chin. "But be forewarned, once they're checked out, they never return."

Obviously squelching a chuckle, the girl rolled her eyes skyward. "And what about a book on social introverts?"

"Adult, non-fiction, second aisle, third row to the left."

"And lastly, a book on sadomasochism?" Her facial expression remained blank, without the slightest grin.

Oh, she's good

Irwin was impressed. "I will assume in the realm of *Fifty Shades of Gray*? Try upstairs, aisle seven. I believe you'll find it lurking next to a book titled, *Angst of an Obnoxious Adolescent*."

"I need a library card."

"Identification?"

Harper produced her school ID.

Irwin stared at the ID. "That'll be two dollars and fifty cents, Miss Harper, unless of course you'd rather I bill your reform school." Irwin slid a form across the desk. "Fill this out and bring it back when you're ready."

Harper shot Irwin a not-so-subtle glare and shuffled back to her seat. He noticed her agitation as she counted and recounted her money, apparently coming up short. After stuffing the coins back in her pocket, he watched her dig in her hobo bag for a pen. She leaned over and began filling out the form, her eyes darting intermittently in Irwin's direction.

Irwin continued to monitor her from afar, pretending not to notice when, in a fit of frustration, she crumpled the paper into a ball and tossed it angrily into the nearby waste can.

Temper, temper young one.

What made this strange, sharp-witted, but most annoying teen person tick?

Irwin pondered. One moment her nose would be buried within the pages of a book, while at other times he'd catch her leaning in the chair grinning, entirely content to sit back and people watch. And for whatever reason, Irwin seemed to fascinate her.

In the Poconos, the temperatures could turn from hot to cool to freezing almost overnight, sometimes fluctuating by the hour. Although the sun had shone brightly throughout most of this day, by early evening the air had grown frigid and rather blustery. Fierce autumn winds tossed torrents of leaves across parking lots and onto roads. People already weighed down by bulky sweaters or hooded sweatshirts dashed into the library. By evening, folks added wool hats and coats to the many existing layers. At the slightest dip in temperatures, they'd rush to don a hat or scarf.

Irwin despised the cold. But then again, he also

hated the heat, the sun, the rain, snow, and ice. And hail. Especially hail. Not this girl, who Irwin couldn't help but notice often showed up at the library underdressed, wearing nothing but an extra baggy sweater or a thin jacket no matter what the temperatures were outside. And while he never heard her complain, she wasn't fooling him. He noticed the way she braced against the evening chill each night, scrunching her shoulders and tucking her chin into her jacket before stepping outside. At least tonight, she had the good sense to wrap that bony neck of hers with a scarf, a much too long and flamboyant contraption equipped with entangled fringes that had seen better days and a host of colorful, mismatched beads.

Each evening the girl selected a different book to place on the side table next to her chair, evidently left for him to find. Tucked inside he'd find an insufferable message, penned in chicken scratch on bright yellow sticky notepaper. The first one read, "It wouldn't kill you to smile more." The second, "I heard somebody call you 'Irwin.' Please help me sleep at night—tell me that's not your real name."

On the third night, she left him a joke—an oldie but goodie:

Q: How many librarians does it take to change a light bulb?

A: Only one, but first you have to have a committee meeting.

PS: The light is out in the woman's

20

bathroom on the second floor.

On the fourth night, the millennial urchin enclosed a single packet of chamomile tea with a note.

You look like you could use this more than me. Enjoy! PS: Total bummer about that little kid barfing near your desk. What a stench! I could smell it from my seat, so it must have been pure hell for you.

Tonight's message took the form of a quote:

"Libraries will get you through times of no money better than money will get you through times of no libraries." – Anne Herbert.

While he had to agree with the sentiments of Anne Herbert, Irwin debated whether or not it was time to confront the teenager about these little missives. But by the time he built up the nerve to face her, she had already hiked her backpack strap over her shoulder, ready to leave.

"See ya later, Mr. Grumpy," she teased, coasting straight past him. Her thick, chestnut brown braid bounced and swayed as if keeping time with each determined step. Without looking back, she strolled through the metal detectors and out the sliding doors before vanishing into the dark hole of night.

"What's that?" asked Roger, peering over Irwin's shoulder.

Irwin crumpled the paper and shoved it in his pocket. "It's called none of your business."

"Wait, is that a love letter?"

"Hardly."

"Then let me see it."

"Go away."

"A secret admirer then."

Irwin nudged him away with an elbow. "And therein lies the crux of your issue."

"I have a crux?"

"You *are* a crux. And you read too many romances."

"Hey, don't put down romance. It happens to be an incredibly versatile genre. One which has successfully warmed many hearts while expounding upon a myriad of societal ills and values."

"Enlightening." Irwin huffed, jostling to get past him. "Don't you have someplace else to be other than in my business?"

Roger chuckled but stood his ground. "You know, Irwin, one of these days, this tough outer exterior you've worked so hard to hide behind all these years will crumble. And when it does, we will all be waiting. Ready to see the real you for the softy you truly are."

"Charming. But until such a never-going-to-happen-in-this-lifetime event occurs, perhaps you could redirect your sage vivacities upon some other unsuspecting patron of the community. I'm sure your wit and talent to foretell the future will have them swooning in awe. However, I must take my leave." Irwin tugged his hat on his head and darted past Roger.

"Suit yourself," chuckled Roger, "but I've got my eye on you."

"Which one?"

***

Irwin stayed only until four on Friday afternoons. Before heading out, he cornered the children's librarian by the children's reading nook with a request.

"Regan."

"Ir—Winnie." Regan, a big lifetime fan of Winnie The Pooh, prided herself in quoting the books and coming up with wretched names to torture him with.

"You know the bohemian rhapsody girl who comes to the library every day? Dresses like she's stuck in Woodstock," he asked, virtually in a whisper.

Regan squinted and blinked before cutting her eyes to both sides of the almost empty children's room. Nobody but a mother and her toddler were remotely in earshot, and neither was paying them any attention, as she had her nose buried in her phone and her son had his finger buried in his nose.

"Why are you mumbling?"

Irwin snapped his fingers in Regan's face. "Stay with me," he snarled. Regan blinked and juddered her neck. "She comes in around four-thirty."

"Oh! Yeah. I know who you mean now." Regan's too-large purple eyeglasses began to slip down her straight nose, causing her to peer at Irwin from over the rim.

Losing patience, Irwin's fingers twitched, itching to shove the purple obscenity back up her beak.

"The one with all the cool rings and wild hair?" she asked.

"Yes."

"Always sits in the chair over there?" Regan pointed to some vague place presumably outside of the children's room.

"Good. You know who I mean. I need you to…"

"I love her rings…"

Irwin growled, pumping his hand in the air. "I need you to…"

"What about her?"

Irwin palmed his forehead. "She left her book here last night."

"Okay, so?"

"Would you make sure she gets it back?"

"Why can't you give it to her?"

"Because I'm running late," Irwin lied. He just didn't want to be around when Harper got handed the book.

Regan pushed her glasses back up her nose and blinked like a lost owl. "Yeah. I guess I could do that, Ir—Winnie."

"Would you *please* stop calling me that?" he

grumbled, already headed to the back room to grab his keys and coat.

CHAPTER 3

Harper

By taking side roads and various shortcuts, Harper Crane made it from the library to home in less than fifteen minutes. The old dilapidated house she called home, with its sagging porch and peeled paint, could have easily been mistaken for abandoned, except for a hazy glow coming from the front kitchen window. The faint flickering light sent shadows dancing against the curtain from inside.

Harper fumbled with her key, dropping it twice. The porch bulb had blown out months before, but neither she nor her mother had bothered to replace it, figuring its absence would help save money on the electric bill. In the moonless night, she felt for the lock's cylinder with the tips of her finger until eventually jiggling it correctly into the lock.

"I'm home," hollered Harper.

"In the kitchen. Just getting dinner started," answered her mother, Olivia Crane, which the end of the month meant a sandwich of either peanut butter and jelly, tuna, or two slices of cheese, sometimes accompanied by soup or pasta.

"Hey, Ma."

"Don't you 'hey Ma' me. It's pitch-black outside, and you should have been home sooner. How many times have I said to you that I don't want you out at night?" her mother reprimanded. "It's dangerous."

Harper kissed the side of her mother's cheek before hooking her backpack and jacket on the rung of the wooden ladder chair. "I'm fine."

"You're fine," her mother muttered. "This time you're fine, but people are crazy. The newspapers are filled with photos of kids gone missing. I bet they told their mothers they were fine too."

Harper groaned and swiped a napkin from the basket.

"I'm not kidding. You can't be gallivanting around like this. You're only fifteen years old."

"Who's gallivanting? I'm walking home from the library. Besides, I'm almost sixteen, and you worry too much."

"Harper…"

Harper reached over her plate to swipe the butter knife off the counter. "How about I carry one of these?" she teased, making an exaggerated, sweeping Three Musketeers' move.

"Put that down."

"Mace?"

"Harper!"

"Okay. Relax. You win. I'll come home before it gets dark and my carriage turns back to a pumpkin. But just stop worrying so much."

Her mother grabbed the nearly empty bag of sandwich bread and stuffed two slices into the toaster. "Cheese or tuna?"

"Nothing for me."

Olivia's head snapped around. "You have to eat something," she demanded, one hand clasped firmly to her hip.

Harper's belly growled in agreement, but by her calculations, her mother wouldn't get paid again until Friday. That meant three more days to make the food in the house last. "I'm okay. I had a big lunch."

"Cheese or tuna? And before you dare open your mouth again, I'm not asking."

Harper grinned. "I'll take the cheese."

"That's better."

Her mother twisted and knotted the plastic bread bag closed instead of pulling another two slices out for herself.

"Aren't you eating?"

"I ate before you came home."

Harper recognized a lie when she heard it, especially since she frequently told the same one many times, but living poor did that. It made you fib to save face, pretending indifference when hungry or cold.

The toaster popped. Harper bounded to her feet, but her mother blocked her. "Sit. I got it."

Even under the glow of candlelight, her mother's face looked pale and drawn. Harper glanced down, worried to see her mother's ankles swollen again from long hours spent working as a cashier, sometimes seven days a week. Despite her mother's selfless efforts to provide, they still found themselves coming up short, forced by circumstance to make hard choices while confronting uphill, endless struggles: to pay the rent over the heat, the heat over food, or food over medicine, and all along scraping by to make ends meet until the next disaster hits…life's little game show. Don't be shy! Step up and spin the Wheel of Existence and see what treats Fate has in store for you.

"I got something for you," Harper said, spinning around in her chair and unzipping her backpack. "Mayo, ketchup, and mustard." It took two hands to dump the impressive pile of absconded single-serve packets onto the middle of the table. "Oh, and for the *pièce de résistance.*" She reached deep down deep and yanked out a small bag of potato chips, one overly ripe brown-spotted banana, and something square and small, wrapped in a napkin. "A brownie, *Madam.* Just for you."

Olivia smiled. "*Merci infiniment,*" she said before kissing the top of her daughter's head. "Something to enjoy with my tea." She pulled a mug out from the cabinet. "Will you join me?"

"Yes, please."

Her mother took the second mug out. "Save the banana for yourself, but after you eat, add the condiments to the jar." Olivia opened the bag of potato chips and emptied them on the plate next to Harper's toasted cheese sandwich. "*Bon appétit.*"

Harper tore through her thin-cheese sandwich, barely chewing between mouthfuls before taking the next bite.

"Slow down before you choke," admonished her mother while she poured the steaming hot water over each of the dollar store tea bags. "Take human bites."

Harper dabbed the corners of her mouth. "That was good," she said, then dumped two heaping teaspoons of sugar into her cup.

"Careful, careful. Diabetes runs in the family."

Her mother placed her mug on the table across from Harper and collapsed in her chair, exhausted. The candle in the middle of the table flickered and sputtered wildly, but Harper didn't mind. She preferred taking their meals by candlelight as opposed to the overhead fixture, which did nothing but emphasize their stark, worn-down kitchen.

"Since this is becoming a habit," said her mother, hunched over her tea, "why don't you explain to me what you're really doing at the library?"

"I don't know." Harper shrank back in her chair. "Nothing much."

Olivia's glare never wavered.

Knowing that unrelenting stare, Harper complied. "I study. Do homework. I read. It's a library." She fiddled with the corner of her napkin, wondering what her mother would say if she told her about the highly entertaining Mr. Grumpy or whether she'd understand her need to be away from this place. Instead, she told her mother what she needed to hear and nothing more. "Sometimes I'll use their computers if I have a project or have a paper to write."

Olivia's eyes burned into Harper's face. "I hope

you're not meeting boys there."

"Oh, pl—eeze."

"I don't want you to become one of those mall rodents."

Harper snorted. "A mall rodent? You mean rat, and not for nothing, but wouldn't I first have to be hanging out at the mall to qualify for the title?"

"I'm being serious."

"Yeah, I get that. But seriously, I'm at a library. Pretty much the safest place for a teenager with no life to hang out."

"Well, it's my job to ask." After a more deliberate sip of tea, Olivia lowered her mug onto the table. "Listen. I need to talk to you about something important, but first, you have to promise me you won't get upset."

Whenever her mother opened up a conversation with that "promise me you won't get upset" bit, Harper braced for the worst. "What is it?"

"Promise me first."

Harper crossed her ankles under the table—just in case she needed to renege. "Fine, I promise. What is it?"

"I got a call today from Mr. Singer telling me Darren got approved for parole." Olivia bit her lip and waited.

"Parole?" Harper's nostrils flared. "There's no way."

"I know."

"But that can't be right. They gave him fifteen something years, right? And he's only done, like what?" Harper wiggled her fingers in the air.

"Six."

"Six! How's that even close to fifteen?"

"It's not, but that's what he told me. Something about Darren earning good time."

"Good time? Him? Are you sure? Maybe Singer made a mistake."

"Harper—"

"You might have heard him wrong."

"Harper, stop."

"This is so unfair!" Harper screwed her lips in a tight pout, then crossed her arms over her chest much as she did as a toddler. "When?"

"Next week."

"Next week?" Harper repeated, pressing her eye sockets with her fists. "Why so soon?"

Olivia glanced down, shame-faced. Her long finger slid absently around the handle of her mug.

"Well, he can forget staying here." Harper was on a full-fledged warpath.

"Singer said that Darren has to stay at some halfway house, so he'll be under supervision."

Harper rolled her eyes.

"He'll be expected to follow the rules."

"The rules," Harper scoffed. "When has he ever followed anybody's rules?" She crushed her napkin in her fist. "And what if he doesn't—then what?"

"Then they'll send his butt straight back to prison, no questions asked. He'll have to finish the rest of his sentence."

"I can't believe this is happening again."

Her mother reached for her now-tepid tea.

"I don't want to see him."

"But Harper—"

"No!"

"He's still your father."

"I don't care who he is." Harper twisted her napkin into a ball. Without warning, she exploded from her chair, almost causing it to topple over. "He's a walking disaster; he hurts everything he touches."

Olivia lowered her gaze. "Harper, if I could do anything to change the past, I would."

"I know that, but this is now, not the past."

"I've changed. It's been six years. Maybe he did too—"

"No!" Harper yelled, stomping her foot. "Not him. People like him don't change, and you know it. People like him stay hurting everyone around them. Always quick to blame everyone else for their problems." Harper sniffled. "He's a parasite." She gulped back the tears. "I…I…can't believe you're even defending this shithead."

"Harper! Your mouth…"

"Sorry, but that's what he is."

"People do change."

"Not that much, they don't."

"I did."

"Because you were never a cruel and vindictive sociopath." The small candle, down to its nub, barely gave off enough light for either of them to properly see. "What if you fall back into that life again?" shouted Harper. "What if he gets you hooked back on drugs? Then what?"

"That's not going to happen."

"But what if you do?"

"I won't."

"But you could with him around—"

"That's not going to happen. Things are different now. I'm different now. Like I said before, I've changed. You're gonna need to trust me when I tell you that." Olivia lowered her voice. "Harper, please, look at me, baby. You've got nothing to be afraid of this time. I got this."

Frustrated tears welled in Harper's eyes. "I can't go through it again," she said, pacing the tiny kitchen. "The last time you almost—" Thoughts of the past collided with her unrequited bitterness and became too much to contain. In a sudden fit of uncontrollable rage, Harper threw the balled napkin at the wall as hard as she could. "I can't do it!"

"I know, baby, but I'm not going to mess things up. Not this time," her mother pleaded, motioning for her daughter to take her hand. "Trust me."

Harper recoiled. As much as she loved her mother, she had yet to learn how to trust her again. She glanced at the door. For a split second, the temptation to flee became almost unbearable. Her mind raced through her limited, if not impossible, options, but each time she came back to the same conclusion. Despite the fear of feeling trapped, regardless of the unknown knocking at her door, she could never leave or turn her back on her mom.

"Now please, just sit down…finish your tea."

Shoulders slumped, Harper slid back down in her chair, defeated, confident that all the bottled-up nightmares that haunted her dreams would come to fruition and there wouldn't be a damned thing she could do to stop them.

Harper had little recourse but to wait and see, but inside, she continued to fume. A wild rush of bad memories flooded her consciousness, leaving her unequipped to face the past.

***

Six years earlier

Awakened by a crash of glass, Harper clenched the threadbare blanket with her little fingers, drawing it closer to her face.

In the adjacent room, she heard a chair dragged across the marked wooden floor, followed by a parade of sloppy giggles and an angry *shush*. Then something else dropped to the floor. Harper couldn't make out what it was.

She overheard an exchange of muffled words, trailed by a shrilled ripple of laughter. Harper cowered even farther under her covers, afraid of getting caught should she decide to take a peek out her bedroom door. Too terrified of what she may see.

Harper trembled. She didn't lift her head out from under her blanket until she heard the familiar creak of the front door opening and closing, turning the house dead silent. She was alone. Forgotten.

Outside the moon still shone, but soon it would be time for her to dress and make the long trek to the bus stop. There she would stand and wait until the bus arrived, dressed in a too-small coat and no hat, shivering. Staring down at her feet to avoid eye contact with the other kids gawking at her from within their parents' cars. Children who knew they were loved, cherished, but most of all—protected.

35

But for now, the welcomed dark silence lured the sleepy child back to sleep.

When she awoke, the morning's crisp, cold air filled the bedroom. Harper yearned to stay in bed, but it was time to get ready for school. She pulled off the covers, shivering and hugging herself to keep warm. The wood floor beneath her small feet felt like ice. She scampered out of the bedroom, totally forgetting about the loud, disturbing noises of the night before. Ready to begin her day until greeted by absolute chaos.

Lifting the edge of her frayed nightgown, Harper tiptoed carefully around the larger shards of glass splayed across the living room and hall floors. She had almost made it to the bathroom unscathed until by mistake, she stepped on a small sliver of glass.

"Ouch," she cried, clasping her foot while hopping with the other. "Mommy?" she wailed out in pain. "Mommy—" She bounced on one foot, but when that did not stop the throbbing, she gave up and limped the rest of the way to her parents' door. "Mommy," she sobbed, knocking softly, but no one answered. Slowly turning the knob, she poked her small face into the dusky room. A thin sliver of light had managed to filter inside through the almost-drawn curtains.

At a quick glance, the room appeared empty except for a tangled heap of sheets and a few soiled pillows strewn across the bed. One corner of the bedroom was filled with a week's worth of dirty clothes while the tops of both her parents' nightstands were littered with an assortment of drug paraphernalia—needles, matches, ashtrays, thick rubber bands, and pipes. Plastic utensils, tipped over soda and beer cans, and a mixture of opened, half-eaten take-out food containers had the room reeking.

Not sure what else to do, Harper eased the door shut but stopped when she heard a faint, muffled moan coming from inside.

"Mommy?" she called out, forgetting her pained foot. "Where are you?"

On the far side of the bed closest to the wall, her mother lay passed out on the floor, wearing nothing but a pair of panties and somebody else's tee-shirt, bunched high above her backside. One side of her face remained squished into the dirty floor where a puddle of drool had collected. Harper froze where she stood, staring with wide eyes at the horridness of the scene before her.

She crouched to one knee. "Mommy, wake up," she cried, shaking her mother's wrist while trying to avoid the upper forearm area where her mother still had a ripped piece of cloth loosely tied in a knot just above a protruding but empty heroin syringe.

Harper leaned in closer, brushing her nose against her mother's face. "Please wake up," she whispered, practically gagging from the stench of her mother's faint, stale breaths. "You're scaring me." Her mother did not respond.

"Mommy," she sobbed louder. "Wake up." Panic-stricken, Harper shook her mother's shoulder harder. "Wake up, Mommy, wake up. Wake up." She screamed for her father, but as usual, he was nowhere to be found, having left nothing behind except a full set of his fingerprints planted around her mother's thin neck.

Harper bolted from the room, screaming. Rocking from side to side, hysterical. The hem of her thin nightgown brushed against the dirty floor, collecting dust and glass as she ran. The heel of her foot left microscopic smatterings of blood in her wake.

"Somebody help my mommy," she screamed as she pushed the front door open, bolting down the rickety porch steps onto the sidewalk. "Please, somebody. Help my mommy." A strong autumn wind blew her nightgown above her knees. "Help me," she cried, frantic, tears trickling from her eyes.

A man on his way to work heard the frantic child crying and bolted across the street to help. After wrapping his coat around the shivering child, he immediately dialed 911. Not long after, the police arrived, followed soon by an ambulance.

From there, the details of the event remain muddled. Over the years, Harper had tried to draw out the particulars from her memory, but without much luck. After all, she had only been nine years old at the time. She did, however, recall a kind-spoken policewoman who bundled her up in a blanket, then handed her over to a medic who cleaned and bandaged her foot. The many faces after that of those who helped her that day remained sketchy.

Harper recalled how the emergency team wasted no time getting to her mother, who they found on the bedroom floor with barely a pulse. Harper remembered pleading with the technicians to let her ride in the ambulance to the hospital, but to no avail.

Once seated in the back of the police car, the same policewoman gently plied her with sweet snacks while asking a ton of strange questions. To this day, Harper had zero recollection of what she might have said to the officer between sips of boxed apple juice and bites of salty chips.

With no family or family friends willing or able to take her, the state stepped in and placed Harper in foster care, moving her from one stranger's house to the next until Olivia got clean enough to petition the courts to have her child returned to her custody. It took over two years before the judge finally agreed—reluctantly, and with the added stipulation that Olivia must remain clean and continue with her rehabilitation.

And Darren Crane, aka Harper's MIA father and all-around degenerate? It took less than a week before the police found him next to an abandoned building's alleyway, cowering like a punk behind a discarded filthy mattress, higher than a kite. They arrested Darren and charged him with drug possession and endangering the welfare of a minor and robbery. Assault charges were later tacked on when an elderly man, who Darren had viciously attacked in an elevator, picked him out of a lineup. The judge sentenced him to fifteen years behind bars.

***

The candle flame sizzled and cracked. Tiny threads of wax slid down the side of its glass.

"Here." Olivia handed Harper a tissue. "Wipe your face," she said, but Harper ignored the offer and rubbed her eyes using her sleeve, smearing new tears across an already damp, miserable face.

CHAPTER 4

Harper

The entire next day was miserable. Harper felt like a zombie, dragging her feet from class to class, exhausted from lack of sleep. A pounding headache had begun to follow her from sixth period on. Most likely the result from the heated argument she had with her mother the evening before. Since she had to pass her block to get to the library, she decided to stop at home to grab some headache medication. She slipped her key into the front door.

"There's a letter for you on the table," called out Olivia. She lay sprawled out on the sofa in the living room, nursing her swollen ankles.

Harper shoved the door closed.

I should have gone straight to the library.

"From who?" asked Harper, clearly annoyed to find her mother home. This was the second time this week her mother had called out for an entire shift.

Her mother's cheeks reddened.

"A-ha." *Him.* Harper swore under her breath.

She dropped her backpack in the hall and marched into the kitchen. She picked up the envelope, confirmed the sender's name, and flung it unopened into the garbage.

Olivia leaned on the door frame for support. "You're not even going to read it?" she said.

"Why should I?"

"We're beating a dead horse here, Harper," Olivia hissed. "He's your father, and he's reaching out to you to make amends."

"How do you know what he's reaching out to do?" Harper snapped, curling her lips in disgust. "Thanks, but no thanks." She pushed past her mother and grabbed her backpack. "I'm leaving."

"Where are you going?"

"Out."

"Harper!"

"To the library! Where else do I ever go?!"

"Be back before dark," yelled her mother as the front door slammed shut.

***

Motivated mostly by irritation, Harper weaved her way through back roads, scaling one small fence and hiking across a few parking lots while successfully skirting careless car drivers. Actual sidewalks didn't start until she hit Main Street. Within minutes she had made it to the library, no worse for wear.

Harper sank into her favorite library chair but didn't feel much like reading or studying. With too much clouding her mind, she instead sat in silence with her backpack resting closed on her lap.

On most afternoons, the library stayed blissfully peaceful. So peaceful, in fact, that Harper often felt relaxed enough to drift off the moment she dropped into her favorite armchair. Exhausted and stressed, she closed her eyes. She was just about to drift off when…

"Excuse me," interrupted a woman sporting the largest round glasses Harper had ever seen. "Love your hair, by the way. So totally retro."

"Ah, thanks?" mumbled Harper, squinting up to better focus.

"Oh, sorry. I didn't mean to startle you."

"No, no, it's fine." Harper sat up straighter, scrutinizing the familiar woman currently wagging a book in her face. *Ah, the librarian.*

"I was asked to give this to you."

"To me?" Harper frowned. "Why?"

"Because supposedly it's yours. Didn't you leave it here?"

Harper, unsure if this was some sort of joke, cut her eyes sideways. "Who found it?"

"One of our librarians."

Harper sat upright. "A guy with tall-cropped gray hair? Always grumpy?"

"Religiously."

"Sarcastic, sardonic, and scathing?"

"Bingo. You win." Regan tilted her head to the side and wiggled the book. "Well…? Do you want it?"

"What? Oh, right—" said Harper. "Thanks."

Regan handed Harper the book and shot her the peace sign. "Sure thing. Take care."

Harper played it cool but chuckled when she glimpsed the title. *The Bookshop on the Corner* by Jenny Colgan.

No way!

She'd read a ton of great reviews about this novel and had wanted to put her name on the library's long waiting list, but without a card, it had been impossible.

Harper opened to the title page, and a small envelope slid onto her lap addressed to "The Juvenile Delinquent."

Very funny.

Inside, Harper found a short note penned in the most perfect, precise handwriting she had ever seen. Paper-clipped to the message was a shiny new library card with her first and last name prominently displayed.

Dear Juvenile Delinquent,

"The library card is a passport to wonders, and miracles, glimpses into other lives, religions, experiences, the hopes and dreams and strivings of ALL human beings, and it is this passport that opens our eyes and hearts to the world beyond our front doors, that is one of our best hopes against tyranny, xenophobia, hopelessness, despair, anarchy, and *ignorance."—Libba Bray*

Perhaps now that you are in legal possession of a library card, you will see fit not to leave books strewn willy-nilly around my library.

Sincerely,

Irwin Abernathy [Irwin is, in fact, my real name. Sleep tight.]

PS: This is not a library copy. It is yours for the keeping. You're welcome.

PSS: Your handwriting is atrocious. Your crumpled-up library card form looked like a toddler on antihistamine had filled it in, so don't dare blame me if your name is misspelled.

Harper giggled.

Yes! A library card.

She stuffed the book and envelope into her backpack, then hoisted the strap over her shoulder and set off in search of the kooky librarian with the oversized purple peepers.

Her search didn't take long. She found Regan in the Children's Room on her knees, leaning over a long, glass tank attempting to feed strips of ripped lettuce to the library's mascot: a thirteen-year-old box turtle aptly named Shakespeare.

"Um, excuse me?"

Regan paused and tilted her head to look at Harper, appearing confused—as if the two hadn't spoken just moments before. "Can I help you?"

"Would you happen to know when the librarian who found my book will be back?" Harper lifted the book in the air, hoping to jog the silly woman's memory. "I wanted to thank him personally."

"Ah, yes. Irwin. I'm afraid he's doesn't work again until Monday." From the corner of her eye, Regan saw Irwin, dressed in a long gray overcoat, dash past her room, making a beeline for the front doors. His trench coat collar was raised high around his ears like some cartoon villain. All he lacked was a black fedora instead of that silly gray wool trapper hat with the brim and floppy ears he insisted on always wearing. "Hold up. Plot twist. Irwin just left the building, but if you hurry, you may catch him in the parking lot."

"Thanks!"

Harper peeked from behind a parked vehicle as Irwin drove the ridiculously short distance from the library to the florist shop across the street and parked.

Lazy old dude.

***

Irwin

"Afternoon, Irwin," called the shop owner standing behind the counter. "I'll be right with you," she said, putting the finishing touches on a massive wedding bouquet.

Irwin took off his hat and stuck it under his arm. He remained standing by the counter, as usual, eyes gazing straight ahead.

"A beautiful day we're having today," said Rosie. She ripped two large sheets of colorful paper from the roll. "Your daffodils will be ready in a jiffy."

Irwin put his hat back on his head and reached into his back pocket for his wallet. Then he placed the exact amount on the counter.

"Wait a sec." Rosie tucked a few extra green ferns around the long stems to compliment the two bouquets. "There. Much better."

"Thank you." As Irwin reached out to grab the door's handle, he hesitated and jerked back. "What the hell?" he grumbled. He could have sworn he saw something dart past.

"I'm sorry," asked Rosie, "did you say something?"

Brow knitted in a perpetual frown, Irwin mumbled a distracted, "Nothing," before he left the shop, the two bouquets nestled in his arms.

***

Harper

Harper crouched as low as she could behind the parked truck, praying Irwin hadn't seen her run across the street like a lunatic. After about fifteen seconds, she peeked around the truck's front window but quickly ducked down out of sight when she realized Irwin was still standing in the middle of the sidewalk glancing around.

After what felt like forever, he eventually gave up, got into his car, and drove off. Harper stood and brushed the dirt and gravel off her jeans. She wished her heart would stop playing the congas in her throat. She scurried across the street and entered the floral shop. The bell on the door jingled, announcing her arrival.

"Hi, there," greeted Rosie, exposing a welcoming toothy grin. "What can I do for you today?"

"Hi," replied Harper, matching the woman's chirpiness. "I wanted to buy a nice flower for my mom. Just one. Something to leave on her, um, desk at work."

"Oh, that's so sweet. What did you have in mind?"

"Not sure, really, but I liked the ones the guy who just left had. They looked nice." The veiled compliment was worth a shot.

Rosie wiped her hands on her apron. "Ah, yes, daffodils. They are a lovely flower, aren't they? From the Amaryllidaceae family. They symbolize friendship."

"Oh. Great. I'll take one of those then."

"Hmmm, I'm afraid I don't have anymore."

"Oh."

"No. Besides not being in season, those two bouquets are a special standing order."

"A standing order?" Harper nodded as if disappointed, but inwardly, she was grateful not to have the pressure of purchasing a flower with money she didn't have to spend.

"Yes. Mr. Abernathy comes in every week. He picks up two bouquets, always daffodils."

"His wife must love that."

"Oh no, not his wife. Fiancé. Well, former fiancé. Not sure what the proper term is, but she died in a car accident. About four years ago." Rosie pulled a roll of string out from the drawer. "A real tragedy too. Nice woman. A teacher at the high school—Gilly…Gilly…something. I forget, but my oldest son used to go to school with her daughter, Dakota. I know the mother's buried here in the town cemetery."

"The one across from the shopping center off the highway?"

"That's the one. The whole town came out for the funeral."

Harper felt creepy prying, but as they say, "In for a dime, in for a dollar." "That's so sad."

Rosie propped an empty vase on the counter. "Sure was. And to make matters worse, her daughter was in the car with her at the time of the accident."

"Oh no! Did she die too?"

"No," said Rosie, "but the poor thing's been in a coma this whole time. And such a beautiful girl too. I remember how upset my son and his friends were at the time. The school brought in a grief counselor to deal with all the…well, you know. A real shame." Rosie's brow creased as she stared through Harper. "You know what? Come to think of it, I think she was about your age when it happened."

Rosie shook her head, self-conscious. "Look at me, telling the world's business like this. I'm not normally such a gossiper."

Harper doubted that but wished she had minded her damn business and never come in. "That's such a heartbreaking situation," she said, hoping to end the conversation.

"Sure is," Rosie agreed. "Brenda—that's my sister-in-law—she works as a nurse's aide where the daughter is. She told me Mr. Abernathy never misses a week. Comes like clockwork and stays for about two hours. Brenda says she's seen him reading to the girl." Rosie rubbed the nape of her neck and mumbled, "I hear the staff adore him."

Harper choked up. The only thing her father ever devoted himself to was drugs.

"Can you imagine?" asked Rosie. "Stuck in a coma for four years."

This conversation was taking a turn for the worst. "At least the girl has Mr. Abernathy," said Harper, glancing longingly at the door.

"True. He may not say a whole lot, but you can tell he really cares."

Harper desperately wanted to leave.

Rosie hunched over the counter and leaned on her elbows. "Listen, I probably shouldn't be telling you all this, but I've been selling flowers practically all my life, and let me tell you, as God is my witness, I have never seen a man as heartbroken as that one."

Harper blinked back tears.

"Anyway, here I am gossiping away like I've got nothing that needs doing. Anything else I can help you with today, young lady?"

Harper had an idea. "You know what? My mom's favorite color is yellow. Do you have another flower that you think she may like? But nothing too expensive."

Rosie slapped the counter with both her palms. "Stay put. I have the perfect flower." Harper watched her waddle to the back room. She heard a wall fridge door swish open and closed. Minutes later, Rosie emerged holding a small but lovely bouquet of yellow and white carnations. She tucked in a few extra ferns to thicken it up before handing it off. "What do you think?" she asked Harper, smiling. "You think your mom would like this?"

Harper's eyes grew big. "She'd love it," she said. "It's beautiful, but I'm not sure if I have enough to cover the cost."

Rosie winked and busied herself with wrapping the bouquet in the same color paper she had used for Irwin's flowers. "Here," she said, handing Harper a tiny card for her to fill out. "No charge. Go home. Kiss your mom. Give her these and make her happy—and remember, sometimes all we get to keep in this life are our memories."

***

Olivia

It was still light outside by the time Harper arrived back home. She found her mother sprawled out on the couch asleep, her feet propped up on a small, square pillow. Tiptoeing across the room, she bent over to lay the bouquet on the coffee table when her mother stirred awake.

"Harper?" she slurred, still half asleep. "You're home. And it's still light outside."

Harper smiled. She bent over and kissed her mother's cheek. "These are for you," she said, handing her mother the bouquet.

"For me?" Olivia rubbed her eyes and adjusted the pillows so she could pull her body to the upright position. "How thoughtful. Yellow and white carnations." She took a big whiff. "And they smell good too. Thank you, but you shouldn't have."

Harper gently placed her pointer finger across her mother's lips to shush her. "I'm sorry for the way I've been acting lately."

Olivia's eyes softened. "You have nothing to apologize for. This is a difficult situation."

"I never meant to hurt your feelings."

Olivia unwrapped the bouquet. "Do you remember the garden we had in the other house?"

"Not really."

"I'm not surprised. And do you know why?"

Harper shook her head no.

"Because barely anything grew. A few dinky tomatoes. I think once I got a deformed cucumber to sprout, but other than that, not much."

Harper rested on the edge of the couch to be closer to her mother. "I don't understand why you're telling me this now?"

Olivia ignored Harper's question and continued. "The garden had been my idea. Just a small patch, nothing big, but I didn't care. I bought a bunch of seeds, tilled and turned the soil myself, and even convinced another local gardener in the area to share some of their manure with me."

Harper inwardly moaned and squared her shoulders.

"Listen," instructed her mother, patting Harper's thigh. "For the first few weeks, I did everything to make my garden work. I pulled weeds. I remembered to water…made sure to cover the plants with a sheet to protect them from frost. You name it, I did it." Olivia shifted in her seat and adjusted her foot on the pillow. "But after a while, I got lazy. I started to forget about watering the plants, and I didn't pull as many weeds out as I should have, and it showed. My plants wilted and died. Most of them burnt up from the sun, looking a lot like Death Valley." Olivia raised her eyebrows at Harper. "Do you understand what I'm trying to say to you?"

"Yes, you have a brown, lazy thumb and you're the reason why we only eat frozen vegetables," teased Harper.

Olivia playfully pinched her daughter's cheek. "You're a riot, you know that?"

Harper laughed.

"My point is that the garden had been my responsibility," she said, softly brushing a wisp of hair away from Harper's face. "I dropped the ball. Nobody else. Me. And I have to own that."

Harper nodded. "I understand."

Olivia lightly squeezed Harper's forearm. "How about you put these beautiful flowers in some water for me?"

"Can't have you killing them too."

Olivia flashed her daughter a playful frown. "There's a vase in the cabinet over the stove."

"Grandma's?"

"That's the one."

In the kitchen, Harper ran the water to fill the vase halfway. "Ma?" she called out, adjusting the flowers in their new home. "Can I ask you something?"

"Ask away."

Harper returned with the filled vase and placed it on the coffee table. "Even though you and your mom had problems, do you miss her?

"Every-single-day."

Harper scooted at the edge of the couch next to her mom. "What was she like?"

"My mother?" Olivia paused. "Funny you should ask. A lot like you, to be honest: tough when she needed to be, stubborn like nobody's business, and super smart. Read everything she could get her hands on, especially memoirs of famous people. I think reading about their lives gave her the peek into a life she couldn't come close to except through their stories."

"Why did you stop talking to her?"

Olivia cocked her head. "I never stopped talking to her. More like the other way around."

"I'm confused."

Olivia inhaled and sat up straighter, re-adjusting her position on the couch before answering. "It's time I told you the truth, but you're not going to like it."

"Tell me."

"When I started to use drugs, things naturally

54

changed between us. We began to argue all the time. I kept my life outside the house a secret, hidden, and your grandmother stopped trusting me, and for good reason."

"But she was your mother. How could she turn her back on you?"

Olivia lifted her pointer finger in the air. "Hold on. You have to understand something, Harper. My mother—your grandmother—was a good person. She tried to reach out to me—on many occasions. Gave me a roof when I had no place else to go. Put food on the table and clothes on my back—and yours."

"But I don't—"

"Hold up. Please, let me finish. My mother hated what I was turning into and felt helpless to fix it. You were a small child at the time. One day, after stopping by unannounced to drop off some groceries, she saw the way the place looked, the way I looked." Olivia shook her head. "Long story short, she lost it. Demanded that I give you to her, but I wouldn't let her near you. It was easier to blame her and make her the bad guy than face the truth."

"I always thought she didn't want me."

"She loved you, Harper. I stole her from you, along with her jewelry, which I pawned for drug money. My thought process at the time was so twisted. I thought nothing of digging into her wallet or lying to her." Olivia twisted her fingers. "I violated my mother's trust, over and over—her own daughter. All she wanted to do to was get me help, but I turned my back on her. Told her to mind her own business and leave us alone. Accused her of interfering in my life. Told her that the only reason she wanted to take you from me was out of jealousy. Accused her of not wanting me to be happy. Can you believe that?" Olivia blinked back tears. "I told her I hated her—to leave and never come back. I'm not making an excuse, there is no excuse for how I treated my mother, but at the time, my addiction took over." Olivia held Harper's hand, kneading the top gently with her thumb. "Eventually she couldn't take anymore. Told me to leave her alone and not contact her until I got clean."

Harper had assumed a major blow-up between her grandmother and mother had occurred, but she had never been privy to the details before now. In her mind, she believed knowing them would somehow ease the pain and emptiness she lived with inside. It didn't.

"By the time the state put you into foster care, we weren't speaking and lost all contact. That's why she never came to get you." Olivia shook her head and lowered her gaze. "I pushed my mother away and hurt the people in my life who cared and loved me, all to get the next fix." Olivia paused to catch her breath, her eyes moist and glazed. She'd tell Harper the truth—or most of it—but would leave out the sordid details no child should ever have to hear. Particularly about the nights faced alone, curled up in a ball fighting the elements and other predators—animal and human. Olivia wanted to forget the countless times she woke up in some random alleyway next to a strange body or below an underpass after wearing out her welcome at a friend's house. She'd purposely gloss over the things done to make ends meet until landing a real job. Olivia swore she'd take those dark memories to her grave.

Deep breath.

Olivia glanced up. There was no mistaking the longing for closure in Harper's eyes. *My baby.*

Olivia weighed her words carefully, not wanting her daughter's pity for something she had brought on herself. Nor would Olivia say anything to make her child carry the burden of her past mistakes any more than she already had. No. Some things were best left unsaid.

Olivia sat up straighter, more determined. "By the time I got clean and got you back, she had already passed away. After all that, I never got to tell my mom how much I loved her and how sorry I was for everything that happened."

Harper cupped her mother's hand in hers. "Mom," she said softly. "Where's Grandma buried?"

Olivia furrowed her brow, puzzled. "At the cemetery. The one in town."

Harper nodded. "Maybe you and I can go visit Grandma together—once your ankles don't look like sausages. Tell her everything you didn't before and wipe the slate clean."

Olivia's face flushed. She hugged her daughter tightly, whispering in her ear. "I am so blessed to have you in my life, you know that?" she said, voice cracking. "I love you so much. I promise I won't let you down ever again."

Mother and daughter embraced, holding onto one another tightly when a loud pounding at the front door startled the pair.

Harper drew back. "Who's that?" she asked, her surprise matched only by her mother's clenched jaw.

"No idea."

Three more insistent knocks followed before Harper stood. "I'll go."

"No. Stay here. I'll go."

"Don't be silly. Your ankles." Harper pressed her mother's shoulder, gently pushing her back down onto the couch. "Rest." Harper darted to the door.

"Ask who it is before you open it!" shouted her mother, but as usual, Harper wasn't listening.

Two more insistent knocks before Harper reached the door and swung it wide open.

"Harper Leigh Crane!" declared the man. "Look at you! All grown up."

There, perched on the front porch stood Harper's worst nightmare with two legs.

"Well? Aren't you going to invite me in?" asked the man, conceit smeared across his weathered, moist face. The face that wore the same cheekbones, the same shaped nose, the same deep-set eyes as hers.

"Shit!" Harper slammed her shoulder against the door, but he moved faster and managed to block the entrance with the heel of his boot, positioning his own shoulder and strength to pry it the rest of the way open.

"Now, Harper Leigh. Is that any way to treat your long-lost daddy?"

CHAPTER 5

Irwin

Irwin replaced the dead, wilted flowers from his previous week's visit with the fresh bouquet. He drew a hanky from his coat pocket and brushed the accumulated dust and occasional leaf off the top of Gilly's headstone before settling in to catch her up on his news. The fact that the gravesite overlooked a highway as opposed to a fancy green meadow mattered less to Irwin than his being able to come and visit as often as he liked, no matter the day, from dawn to dusk. However, it did little to alleviate the grief or mask the loneliness that shadowed his now almost reclusive existence. Today's news would be especially painful, and although Irwin didn't consider himself a religious man, it was the one time in his life he wished he could find solace in prayer or supplication.

Irwin stood, fixed his posture, and cleared his throat. "Winter's coming, Gilly. There's a brisk cutting chill in the air. I can feel it in my bones.

59

Remember how much you loved a good snowstorm? What did you use to say?" Irwin snapped his fingers. "Ah…yes. I remember. 'A fresh coat of fallen snow has the power to blot out the world's imperfections—at least for a little while.'"

Irwin bent over and massaged his knee. "These days, my old bones refuse to cooperate. Takes all I have to roll out of bed and get to work on time, not to mention having to deal with people. There's no shortage of crazy these days. People complaining, griping about their life, talking to themselves." Irwin tugged a few weeds from the bottom side of Gilly's headstone and glanced up. "Okay, I agree. That does sound like me, but you'd gripe and complain too if you had to work with Ledbetter. Something about that guy rubs me the wrong way—and he never shuts up."

A car horn sounded in the distance. A breeze lifted his coat collar.

"Windy day this past week. Most of the leaves at the house are down. I'll probably spend a good portion of tomorrow raking and bagging." He plucked a small pebble from the earth and rolled it around in his palm before tossing it to the side. "You would think that with all the leaves on the road, people would be smart enough to drive slower, but not these idiots around here. They think they're a bunch of road-racers, spinning out in minivans. Matter-of-fact, just the other day, I saw a deer dart in front of a car way ahead of me. The driver tried to swerve, but since he was speeding, he wound up skidding on a pile of wind-swept wet leaves and into an oncoming truck. The truck driver turned so as not to have a complete head-on collision but wound up hitting a light pole instead. I'm thinking he must have cracked something in his undercarriage because gallons of animal waste came pouring out all over the road." Irwin shook his head. "You should have seen it. Chicken blood, everywhere, gushing down Main Street. It looked like something out of a horror movie. Of course, you know the local paper. They had to have a field day with that. Coming up with witty headlines like, 'Red River Flows on Main Street' and 'Red September Comes to the Poconos' or some such foolishness."

Irwin enjoyed sharing funny anecdotes with Gilly about the people he worked with or came across at his job. During the warmer months, he'd bring a blanket and sit and read to her for hours. At other times, he came to talk or ask her for advice. Today would become the latter.

The air felt nippy. Irwin put his hat back on and stuck his hands in his pockets. "I have a strange situation going on that I wanted to run by you. I'm honestly perplexed. You taught teenagers. You understand how they think." Somewhat disconcerted, Irwin felt his cheeks redden. "There's a young girl, I'd say about fifteen, sixteen, no more. She comes to the library every afternoon and stays until closing. No parent, no friends, not even a cell phone from what I can tell. Nothing. She just sits in the chair facing the reception desk and reads or, when she's bored and has nothing better to do with her time, stares at me. I've caught her laughing at me." Irwin shrugged. "Personally, I find her outfits rather painful to look at, but you would like her. I'd say her style is a cross between biker girl and a hippie gone rogue. Oh, and she wears work boots all the time and has this weird, wild hairstyle down to her waist. And the rings…wears one on every finger—and I wouldn't be surprised if she's got them on her toes." Irwin tugged his earlobe. "The thing is, she's, I don't know…sad maybe? Lonely. Always has her face planted in a book. Thin thing. Too thin. I don't think she gets enough to eat." Irwin lifted his hand as if stopping traffic. "And yes, before you say it, I know, she sounds like a mini-me, all but the too thin part."

Irwin crossed his arms over his chest. "Interesting." He nodded. "I thought about that too."

She could be a runaway or maybe has a hard home life.

"Like I said, she's a skinny thing, and I never see her eat, and don't forget, we close at eight." Irwin rubbed his hands together. "She's obviously smart if one goes by the books she reads."

In the far distance, Irwin noticed a young man kneeling by a grave. He watched as he placed a hand on the top edge of the headstone, bowed his head, and openly wept. Irwin diverted his eyes.

"And so, why am I bringing this up now? For starters, because this girl scares me half to death. Don't laugh, Gilly. I'm serious. This girl is forever invading my space. Sends me these strange, cryptic messages and then hides them in books with a supposedly enigmatic meaning in the title. Why can't she bother somebody else? Regan, for example. She'd be a perfect specimen to annoy—or better yet, why not that arrogant, supercilious scoundrel, Roger? He deserves to be harassed."

Irwin lifted his head up to the sky. "Fine," he moaned. "I admit it. I'm sort of amused by her, but honestly, I don't know what to do. I am a single, old man." Irwin chuckled. "You're a riot, but you're right. That does practically give me pariah status." Irwin shrugged and plucked a brown, crisp leaf from the ground and crumpled it in his hand. The wind whipped the particles about.

"Okay, but listen to my side first. You and I both know I have no business whatsoever befriending a rebellious, strong-willed, smart-ass teenager. That's a no-no in any civilized society." Irwin readjusted his hat. "Look, I'm not up for this kind of drama in my life, Gilly. Not me. No, sir. There are hordes of underpaid social workers better trained for this kind of thing, and besides, the kid has trouble written all over her. More problems I don't need. I've got enough of my own to contend with."

Irwin edged closer to the headstone, waiting for his lonely heart to sense a reply.

"No, I'm not like you, Gilly. I have no compulsion to save the world. And I certainly don't make a habit of bringing home strays, if one doesn't count Cornelia and Bones."

Irwin rolled the bottom of his shoe over another small pebble peeking up through the grass. "I wish I had the power to push rewind and set everything that went wrong four years ago back on course." Irwin took a deep, cleansing breath. "Enough of that madness. I need to change the subject now." This was the conversation he dreaded having. For years, he had practiced in his head what he would say when the time came, and now that it was here, he felt at a loss for words.

"I spoke to Dakota's doctor yesterday," he started. "She's been trying to reach your..." Irwin quickly corrected himself, "Dakota's father. The last number she had for him no longer works. Big surprise, right? She thought I might have an address or phone number for him, which we both know is ridiculous at best."

Not long after Gilly died, her then almost ex-husband, Stanley the Slime Ball, couldn't claim the substantial life insurance payout fast enough. Without so much as a goodbye, he hightailed it out of state, his twenty-four-year-old secretary in tow, leaving behind his helpless, comatose child to fend for herself. Irwin dreamed of running the bastard over with his car and feeding his remains to the bears.

"I've tried my best to keep an eye on your little girl, but the doctors say her body's tired, Sweetheart. She's having difficulty breathing on her own and had to be intubated last night." Irwin stopped, the words lodged in his dry, scratchy throat. "I'm so sorry, Gilly. I know this isn't the news you were hoping to hear." Irwin inhaled another deep breath and blew it out slowly. "I guess what I'm trying to explain, but not doing a good job of it, is that it's time." Irwin lowered his head as if in prayer. "They want to go over final options."

No further words were needed; the implication of

his delivered message hung in the air painfully clear. Irwin stood stiffly at the foot of Gilly's grave, silently brooding. He had done what he had promised to do, but the outcome ripped him apart, nonetheless.

Please forgive me.

Irwin kissed his two fingers and placed the kiss on the top of Gilly's stone.

Next stop: the center to visit Dakota. To reach his car, Irwin had to pass the weeping man still kneeling, lost in his own cycle of hell. For a second, the younger man glanced up at Irwin and their eyes locked. Each offered the other the briefest of nods before both turned back inward. But in that almost infinitesimal exchange, they had shared it all.

As Irwin walked back to his car, he couldn't fathom the cruelty of love and why he couldn't have vanished on the day Fate wrenched Gilly from his life.

***

That evening, Irwin relaxed in his favorite reading chair, allowing memories of Gilly and Dakota to wash over and consume him. Gilly had given him so much when alive and, in many ways, even in death. The inexplicable closeness he felt for her child had always been something Irwin had a hard time processing, especially given the fact that he only knew Dakota through her mother's stories, photos, and aspirations.

With Dakota's absentee father living somewhere on the planet, Irwin felt obliged to honor Gilly's memory through the care of her daughter. On the day Gilly died, he made a solemn vow to be Dakota's caretaker, no matter what the outcome. For four years, he sat by Dakota's bedside, every week without fail.

In the beginning, his visits were for Gilly, but then, inexplicably, something changed, and Dakota became so much more to Irwin than a guilt-ridden promise or a deathbed obligation. In Irwin's heart, Dakota became his child. His little girl. She'd never know how even prior to the accident, Irwin had cheered for her success from afar—much like a proud papa. He would have gladly stepped up and become the dad she needed—and wanted—*if* she would have had him. And now, he would have to say goodbye to her as well.

Shortly after he'd arrived at the center, Dakota's doctor had stopped by to speak to him. "Sorry to interrupt," said Doctor Rollins after tapping at the slightly jarred door.

Irwin motioned to stand.

"No, please, sit," she said, waving him back down. "I wanted to let you know, we think we've found Dakota's father," she confided. "I had my secretary leave a message with his wife." Due to the extenuating parameters of this highly delicate situation, the staff over the years, including Doctor Rollins, had pretty much dropped protocol. While technically, Irwin didn't have the legal rights to make medical decisions for Dakota, the fact that she had literally nobody else willing, didn't go unnoticed.

Irwin solemnly nodded and placed a bookmarker

between the pages of the latest novel he chose to read to Dakota. He had already finished reading *Pride and Prejudice, War and Peace, Doctor Zhivago,* and *Gone with the Wind* to her, as well as a few other rather long novels. This time, Irwin chose a shorter contemporary fiction story, something not too long given time was no longer on their side.

Face stone cold, he asked, "And?" Irwin worked hard to contain the overwhelming loathing he held for the man he had never met. Irwin despised anyone who deserted their children. He'd known firsthand the lasting devastation, neglect, and abandonment produced.

"Nothing yet," Doctor Rollins answered, "but we'll let you know what's decided after I speak with him. There's a bit of paperwork we need to discuss first. More than that, I'm really not at liberty to say. I'm deeply sorry, Mr. Abernathy. If there were any other way…"

Irwin held up his hand to stop her from continuing. He didn't want her pity. "I understand. Please, all I ask is that you don't do anything until I'm…" Irwin choked back tears. "I want to be here when it happens."

Doctor Rollins squeezed Irwin's arm gently. "I've got rounds to make, and I'll let you get back to your reading. Take care of yourself," she said to Irwin. "See you later," she called out to Dakota, but only the clicking, metallic sounds of Dakota's life support machines busy at work dared to respond.

"Now, where were we?" Irwin opened the book to the last page read of *Tuesdays With Morrie* by

Mitch Albom. Irwin cleared his throat and began to read aloud, but the pressure from tears threatening to splat on the page became too much for Irwin to hold back, so he closed the book and sat in silence. His sad, weary eyes fixated on the lifeless shell named Dakota, while his dark, agonizing thoughts remained stuck in an endless loop. Falling.

***

After Irwin arrived home, he paid a few bills and poured a bowl of milk to leave outside for his neighbor's cat, Mr. Bones. Then he put up a load of laundry. Lastly, hungry himself, he threw a frozen chicken pot pie into the oven.

Irwin set the timer, poured himself a brandy, and sank down into his favorite chair to read. He plucked from the top of the pile the book he had attempted to read from the evening before, leaned back in his comfy chair, and took a long swig of his drink. "Ah, much better." Irwin closed his eyes and started to drift off just as the phone blasted him awake.

Birring.

"Oh, what now? he grumbled, adding a few extra colorful expletives as he slapped the book down and stomped to the phone, swearing the entire way.

"You had better not be a telemarketer," he warned, lifting the receiver. "Irwin Abernathy here. Speak!" he barked.

"Irwin, it's me…Regan."

"Regan?"

"Listen, I hate to bother you, but you know that

girl you asked me to give the book to?"

"Yes…"

"Well, she's here."

"Here, as in at the library, here?"

"Of course. Where else?"

Irwin rolled his eyes. "And this is news because…"

"Because she's in the women's bathroom, crying." Regan held the phone in the air. "She refuses to come out until she speaks to you."

Irwin stared at the phone in utter disbelief.

"Irwin?" said Regan. "Hey…Irwin! Are you still there?"

"I'm here."

"Well, what do you want me to tell her?" Regan asked, sounding fraught with desperation.

"Tell her to go home," he grumbled into the phone.

"Irwin, this is serious," admonished Regan. "The girl's really upset." A loud banging could be heard over the line.

"What the hell was that?" Irwin was already removing his semi-frozen pot pie from the oven.

"Presumably, her father. She says she doesn't want to speak to him and refuses to leave until he does."

"He's a monster," shouted Harper, her voice echoing against the tiled bathroom walls. "I never want to speak to him again."

"Did you hear that?" asked Regan.

"The entire block could hear that," snapped Irwin. He stared into space, nearly choking the receiver. "Why me? Would you at least ask her that? Why me?"

Regan repeated Irwin's question to Harper. The girl's muffled reply split open the already seeping, raw wound left behind by Gilly and Dakota.

"Because I trust you."

"Did you hear her?" asked Regan.

"I heard her."

"So, you're coming, right?"

"Fine…I'll be there shortly."

"Thanks, Irwin. I'll let the police know."

"The *who*?" Irwin shouted, but by then, Regan had already hung up. "Damn it all."

CHAPTER 6

Harper

Harper and Regan exchanged conspiratorial looks as they huddled together behind the cracked open door, snooping on Janice giving Darren a good dressing down outside the women's bathroom.

"Janice can get a bit carried away sometimes," whispered Regan.

"Darren deserves it," mumbled Harper, impressed and eager for somebody to stand up to that guy.

"Who do you think you are, trying to barge in there?" scolded Janice to Darren. "This is a public library, sir, not some saloon. For your information, people come here to read and to expand their minds. They bring their children here precisely because there's an assumption, a well-deserved assumption, mind you, that it's safe. What they don't come for is your vulgar brand of street thuggery and soap opera drama."

Saloon?

"Totally savage," muttered Harper, impressed, her chapped lips twisted in a grin.

"Janice," interrupted Roger. He yanked her sleeve, but Janice, too deep into her speech to catch air, wasn't paying him the slightest bit of attention.

"Save your family dysfunction for the mall—but not here, my friend. Not in my library you don't!" Janice roared, lifting her stately nose haughtily in the air.

Harper stifled a giggle. "She's good." Regan nodded.

"Janice," murmured Roger louder. "I don't think this is helping," he said and shifted his body intentionally between Harper's furious father and Janice.

"Nonsense, Roger," admonished Janice, undaunted and raring to go.

As if by cue, a tall, strapping Area Regional police officer with a face that belonged splayed on a fashion magazine cover arrived on the scene. Janice saw him enter first.

"Now you're in for it," Janice threatened, thrusting her long-manicured talon in Darren's chest.

"Now he's in for it," repeated Harper under her breath, cracking the door a little wider to get a better view.

The police officer walked up to the trio and gave each a tentative nod. "What seems to be the problem?" he asked.

Darren, Janice, and Roger began speaking at the same time.

"Whoa now," said the officer, holding up his

hands. "One at a time." He glanced at Janice. "Why don't you go first, Miss…"

"Stroop," offered Roger. "Janice Stroop. Our glorious leader and Sergeant in Arms."

Janice shot Roger the side-eye. "I'm Head Librarian and Branch Manager," she said, not finding Roger the least bit amusing.

"And who phoned in the disturbance?"

"I did," confirmed Janice. "This ridiculous man is disturbing the peace, and I want him removed."

The officer gave Janice a slight head-bob. "One thing at a time, Miss Stroop." He looked towards Roger. "And you are?" asked the officer.

"Roger Ledbetter. Librarian and Circulation Supervisor." Roger had worked at the library since straight out of college. He loved nothing more than to tout his title at every opportunity.

"And you?" asked the officer, jutting his chin in Darren's direction.

"I'm the father."

"Of the girl refusing to come out of the bathroom," confirmed Moore.

"Father my ass," groaned Harper in Regan's ear.

To his credit, the handsome officer didn't seem at all fazed by the bizarre situation. "Miss Stroop, if you could, I'd like you to please wait over there by those tables—you too, sir," he said to Roger. "I'd like to have a word with the father."

Roger left first, while Janice, who apparently didn't take kindly to being dismissed, grumbled her disapproval loudly with each subsequent footstep.

Harper quietly cracked the door open a little bit more—just enough to comfortably keep snooping.

This was too good to miss.

"Thank you," said Officer Moore to the parting pair. Turning to Darren, "You said you're the father?"

"Yeah. That's right."

"Can you explain to me why your daughter decided to lock herself in the bathroom?"

"No idea," asserted Darren, much too coolly. "I saw her run into the library bawling and then she headed straight into the bathroom. I wasn't trying to cause a scene like that screwy woman just told you. I just wanted to make sure my kid was okay."

Incensed, Harper poked her entire face out the slightly ajar door. "Liar!" she yelped. "He's a liar, Officer. Don't believe a single word that slime ball says."

"Harper!" Darren bolted for the door, but Harper was quicker and managed to slam and relock it by the time he got there.

Darren pounded the door with his fist. "Come on already—I just want to talk to you," he shouted.

"Go away and leave me alone," yelled Harper.

Darren hissed. "Harper Leigh, if you don't open this door…"

"You'll what?" she challenged her father.

"Sir, step away from the bathroom door," instructed the officer. "Now!"

"I just want to speak to my daughter."

"I understand that, but she doesn't want to talk to you, so for now, I want you to step away. Let's give her some space and see if we can sort this mess out." While delivered with flair, to all those present the officer's request sounded closer to a command.

Harper heard the voices fade as they moved away. She waited a few seconds more before cracking the door open enough to watch the circus outside unfold. She watched Darren, under the stares and glares of a small but gathering group of curious library patrons, walk past Janice. Harper had to contain a laugh when Darren shot Janice a dirty look. Unfazed, Janice matched and raised her countenance as only Janice could.

"Show's over, folks," said the officer, turning towards the small crowd. "Please go back to what you were doing." To Darren, he crooked a finger. "Follow me," he said and escorted Darren farther down the hall. "Now, let's start from the top. You said your daughter was upset and ran into the library, correct?"

"Yeah. That's right."

"And then what happened?"

"I told you, I followed her inside, but by the time I got in, she had already locked herself in the women's bathroom."

Officer Moore scribbled something in his notebook. "Did you come to the library together?"

"What do you mean by come together?"

The officer, already exhausted from pulling a double shift, had no energy left for Darren's stupid games. "Did-you-arrive-in-the-same-vehicle?" he enunciated, spittle forming at the corner of his mouth. "Did-you-walk-here-together? Did-you-plan-in-advance-to meet here?" His patience had obviously petered out.

"No. Not really."

The officer cut his eyes and rubbed his temple.

"To which one?"

Darren, not always the sharpest tool in the shed, as far as Harper was concerned, shrugged. "All of 'em?"

At this point, the officer cocked his head towards the ceiling and counted to five before responding. "Let's try this again, shall we? What led up to your daughter locking herself in the bathroom?"

Darren frowned, clearly calculating his response.

The officer waved a hand in Darren's face. "Hey, buddy, I advise you to stop playing games and jerking me around. I'm tired. I've had a long day and night. The last thing I want to do right now is dance with you. Now, I'm going to ask you this one more time. Why is your daughter upset?"

Darren pinched the bridge of his nose and ran a chafed hand over his five o'clock shadow before committing to a response. "Okay. I'm going to level with you."

The officer, his fist planted on his belt, stood tall. With his legs spread apart, he looked like a superhero ready to burst into action. "Go ahead."

"I'm not gonna lie. Harper's mother and I haven't exactly been together for a while. I'm talking years. You get me?"

The officer nodded. "I got you. And?"

"And I came over to her house this afternoon—just to talk to Olivia. That's my ex's name—who is also Harper—my daughter's mother."

"Okay…"

"I went over there to see if I could patch things up between us. See if she'd be willing to give me another shot. I mean, what do I have to lose, right?"

The officer recoiled but nodded for Darren to continue.

"Thing is, the kid overheard us. One thing led to the other, and Harper freaked the hell out. She started screaming her head off, calling me terrible names, and ran out of the house before I could explain. I tried to get her to come back inside, but by then, she was too pissed off to listen. Olivia got worried, so I offered to track Harper down and bring her back home. That's how I wound up here. End of story."

The officer turned his pad to a fresh page. "Your full name?" he asked, continuing to take field notes.

"Darren Crane."

"Any middle initial?"

"E, for Elliot."

"Daughter's name?"

"Harper Leigh Crane."

"Age?"

"Hers or mine?"

"Both."

"She's..." Darren squinted and started to mumble, seemingly doing the math in his head. When that apparently failed, he began to count backward using his fingers. "I'm thirty-six, so that would make Harper sixteen."

The officer sighed. "Address?"

Darren dithered.

The officer peered up from his pad. "Address?" he repeated more forcefully.

"East Stroudsburg." Darren lowered his voice. "I'm staying at the half-way house."

The officer narrowed his eyes. "Parole?"

"Yeah."

"Working phone number?"

"Not at the moment."

"Parole officer's name?"

Darren slipped his hand into his back pocket and produced his parole officer's business card.

The officer copied down the information.

"Here," said the officer, handing the card back. "Last question for now—and I warn you for a second time, you don't want to lie to me."

Darren nodded.

"Is there a restraining order in place?"

"Like that says I can't see my own kid or something?" asked Darren, crossing his arms over his chest.

"Your kid, your ex—either one."

"Then, no. None of that."

"Fine." The officer snapped his notebook shut for the moment. "Hang tight here. I'm going to speak to your daughter." The officer passed Janice and Roger, still huddled together, conversing in whispers. "Thank you for waiting. I'll be with the both of you shortly," he said and headed straight to the bathroom door and knocked twice.

"Harper? I'm Officer Moore. Can I talk to you for a minute?"

No response.

Behind the door, Harper gnawed on her bottom lip, but she refused to speak, uncertain that anyone, including a seasoned police officer, would understand how much she loathed the man calling himself *her father*.

"Come on, Harper. Look, I get you're upset. But

I just want to make sure you're okay. And I'd like to hear your version of events." Officer Moore air-snapped his fingers at Janice, making the hand sign for key. She gave him the thumbs-up and sprinted toward the office. Then to Harper, "I want to help you if you'll let me."

"I'm not coming out," shouted Harper, this time emphatically.

"Then can you at least come to the door, so we can talk instead of all this yelling?" he asked. "The Head Librarian's giving me the evil eye. I hear she's pretty strict about using inside voices."

A moment passed. "Fine, but I won't come out until *he* leaves," she sniffled, followed by a muffled sob.

"Harper! Enough screwing around, already!" hollered Darren, who had somehow managed to slither his way back behind the officer. "Get out of there already and let's talk this out. You and me."

"No!" Harper yelled from inside. "Leave me alone!" She pressed her entire body against the door frame.

"Harper!" Darren reached around the officer and pounded on the door again.

"Sir, step aside and go back to where I told you to wait," ordered Officer Moore.

"Stop yelling at her, you-you mean man," admonished Regan from behind the locked door.

The officer's ears perked up at hearing an unfamiliar voice. "Is there somebody else in there?"

"Yes," answered Regan and Harper jointly.

Officer Moore spread his hands confused. "And who are you?" he yelled at the door.

"Greetings from inside, Officer Moore. I'm Regan Vanhorn."

"Who?"

"Regan Vanhorn. I'm the librarian for the children's room."

"Of course you are," mumbled Moore. He rubbed his weary eyes. "And why are you in there, Miss Vanhorn?"

"Yeah." Darren nodded, standing over Moore's shoulder. "I'd like to know the same thing."

Moore twisted his body slightly towards Darren and clapped his hands. "Hey! I told you to stay over there. Now, go. Move it. Over there."

"But…"

"Mr. Crane. I swear to…" The officer bit his bottom lip. "Would you just stand over there, already?"

"But I…"

"Don't make me handcuff you to a table."

Darren seethed but kept his cool; it would only take one slip-up to send his ass back to prison. "Whatever," he grumbled and stepped away, although not nearly as far as the police officer had directed.

Officer Moore lowered his voice. "Harper, I would really like to speak to you."

"I only want to speak to Mr. Abernathy," said Harper.

"I'm sorry, who?" asked Officer Moore. He turned around, his eyes darting from Darren's blank expression to Janice's knowing scowl.

"Officer?" shouted Regan, tapping on the other side of the door. "Excuse me, Officer?"

"Yes, Miss Vanhorn?"

"Irwin…um, I mean, Mr. Abernathy…he also works here."

Officer Moore shrugged. "I bet he does."

"But not today."

"Right." The office's shoulders dropped. "I don't get paid enough for this," he mumbled under his breath.

"But I called him a short time ago, and he's on his way." Regan checked her watch. "Matter of fact, he should be here any minute."

The officer rubbed his tired eyes. "And what, pray tell, does Mr. Abernathy have to do with any of this?"

"Absolutely nothing," growled Irwin, trudging onto the scene.

"Irwin?" called Regan. "Is that you?"

Irwin sighed.

"Come to the door, and I'll let you in," said Regan,

Irwin rolled his eyes then glanced at the officer, seeking for his permission to enter.

"Go ahead," said Officer Moore. "Good luck."

"Wait a damned minute," demanded Darren, now back at the door with a vengeance. "I'm her father. Why does this guy get to go inside and not me?"

"Because, sir," declared Irwin, unfazed, "I am her librarian." Neither Irwin's face nor eyes revealed even the slightest hint of irony.

"Her who?" asked Darren, perplexed. "What the hell is going on here?"

"For the second time, watch your mouth,"

chastised Janice from the far corner, covering her own ears.

For the next five minutes, further mumbling and arguing ensued, much of which neither Regan nor Harper could make out with their ears pressed to the door until they heard Irwin's voice rise above the fray. "Stand aside. I'm going in."

From inside the bathroom, Regan signaled Harper to scoot over, but even then, she couldn't open the door nearly wide enough for Irwin to pass through comfortably.

"Oh, for God's sake," grumbled Irwin when his coat pocket caught on the door handle. "Who the hell are you pretending to be?" he barked at a squinting Regan. "An MI-5 agent or something? Open the damn door!"

Regan pulled the door open slightly wider and tugged Irwin in by the shoulder. Then she poked her owl eyes out. "Uh oh," she yelped. Everyone outside the bathroom door stood gawking at her with stunned open mouths. "Sorry," she screeched then slammed the door shut.

Irwin huffed and clasped his hands. "I'm here, and this had better be good," he said, face glowering. "I'm missing out on a perfectly defrosted chicken pot pie for this." Irwin glared down at his feet where Harper sat crossed legged. "Kindly explain to me why I have been summoned."

Harper rose to her feet and crossed the bathroom. She was just about to start talking when she cracked up hysterically laughing.

Irwin recoiled. "I'm sorry, but how is rousing me

from the comfort of my home to deal with your personal issues the least bit funny?" he declared, slightly put off.

"I'm sorry," Harper giggled, holding her belly. "But your outfit..." Harper waggled a finger at Irwin's attire.

"What about it?" he asked gruffly.

Harper glanced at Regan, and they both giggled, which soon turned into fits of uncontrollable laughter.

Brow furrowed, Irwin appeared confused until he peered down at his ensemble. With as much dignity as he could muster, he began to pluck a few cat hairs from his sleeve. "I was in a rush," he mumbled, using one hand to smooth wrinkles that didn't exist.

"In the dark?" teased Regan, still yukking it up.

"And that hat!" Harper giggled, clutching her stomach. "Who was the poor, unsuspecting beaver trapper you mugged for that ugly thing!"

Regan abruptly stopped laughing, frantically signaling Harper to be quiet, but Harper, not comprehending the urgency in Regan's hand signals, just shrugged.

"A friend gave it to me," Irwin grumbled, none too happy. He tugged his hat off and shoved it into his pocket.

Regan cleared her throat and wagged her fingers in the air like Tweety Bird. "Um, excuse me, but since Irwin's here, I can leave, right?"

"Yes," agreed Harper.

"No!" yelled Irwin louder.

Regan glanced rapidly between the two, looking

baffled as to who to listen to.

"Miss Vanhorn will remain," said Irwin, leaving no wiggle room for further discussion. "For propriety's sake."

Harper shrugged. "Whatever."

"Whatever," mumbled Regan, leaning back on the edge of the sink. "Oh, darn it all," she screeched, slapping her now-soaked butt, drenched with splattered water and soap suds.

The door handle jiggled. "Hey! Is everything okay in there?" inquired the officer.

"Yes," shouted all three in unison.

"Just give us a few minutes, officer," said Irwin, shooting Regan a death glare. No interpretation necessary.

Outside the door, Harper's father could be heard bombarding the officer rather brashly with his account.

"I just wanted to talk to her is all," complained Darren.

Harper rolled her eyes. "He's such a freakin' two-faced liar," she said.

"No. I have no idea why Harper's acting like this. I just wanted to make sure she's okay."

"Oh, please," scoffed Harper. "You hear him? He's lying through his yellow, nicotine-stained teeth," she said, clearly not amused.

"Ignore him. I want you to tell me what's the truth," Irwin said, "and I want to hear it from Harper—not you," he said jerking his head slightly at Regan.

Harper slid back down onto the tile floor. She pressed her back against the wall. With both elbows resting on her knees, she clasped her hands and peered up. "I don't feel like talking about it."

Irwin exaggeratedly blinked twice, not sure he'd heard right. "I'm sorry, what?" He stared down at the girl like she had lost her mind. Harper played with the zipper on her jacket.

Irwin threw his hands in the air. "You know what? That's fine," he said. "Have a nice life," and he reached out to open the door.

"No! Don't go!" cried Harper, leaping to her feet. "Please don't go."

Irwin paused.

"You don't understand…"

"Then make me."

Harper clenched her hands into tightly balled fists. "Darren—the guy outside—he's my sperm donator. To be honest, I don't really know him."

"And why is that?"

"Because he's been away a long time."

"For how long?" countered Irwin.

"Five, almost six years."

"You said away. Away meaning?"

"Prison."

"And now he's…?"

"Out. Sort of. On parole."

"What did he do to get sent away?"

"Drugs, assault, child endangerment. In general, being a degenerate lowlife jerk."

"And he lives with you?"

"No, he's staying at a half-way house for now, but that's what set this whole thing off."

"You'll have to do better than that," said Irwin, tucking his crossed hands under his armpits.

Harper ran her ringed fingers through her tangled mop. Voice low but steady, she began to explain. "Darren got released a few days ago. He decided to come over to the house uninvited to inform, not ask, my mother that he's moving back. Claims on a stack of hotel bibles that he's clean, but he's a liar and not right in the head."

"Is that your opinion?"

"It's the truth. I don't want him around, especially near my mother. She's not…strong enough around him."

"Speaking of your mother, where is she and what does she want?"

Harper's eyes flashed a disconcerted fusion of fear and rage. "She's still home, I guess, I don't know. That's where she was when I left. Concerning what she wants? She doesn't have a clue. Likes to tell me she can handle things now." Harper made air quotes. "That she's changed."

"And by that you mean you don't believe her?"

"I believe she believes what she's saying, but I'm not convinced she can follow through. Things have been rough for her, and I think she'll slide right back into trouble the minute Darren barks. I don't get it. What does she see in him? He's such a loser; everyone knows that, but he has some kind of hold on her. It's hard to explain."

"You're doing fine. Continue."

"When I was smaller, they both got heavy into drugs. I mean really bad. Hard stuff too. Back then, he used my mom's drug habit to control her. Got her to do whatever he wanted."

"And why is that?"

Harper pursed her lips and stared straight into Irwin's eyes. "Because she's scared of him."

Irwin nodded. Insightful, but still, why involve him? "And so, you decided to lock yourself in a library bathroom and call me. Why?"

"Yeah, about that. I'm sorry. It's just that I didn't know who else to call," said Harper, her wet eyes affixed to Irwin's face. Neither one of them said another word.

Irwin's eyes dropped first, his fingers fidgeting with the buttons on his sweater, deliberating on his choices while attempting to ignore Gilly's voice yelling in his head. Besides Dakota's situation, he knew any involvement with this girl and her family dysfunction would only bring trouble. Trouble he certainly didn't want or need.

"She needs your help," insisted Regan, poking Irwin hard in the arm. "And remember, Irwin, a little consideration, a little thought for others, makes all the difference."

Harper shrugged. "Huh?"

"Winnie The Pooh," Irwin clarified. "Ignore her." Irwin directed his long-suffering attention back to Harper's situation. "What exactly do you think I can do to help?" he asked.

Harper gathered her belongings. "Well, for starters, could you arrange safe passage out of this bathroom for me?"

CHAPTER 7

Olivia

Swollen ankles or not, Olivia took off in search of her daughter. She threw on a coat and slipped her bloated feet into a pair of scruffy sneakers, locking the front door behind her. She assumed Harper had headed to her safe place—the library. She plodded along, hoping to beat Darren there, but with a gimp and no car, Olivia seriously doubted it. Darren had been in full form after he left the house, yelling and blaming Olivia for turning Harper against him.

"I should have known you'd badmouth me to my own kid," accused Darren, his fists clenched tight. "I rotted behind bars for close to six years in that stinkin' prison, not knowing a thing about what was going on out here. Not once did I receive a single letter from you. Hell, you even refused my collect calls. You're evil. You know that, Olivia? Pure evil."

"You want to talk about evil?" countered Olivia, her voice shaky but determined. "You left me for dead six years ago, lying in a puddle of puke."

Darren leered, but Olivia kept talking. "Harper was the one who found me. Can you imagine? A nine year old had to find me like that. On top of that, they took her away from me. I had to get clean so I could fight to get her back—all by myself. Who knows what Harper endured in those foster homes?" Olivia seethed. "And you know what? Since then, she's never been the same. Since then I have been making it up to her any way I can, but where were you all that time I detoxed, went to court, dealt with social workers, huh? Speak, Darren."

Darren bit his bottom lip.

"Oh, that's right. How could I forget? You were probably holed up somewhere, drugged out of your mind, beating and robbing the elderly for their pocket change."

Darren lunged for Olivia, but she anticipated his move and had already snagged one of the pillows from under her feet to block him. "Go ahead, I dare you," she seethed. "Let's see how fast they throw your ass back in jail."

Darren tried tugging the pillow away, pulling Olivia's wrists to release her tight grip, but Olivia refused to relent.

"I'm not afraid of you anymore, Darren," she cried from behind the pillow, attempting to put up a strong front. "You can't do to me what you used to."

"You lying bitch. I didn't do a damn thing to you that you didn't want done." Darren lifted his leg and snap-kicked a nearby chair, causing it to fly across the room and topple over on its side. "And you better keep your mouth shut and stop spreading your lies."

Olivia, knowing better than to drop the pillow from her face, glimpsed Darren scanning the room for something else to destroy.

"Always blaming me for everything," he grumbled, head twisting left, then right, then left again.

Olivia caught Darren's eyes register the bouquet of flowers. She watched in horror when his lips sneered.

"NO!" she screamed, but she was too late. Darren tore the flowers from their holder and flung them on top of her head. Stems, petals, and droplets of water scattered and landed in every direction.

"I'm out, Olivia. Deal with it." As Darren headed for the door, he passed Olivia's handbag. With a calculated, cruel smile plastered across his face, he swiped the bag and began to rifle through its contents, pocketing a chapstick, a pen, and the few dollars left in Olivia's wallet. "Thanks," he said, folding the bills and stuffing them in his jacket.

"Just take what you want and leave," she threatened, sounding braver than she felt.

Darren turned to face her. "I'm going, but remember this—Harper's my kid, and there's not a damn thing you can do to change that."

Olivia's eyes drew into killer slits. It had been six long years, and the self-serving bastard still never missed an opportunity to hurl threats at her.

"Leave her alone!" hollered Olivia, her body racked in fury. She understood all too well the vile game he was playing. Access to Harper would be the ticket he needed to regain control over her, his way of forcing her back into compliance. "I'm warning you, leave her alone. Harper's been through enough hell because of us, and I won't let you hurt her again."

Darren cackled. "Why look at you, Olivia. All big and bad, and thinking you can threaten me," he taunted. He held his hands high in the air in mock surrender. Darren sauntered back into the room and over to the coffee table, taking aim for the glass vase.

Olivia leaped to her swollen feet, trying to snatch it away, but Darren, who had her by a good four inches, held it above her head and laughed, taunting her while using his free hand to cuff her in the face every time she reached out to grab it.

"Don't!" she implored, arms flailing. "That was my mother's…"

"I know." Darren pulled back his arm and launched the family heirloom smack at the wall, shattering the vase and, with it, all of Olivia's hopes, into a thousand, fragmented pieces.

***

After a painful and arduous hike, Olivia limped up to the library's front desk, ready to inquire about Harper, when she heard a loud commotion taking place around the hall's bend, closest to the bathrooms. Without missing a beat, she limped over, favoring her left ankle over her right.

Rounding the bend, she glimpsed Darren pouting. She laughed after realizing that he had his back pinned to the wall, seemingly being lectured to by an older, irate woman wagging a finger riotously in his face. On Darren's other side stood a much younger man with a head of shaggy brown hair, slumped over and gripping his head as if fighting back a migraine. Down the hall by the bathrooms, Olivia spotted her daughter standing with both arms crossed over her chest, flanked by a police officer, a younger woman, and a tall, older gentleman.

"Harper!" Olivia called, rushing down the carpeted hall the best she could.

Everyone stopped mid-sentence.

"Mom," sighed Harper.

"Are you all right?"

"I'm fine."

"Ma'am, I'm Officer Moore."

Olivia, eyes darting between the officer and her daughter, gave him an uncommitted nod.

"Glad you're here," said Officer Moore. "I was about to contact you."

"What happened?" Olivia pushed through the group and wrapped a protective arm around her daughter's slumped, unresponsive shoulders.

Darren approached from down the hall and sent Olivia a clear warning to tread carefully. His non-verbal threat may have gone unnoticed by the police officer whose back faced in the other direction, but it hadn't gone unobserved by the tall, older gentleman.

"Harper," said Officer Moore, "I'd like for you and your mother to stay here with me, while Miss Vanhorn and Mr. Abernathy, please wait at the tables over there." He pointed.

"I hate to run, but I really have to get back to work," said Regan in a slight, shrilled panic. "Pamela, our other children's room assistant, called out sick today. Supposedly the flu. I told her two weeks ago to get her flu shot, but did she listen to me? No, of course not. Nobody listens to me, and now there's no one to man the children's area."

Irwin groaned, his hands cupped in supplication. "Officer, please dismiss Miss Vanhorn. I'll be forever in your debt."

The officer side-eyed Irwin before addressing Regan. "That's fine, Miss Vanhorn. If I have any further questions, I know where to find you."

Irwin cleared his throat and pointed his finger in the air. "If possible, I would also like to take my leave, so I can go home to feed the neighborhood feral cat my now ruined, cold dinner."

"No, stay!" interrupted Harper, reaching out to grab Irwin's sleeve. "Please stay," she added.

Olivia frowned and leaned into her daughter. "Who's he?" she whispered loud enough in Harper's ear for Irwin to respond.

Irwin drew in a long, tortured breath. "Irwin Abernathy, ma'am. Resident librarian. Nice to meet you." He offered a slight bow of his head instead of reaching out to shake Olivia's hand.

"Nice to meet you, too," she said, embracing Harper even tighter.

"Ma'am," said Officer Moore. "Your daughter locked herself in the bathroom, pretty upset. Miss Vanhorn, the lady who just left, and Mr. Abernathy agreed to stay with her until she felt ready to come out."

"Oh, Harper," murmured Olivia, embracing her daughter's shoulder.

No longer willing to be discounted, Darren shoved his way past Janice and Roger to stand next to his daughter. But Harper, unwilling to be sandwiched between the two, jerked away from her mother's firm grasp and moved next to Irwin clear on the other side.

"What do you think you're doing?" Darren asked Harper. "I told you, I only wanted to talk."

"Well, she obviously doesn't want to talk to you," spat Olivia.

"That's because you turned her against me," snapped Darren. "Can you arrest her for that?" he asked Officer Moore.

Officer Moore spread his arms wide, forcing them to keep their distance. "No laws have been broken—yet," he said, glaring straight at Darren. "But I strongly suggest you leave, sir, before I have to take you in for disturbing the peace."

"For shit's sake," Darren snarled. "And what about her?" Darren asked, chin jutted at Olivia, nostrils flared. "Why am I the only one in trouble?"

"Mr. Crane…" warned the officer.

"This is some bullshit," mumbled Darren. "And I don't know who you are, mister," he said, facing Irwin, "but you better stay away from my kid."

Irwin, never one to be easily intimidated, stood taller. "Oh my," he said to Darren as he rolled up his sleeve, making a big hoopla of looking down at his watch. "Would you look at the time? You'd best be running, Mr. Crane," he said, apparently unfazed by the man's surly stares and threatening glares.

"You wouldn't want to be late checking in with your parole officer. Or perhaps I can assist and make the call?"

Darren's face blanched. His piercing eyes darted from one face to the next, ready to counterattack, but Officer Moore beat him to the punch.

"Good advice, Mr. Crane," advised Officer Moore, one hand resting on his holster. "I strongly suggest you take it."

Beaten, Darren took a step back. "Fine. I'm going," he said to the group, "for now." He pointed a dirt-stained finger in Olivia's face. "You can't keep me away from Harper forever. She's my daughter, and I have rights."

The group watched Darren stomp off, mumbling and cursing, shoving chairs not even in his way and basically acting like a petulant child. At one point, they saw him knock down a few books on display just before bolting out of the building. A few startled library patrons quickly moved out of the disgruntled man's path as he continued to yell his way out of the building.

Harper sighed. "Thank you," she murmured to Irwin, but Irwin didn't hear her; he was too weighted down by the realization that somehow, and only God knew how, he had just inherited another wayward teenager burgeoning with father issues.

Irwin wasn't the only one concerned. With everyone else seemingly transfixed by Darren's appalling display of dysfunction, Olivia concentrated her attention on Harper and whoever this Mr. Abernathy person was. With eyes narrowed into crinkled slits, she studied Irwin's unremarkable face, mesmerized by his off-beat, somewhat ill-conceived get-up. Most of all, she questioned what Harper saw in this man's blatant, ornery disposition, who looked as uncomfortable in his skin as a leper does in theirs...yet Olivia had to give it to the old guy—especially when Darren tried to force his way next to Harper. However, the fact that Harper chose to stand near Abernathy over her had hurt.

For the longest time, Olivia would have sworn up and down that Harper was incapable of open displays of trust, but apparently, she had been wrong. And not only trust but appreciation. But there had been no mistaking Harper's softly offered *thank you* to Abernathy. For whatever reason, Olivia saw that her daughter trusted this strange, contentious old man.

There better not have been any funny business going on. I'll castrate him.

To Irwin, she said, "I want to thank you for helping my daughter." Olivia made the first move and reached out to shake Irwin's hand. "I hope we can meet again," she said disarmingly, pumping his hand but not letting go. "But under better circumstances the next time." She had been all ready to ask Irwin to speak to her for a minute alone when Harper jumped in.

"I have to study," Harper announced to her mother. To Irwin, she gave a slight chin-nod. "Thanks again."

Plan foiled.

Olivia offered Harper a strained smile. "Good night, Mr. Abernathy," Olivia called out after the departing old man, already lumbering away with his head bowed and his coat collar tucked high around his ears.

***

Mother and daughter took their time walking home, stopping along the way for Olivia to rest her sore feet. At one point, Olivia tried to pry Harper for information about Mr. Abernathy, but the girl shut her down quick.

"Let's not do this right now, okay, Ma? I'm tired and just want to go home."

Upon arrival, Harper sprang ahead, taking two steps at a time, even getting her key to work on the first try. She held the door open for her mother, who lagged behind, using their rickety stair railing for support.

Without lights, the place looked pitch-black. Once inside, Harper dropped her backpack on the floor, flipped the overhead light on, and hung up her jacket. When she turned around, she gasped. "What the hell…" She stopped dead in her tracks, ashen face frozen in utter disbelief.

Damn it!

In all her rush to get to the library, Olivia hadn't bothered to clean up the chaos caused by Darren. It had been pretty awful when it happened, but now coming home and seeing the destruction in bright, glaring light made the room look all the worse. Glass shards from her treasured, broken vase were scattered everywhere. Torn, mangled flowers littered the couch and floors. A massive wet spot

97

remained prominently on the wall where Darren had flung it. A standing testament to the horror that transpired in Harper's absence.

Immobilized, Harper stood trembling, unable to speak. Her eyes toured the room. Harper looked down. A broken piece of the vase near her boot triggered a flash of terrifying memories to resurface. The room began to twirl and spin. She no longer had control over her legs, and her knees started to buckle. Without warning, she collapsed to the floor, tearing at her hair and moaning.

Olivia watched in fear as her stubborn, determined, fifteen-year-old, strong daughter transformed back into the terrified nine-year-old kneeling at the foot of her mother's bed, while she begged her to wake up to breathe. "Harper!" Olivia cried, rushing forward to envelop the quivering child in her arms. "I'm sorry. I'm so sorry, baby." Olivia couldn't stop apologizing. "I should have warned you, but I left in such a hurry...I wasn't thinking..."

"Leave me alone," Harper shrieked through fast, shallow breaths. "Don't touch me," she screamed, thrusting her palms out, squirming out of her mother's embrace. "You promised..." Harper crawled towards her backpack and hugged it close to her chest, rocking. "You promised, you promised."

Olivia snatched Harper's sweater, attempting to tug her back, but all it did was stretch. "I know how this looks, but I swear to you, I *swear* to you, I didn't break my promise. If you'd just let me explain..."

But Harper couldn't hear her mother. Too trapped behind a wall of grief. "It's happening again," she moaned, slumped over, swaying. She pressed her pallid face into her bag, hiding from the destruction surrounding her. "Just like I said it would...all over again," she sobbed. "All over again. It's happening," Harper kept repeating between large gulps of choked air.

Olivia leaned forward, edging as close as she could to Harper without actually touching her. She so badly wanted to soothe her daughter's pain away. Comfort and protect her from the terror threatening to steal her lucidity.

Come back to me, Harper, Olivia's eyes pleaded. *Let me be here for you.*

Olivia thought about how quickly everything could change. How only hours before she'd felt that she and Harper had finally gotten past some of the hostility plaguing their tenuous relationship. But now, that all vanished as if it never happened. The two remained seated amongst the splintered glass and strewn debris, close but not close enough. Within reach, but not touching. Hearing, but not listening.

"Please," Olivia whispered through pleading, quivering lips, but Harper would neither move nor respond to her mother's appeals, much too lost in a netherworld of hurt, *just like before.*

CHAPTER 8

Cornelia

Irwin tugged the garage door down. As usual, Bones, named by his owner's unhealthy obsession with Star Trek and all things sci-fi, lay waiting for Irwin by the side entrance of his house, in anticipation of his daily bowl of milk and nibbles. His long tail flitted and curled. His penetrating, judgmental, emerald eyes remained glued to Irwin's every movement. Usually, Irwin would have already fed the small, not-homeless-but-acts-like-he-is-cat, but normal no longer applied to any aspect of Irwin's tumultuous life.

"Don't blame me," Irwin grumbled at the cat as he inserted his key into the side door. Unfazed, Bones continued to wrap his furry body around Irwin's lower leg. "Would you please stop that? And where is your human mother?" Bones purred in response. "And why doesn't she feed you?"

"I am here, and I do feed him," responded Bones's human companion, Ms. Cornelia Parish—

writer, author of cozy murder mysteries, and local historian. "He's just greedy and plump." Of course, this fact made the cat's name more nonsensical.

Cornelia labored up the stoop steps, trailing Irwin inside. She lifted a stack of unopened mail and began sifting through it, making herself at home at his kitchen table. "You might want to open a few of these sometime soon," she said, indicating another growing pile of unopened envelopes shoved in a napkin holder.

"I pay my bills."

"Bully for you, but I wasn't referring to your bills." She waved a pale cream envelope in the air. "This one looks mighty official. Says here it's from the Law offices of Mun…"

Irwin plucked the envelope from her fingers.

"Testy." Cornelia dropped the mail where she had found it to fetch mugs from the cabinet for tea. "Having any?"

"Might as well. I didn't get a chance to eat yet." Irwin turned on the kettle, then stuck the envelope between the pages of his leather journal. The same journal used for all the notes he took for a book he swore he planned to write but hadn't actually started. Irwin lifted the semi-cooked, room-temperature potpie to his nose and took a whiff. "Safe enough." He placed it on the floor next to a bowl of milk. "There you go, you conniving, self-absorbed, hairy interloper."

Bones circled and purred.

"You're welcome."

"What?" asked Cornelia, standing by the counter, staring off into space.

"I was talking to the cat."

"The who? Oh. Right. Him."

Irwin turned the flame under the kettle higher. "Where were you just coming from?"

"Who me?"

"No. Bones."

Cornelia rolled her eyes. "Doctor's appointment."

"Oh? Rather late. Is everything all right?" Irwin noticed Cornelia's lips pucker.

"Just my yearly check-up," she said, averting her eyes.

Something was going on, but Irwin, already drained, didn't press her. Without further discourse, Irwin and Cornelia each settled into their regular routine, setting the table like an old married couple. Cornelia placed an Earl Gray tea bag into each of their cups, their agreed favorite. Irwin preferred his tea with two heaping teaspoons of sugar and no milk, while she fancied her cuppa super light but without sugar.

Cornelia popped opened a tin of Danish butter cookies while Irwin set out two small dessert plates, napkins, and two spoons. "Ew," she groaned, face scrunched up. "These cookies don't taste right." She turned the tin over to check the date. "Not expired. Still, sort of stale."

"I just bought them," said Irwin, grabbing one for himself. He took a bite. "No, they taste fine. Are you coming down with a cold? That can change your taste buds."

Cornelia sniffed the cookie and took another bite. She wrinkled her nose. "Are you sure? They taste weird to me."

Irwin popped the rest of the cookie into his mouth. "Nope. They taste perfectly fine to me. You may be coming down with the flu. Touches of flu can get nasty this time of the year. I really think you should give your doctor a ring."

"Enough already," she unexpectedly snapped. "I heard you the first time."

Irwin didn't respond.

"Change of subject. Did you go today?" Cornelia asked, much like she did every Friday evening over tea and cookies.

"I did."

"And? Did you tell her?" Oddly enough, Cornelia never spoke of Gilly in the past tense, endearing her to Irwin more. After Gilly had died, many of their mutual friends stopped coming around or asking about her or Dakota. The absence of hearing her name spoken aloud hurt, but the erasure hurt more.

Cornelia had known Gilly before Irwin and had been the one to introduce them. The two women met back when Cornelia volunteered at the high school where Gilly taught. The school had been on the lookout for volunteers to help run the student theater group. Gilly, always resourceful and outgoing, weaseled Cornelia's name and information from a mutual associate and made her pitch.

Initially, Cornelia had not been enthused by the idea of working with amateurs, much less teenagers, but by then she'd been widowed for over three years, and the loneliness and boredom had been particularly stifling. Moreover, her authorship didn't do much to curb the feeling of isolation since she mostly worked from home, stuck behind a computer screen. Except for the occasional luncheons or her monthly interactions with the historical society, Cornelia socialized little—not counting time spent with her neighbor and close friend, Irwin. Another introvert—of a degree that put her life of loneliness to absolute shame.

And so Cornelia half-heartedly agreed to Gilly's request, but it had turned out to be one of the best decisions made in a long time, propelling her back into the world of the still living.

The two women, Gilly, the perky and pretty high school English teacher turned stage director, and Cornelia, the flippant murder mystery writer, trying her hand at scriptwriting, wound up working closely together. The pair had hit it off from the start, becoming fast friends. For the duration of the play, the two women remained inseparable, spending rushed bag lunches in the school's auditorium, munching on sandwiches and chips, and swapping intimate details of their less than perfect lives.

Cornelia often confided in Gilly about the lonesomeness of widowhood.

"Since Bill died, I barely hear from any of our mutual friends." It had made Cornelia sad how most people couldn't handle death, choosing to trickle away as if widowhood, by proximity, was something to fear, something contagious. "When he first died, I'd wake up feeling disoriented, my nightgown drenched in sweat. During the day, I could put most of my fears to the side, but at night, alone, my imagination would kick in, and I'd get scared thinking about what would happen to me, if say, I ever became seriously ill or disabled. Even facing the most mundane tasks overwhelmed me. My throat would contract, and my head would begin to pound. In all probability, I probably had a full-fledged anxiety attack. Scary as hell. Feels like a heart attack. Shoot—I remember once how a broken window latch or single drip from the faucet brought me crashing to my knees, sniveling. Can you imagine? Over a broken window latch!"

In fits of laughter, Cornelia shared with Gilly how scared she felt the first time she brought her car in for an oil change and inspection. Cornelia had known, of course, where to go, taking it to the same place her husband brought both their vehicles for years, but for the entirety of their long marriage, that had been Bill's understood "job." So, not wanting to appear stupid, Cornelia practiced car-mechanic speak in her head as if she were writing dialogue for one of her mysteries with her playing the role of protagonist. She spent countless hours researching automotive maintenance as if studying for an exam. As it turned out, all her energies had been for naught since the mechanic, after a polite hello, barely said five words to her the entire time.

Gilly disclosed specifics about her marital difficulties, the humiliation that came from dealing with a venal man, known in closed circles as a shameless philander who favored younger women's beds over hers. She explained in painful but exacting detail how Stan barely helped around the house or with their daughter. "He barely comes home. Most of the time you can find him playing multiple rounds of golf with his work buddies or sliding his ass on some barstool, smelling like a bottle of cheap cologne."

Cornelia put down her bag of potato chips to search in her purse. "Bingo." She handed Gilly a tissue.

"Stan cheats on me with anything with two legs. The younger, the blonder, the stupider, the better."

Cornelia despised Stan. She'd heard the rumors and seen him on occasion. Gilly wasn't exaggerating. The man was a malignant adulterer. "You deserve better than him."

Gilly snorted. "Yeah, well, if you know anyone who's a real man…who can hold down a job, has minimal emotional baggage to contend with, is trustworthy, loyal, gentle on the eyes, and wouldn't mind a teenager thrust down his throat, let me know. I filed for divorce last week. Stan will probably try to contest it, but if he doesn't, I'll be free in ninety days."

"Oh, Gilly, divorce? That's a big step."

"One I should have taken years ago. I wanted to stay together for the sake of Dakota, but it's so tense in the house now that even she is begging me to be done with him."

"I'm so sorry." Cornelia popped a chip into her mouth. "No. I'm not. I mean, I'm sorry that your marriage didn't work out, of course, but you deserve so much more than Stan can give."

Gilly stuck her hand in the proffered snack bag and snatched a handful of chips. "I never wanted to be a single parent."

Cornelia smiled. "You might not have to be once I introduce you to someone who I think would be perfect for you."

"What are you talking about?" Gilly grinned. "I'm not even divorced yet."

"Technically. You've been alone for years."

Gilly shrugged. "True, but still. Who would want a middle-aged woman with a degenerate ex-husband and a teenage girl?"

"Yes, Stan is a degenerate, but you're a beautiful, smart, and wonderful person with a lovely daughter. A catch in my book, and I know the perfect man for you."

Gilly rolled her eyes and shook her head. "Yeah. Okay."

"I do!"

"Uh huh."

"Do you trust me?"

"You know I do, but…"

"Then let me do my thing."

***

Cornelia reflected on the friendship the two women had and missed Gilly all over again. Gilly had been a beautiful person. Trustworthy. Easy to talk to and smart. She'd been passionate about her pupils' lives but, most of all, a fantastic mother to Dakota. The whole package in human form and, precisely what drew Cornelia to believe, a more than perfect match for Irwin. And although technically still married at the time, that did little to dissuade Cornelia from dropping hints to Gilly about her neighbor-buddy on the sly while executing a steady stream of stealth matchmaking techniques.

Irwin cleared his throat, jarring Cornelia's attention back onto him. "Irwin to Cornelia, do you register?"

"Sorry," she said. "And?" she asked, where she'd left off.

"And what?" Irwin pretended not to know what she meant.

Cornelia frowned. She loved the man with all her heart, but honestly, she could choke him half the time.

"Fine," he grumbled. "I told Gilly all I knew. I'll fill her in once I hear more from the doctor, but from what I've been told, nothing can move forward until Stan signs off on it. Legally, he still gets to call all the shots about what's ultimately done with the child he neglected and abandoned. That's if they can find him."

"And what if they don't?"

Irwin rubbed his temples. "That I don't know," to which he added sadly, "but what I do know is that Dakota's body is giving out. She's dying, Cornelia. Can't even breathe on her own anymore." Irwin closed his eyes. "At least the doctor had been kind enough to fill me in, but at the end of the day, and as selfish as this sounds, I'm not ready to lose her too."

The kettle whistled, jarring the pair. Cornelia stood and placed a hand on Irwin's shoulder, giving it a gentle squeeze. No more words were necessary. Old friends didn't always need to elaborate when it came to circumstances like these. Their pain, collective loss, and old haunts often spoke volumes.

She poured hot water into each mug and placed them on the table. She'd wait Irwin out, having learned a long time ago that when faced with tribulations as enormous as these, he often needed the extra time to process before discussing. After Gilly died, it had taken Irwin months before opening up, and even then, he never was quite the same.

"Oh," said Irwin, distracted. "Thanks." He slid his cup close to sweeten his tea.

Cornelia sank back into her chair. She glanced over at Bones, currently stretched out on Irwin's sofa, licking his paws and grooming his shiny coat. Irwin liked to joke that he had adopted the two of them, while Cornelia knew for a fact it was more like the other way around. "Why were you so late tonight?" she asked. "Mr. Bones had a conniption waiting for you to show up."

Irwin placed two cookies on the edge of his plate. Vanilla wafers filled with crème, his guilty pleasure. "Where do I begin?"

"Preferably at the beginning, if you can swing it."

"The beginning it is." Irwin propped his elbow on the table, resting his chin on his palm. "I'm faced with a dilemma, if I choose to accept the assignment."

Cornelia sipped her tea. "You have piqued my interest. Elaborate."

Irwin tasted his tea, then placed his cup down on the saucer. "There's a young girl, I'd say about fifteen years old, give or take. I can never figure ages out. Anyway, she comes to the library after school lets out, every single day, and stays until closing. Until tonight, I wasn't entirely sure why."

"Why what?" asked Cornelia. "That she comes to the library?"

"Every single day?"

Cornelia seemed ready to say something, but Irwin interjected first.

"Don't misunderstand me, I've seen my fair share of loners and manic super students working at the library, but this one never gave me that impression."

Cornelia sighed. "What's the big deal? Maybe the kid likes to read."

"It's not that."

"Then what exactly is the conundrum?"

Irwin drummed a lone finger on the table. "It's her home life, or more accurately, her 'sperm donor'—her description, not mine. I had the displeasure of meeting him this evening. And as a result, I now believe I might have discovered why this kid avoids going home."

Cornelia leaned forward. "This sounds serious."

"I agree," Irwin said, his lips twisted in a scowl. "Turns out that her...um..."

"Sperm donor."

"Yes, thank you. He just got released from state prison, and he's out on parole."

"Messy."

"He's a real piece of work."

"And the mother?"

"Tricky. I met her tonight at the library as well."

"What's she like?"

"She seemed 'normal' enough," he said, making air quotes, "much more personable than her ex."

Cornelia shrugged. "At least the girl has her mom."

"Ah, well, this is where the plot thickens because I have also come to find out that she too has a murky past."

"Murky as in?"

"Former drug addict. They both were. Actually, daddy dearest may still be. It's hard to tell. Harper said he got time for assault and drugs."

"Harper? I assume that's the wife?"

"No. The kid."

"Ah. That's rough," agreed Cornelia. "The stress Harper must be under—no wonder she camps out at the library. Poor thing lives with nothing but chaos and unpredictability."

"That's what I thought as well." Irwin drank his tea

"And what about friends?"

Irwin shook his head. "I've never seen her with anyone her age. In my humble and limited opinion, I think she prefers it that way."

Cornelia grimaced. "That's a strange comment to make."

"If you met her, you'd know what I mean."

Cornelia plucked another cookie from the tin. "And what part, if any, do you play in this family tragedy?" She bit down. "Ewww, I swear! Something's wrong with these damn cookies." Cornelia dropped the cookie on her plate.

"Good question. And to be honest, I'm not sure,

except the kid has latched onto me. For whatever reason, Harper's got it into her head that I can do something to help her." Irwin threw his palms in the air. "I've barely spoken to this kid if you don't count our daily exchange of obnoxious notes and verbal potshots."

Cornelia laughed. "There's got to be a good story in there. I'm sure of it."

Irwin ran his fingers through his gray, coarse hair. "I need a haircut."

"You do unless the homeless look is what you're aiming for, but don't change the subject. How did you get pulled into all of this?"

"Oh. This gets better. Regan."

"Regan?" snorted Cornelia. "The silly Pooh Bear girl?"

"The one and only. She phoned me this evening saying that Harper had locked herself in the women's bathroom and refused to come out. He, the father, followed her to the library after showing up at her house unannounced and threatening to move back in."

"Where's the guy staying now?"

"Harper said at a halfway house, but she doesn't know for how long."

Cornelia winced. "Hmmm, I sort of recall those places were called something else now…residential rehabilitation centers? Or was it a community correctional center?"

"I have no idea and care even less."

"Is there any chance the mother will let daddy dearest back in?"

"Not from what I've gathered, but who knows?"

Cornelia tapped the table with her finger. "If I'm not mistaken, if he's on parole, he's not allowed to do that."

"What do you mean not allowed?"

"I mean that he's still considered a prisoner— just out on parole. From what I've heard, those places have strict rules in place."

Irwin appeared perplexed.

"In other words, he can't be just popping up all over the place like that. Don't quote me, but I'm almost positive they need permission from their parole officers to go visit family. I suggest you look into that."

Irwin nodded. "Good idea."

"That would be a good start, right?" Cornelia asked optimistically.

Irwin shrugged. "Again, this is only speculation on the part of a troubled girl. Every story has two sides, and then there's the truth."

"Maybe." Cornelia reached towards the tin to grab for another cookie then stopped. "And maybe not."

Irwin slid the tin closer to her.

"No." She waved him away. "I'm done."

"Are you sure?"

"I'm sure."

Irwin covered the tin.

"You know, Irwin, back when I volunteered at the high school, there were more students than I care to admit who came from these same types of challenged households. Good kids with a ton of potential but saddled with messed-up home lives. Their behavior would become erratic. Warmhearted

SAHAR ABDULAZIZ

one minute, withdrawn the next. I'm sure this Harper child loves her mother, but she's probably feeling angry. Maybe hurt as well. Many of the kids I worked with blamed themselves for their family issues, upset that they couldn't cure their parent's substance abuse problems, which, besides being impossible, was not their job."

"She did seem frightened of the father," Irwin agreed. "I suspect he hurt her."

"I wouldn't be surprised. Drug abuse and domestic abuse go hand-in-hand. Let's pray it wasn't sexual."

Irwin flinched. "Must you?"

"Yes, I must. It's a real possibility and one you better be prepared for."

"Me? Oh no, not me," he said emphatically, shaking his head. "What can I do? I'm a librarian, for goodness sakes. Not a social worker."

"Harper's obviously reaching out to you, Irwin."

"Then she's reaching in the wrong direction."

"There you go again."

"What?"

"Crawling back into your hole to hide."

Miffed, Irwin frowned. "For your information, my plate is full—practically overflowing. I can't handle anything else right now."

"Oh, poo. Utter nonsense. The girl picked you to help her. You can't just turn your back."

Irwin scowled.

Cornelia tried a different tactic. "Is she nice?"

"Who? Harper?"

"Who else are we talking about, ya big dope?"

"How would I know?" Irwin huffed. "She's a

114

teenager."

"She's also a victim."

"She's also an impertinent juvenile delinquent."

"I seriously doubt that."

Irwin moaned.

"Okay, maybe so, but at least this kid is awake and breathing on her own." Cornelia faltered. She hadn't meant to sound unsympathetic, but the words had slipped out before she could rein them back in.

Irwin pretended to pull a knife out of his chest.

"Sorry," she said. "I probably went too far." Cornelia appreciated how Irwin cared and oversaw Dakota's care for years without complaint or fanfare. She respected how he made double and triple sure that anyone who worked at the hospital knew somebody loved and cared about the girl. Cornelia had suspected for the longest time that the weekly bouquets were only the tip of the iceberg. Over time, Irwin's attachment had become a sort of tunnel vision, a way to keep his connection with Gilly alive. But now, as his sleeping princess neared the end of her physical journey, Cornelia had noticed Irwin entering a dark depression, and she was worried.

Coma or not, Cornelia knew Dakota had filled a vacant, lonesome void in Irwin's stunted personal life, albeit one-sided. She provided Irwin with a purpose; she was the consummate listener. Uncomplaining and unclaimed. As horrifying as Dakota's long suffering had been over the years, her existence still provided Irwin with constancy. However, what Cornelia felt Irwin failed to realize was how his attachment to Dakota had succeeded to dominate his life to the point that he could no longer separate himself from the outcome, even if he tried.

Harper, on the other hand, was very much alive. And a real handful, from what she had gathered, more from what Irwin left out of their conversation. As far as Cornelia was concerned, the more obstinate and head-strong the kid was, the better, trusting that Harper could be the ticket Irwin needed to rejoin the world of the living as an active card-carrying member. Perhaps even the catalyst to help heal his shattered heart. "You can help this kid, Irwin."

Irwin sardonically chuckled. "Like I helped Dakota?"

"Dakota is an entirely different situation, and you know it. Completely out of your control."

"For all the good it did."

"No!" Cornelia yelled. "I won't let you do this to yourself. You never abandoned Dakota. You've been by that girl's side through thick and thin, and that's a lot more than I can say for her worthless tool of a father." Cornelia despised Stanley Satterfield and didn't care who knew it.

"You're forgetting, Cornelia, Harper's got a mother and father."

"But she doesn't have anyone to count on, which is why she reached out to you. Be an example for her. Show her that there are still adults in the world she can trust. Prove to her that not everybody's out to use and abuse her. You can reach her, Irwin."

"I don't know how."

"She'll teach you. You just have to be willing to open yourself up to try. The rest will take care of

116

itself." Cornelia hated watching her good friend beat himself up for a crime he never committed. Languishing under some self-imposed punishment, guilt-ridden. It seemed beyond cruel. And as much as she hated to admit it, despite how much she loved Gilly, there were times like now when Cornelia wished she had never introduced them.

Just then, Bones sauntered his lazy self across the room over to his bowl.

"That reminds me—can furry dude stay with you tonight?" asked Cornelia. "I'm meeting some friends downtown for brunch tomorrow, and I'd rather not leave him alone. He's been acting kind of clingy lately."

Irwin glared down at the supercilious cat. "Sure."

"Great."

Irwin walked the dirty dishes to the sink.

"Well, time for me to pack it in for the night." Cornelia feigned a yawn. "I'm exhausted, and I have a big day tomorrow." She stood and stretched. "Remember, Irwin. Harper needs a friend right now and like it or not, you're it."

Irwin groaned and began washing out the mugs.

"Stop with all the moaning." Then Cornelia knelt to whisper in Bones's ear. "Keep an eye out on our mutual friend for me." She scratched behind his ear. "I suspect he's going through another rough patch. He'll need us more than ever, even if the big dope doesn't know it yet."

Bones purred. Cornelia could have sworn that darn cat understood his mission and had to hold back from laughing as she watched him nestle in for the night, with one lazy eye glued on Irwin's every movement.

CHAPTER 9

Darren

"You're late," said Jay McCloskey, the resident supervisor. He waited in the hall, his arms crossed over his chest, leaning casually on the door frame. "You missed your call-in. Where were you? Answer in that order."

"'You're late' and 'you missed your call-in' are not questions," answered Darren.

Jay didn't seem to be in the mood to volley. "We have rules, programs, work requirements, and curfews. Are you with me so far, Crane?"

Darren nodded, slouching.

"That means you not only have to ask for permission before you leave, but you have to check in at specified intervals." Jay gave Darren a tight-lipped smile. "If this is a problem for you, let me know now."

Darren shoved his hands into his pockets. "I don't have a cell phone."

"You don't have a cell phone," repeated Jay.

"Then I suggest you get one. No money? Get a job. Notice the common denominator?"

Darren nodded.

"Unless I know where you are and what business you have there, you don't leave the premises, which frankly defeats the purpose of you being here."

"What do you mean, purpose?"

"To re-enter society. Not as the resident parasite and malcontent you obviously are, but as a successful, contributing member of society. Now follow me." Jay didn't wait for Darren to respond and headed towards the back of the building to his office. "Crane!"

"Coming," mumbled Darren, lagging behind. He fingered the worn, torn self-help posters on the wall with disdain, wishing he could make a damn decision for himself again.

"Take a seat." Jay pointed to the single plastic-metal chair facing his desk.

Darren sat. He bent over, leaned his elbows on his knees, and ran his bony fingers through his short, cropped hair, preparing for the speech.

Darren hated the talks. Had them directed at him for most of his life, from grade school to middle school, and all throughout high school. Where high school left off, prison took over. What pissed him off more than anything else was the fact that the talks weren't talking at all. More like one-sided reprimands lauded above him with the sole intention of making him feel small and inconsequential. His existence remained outside his control, but most definitely within theirs.

High school had been a breeze compared to

prison life. While inside, Darren left the correctional officers alone. He didn't want any trouble with them or the other inmates and kept mostly to himself. Which was not an easy feat considering the severe overcrowding issue, not to mention the rash of daily unprovoked violence and fights.

It hadn't taken long for Darren to lose his damn mind. By his second day on the tier, they assigned him a cellmate. The mere thought of sharing tight quarters with another man drove him berserk. The correctional officers gave Darren a stern warning to tone his irrational behavior down before he wound up doing the rest of his time in solitary confinement.

Darren soon learned a hard lesson: prison staff didn't give a damn's worth about his or any other inmate's accommodations. Their comfort didn't register. Nor did most of their complaints. Their house, their rules, applied. Eventually, Darren grew accustomed to York, his celly—short for a cellmate—being around. York turned out to be the best kind of celly a guy could not ask for. He was quiet, unassuming, minded his own business, and left Darren's stuff alone. York didn't want to stir trouble and kept mostly to himself. With only four years left to finish his sentence, York refused to make it stretch for a minute more.

For the most part, York had been easy for Darren to talk to since he didn't need to qualify his frustration or hopelessness to York. They were both wallowing away on the same sinking boat: facing time, surrounded by other screw-ups, rejected by society, and branded as losers, but most of all, saddled with families who had long ago written them both off.

At the beginning of his sentence, Darren wrote Olivia countless letters apologizing and begging her to visit him. "Just let me make it up to you," he'd write, but she returned them, mangled but unopened. He also tried phoning but had to do it collect. Olivia wouldn't budge, blocking any calls that came from the prison.

"The first thing I do when I get out is bang on this woman's door," he'd confided in York one evening after getting his last letter returned unopened.

York had put down the book he had been reading. "You may want to rethink that strategy, my man."

"She's my wife."

"She *was* your wife. You gotta let it go. You've got too much time ahead of you to be obsessing over what you're gonna do when you get out— especially to her. She's not the reason why your ass is in here. You and I both know that."

In desperation, Darren wrote to his mother. As expected, she never wrote or came to visit him. No surprise, with her being a life-long career addict herself. For all he knew or cared, she could have been in prison herself. He never bothered to contact his father.

Jay tapped a pen on his desk to get Darren's attention. "Speaking of…job hunt. Status?" Jay's art of conversation gravitated towards a vernacular consumed primarily of staccato quasi-sentences.

Darren stared at the ground, buying time to

formulate a good enough response in his head. Running a bunch of different scenarios and weighing out which reply would produce what reaction. A complicated game of Cat and Mouse but with high stakes. One slip-up, that's all it took to send him back inside. The fact was, Darren hadn't looked anywhere. Too busy trying to get Olivia to give him a break and let him come back home, but there was no way in hell he would admit to that, so he colored his dishonesty with half-truths and hoped for the best.

"I went to the library. Heard they were looking to hire a handyman or something, but no luck."

Jay jotted that fabricated tidbit of misinformation into his notepad. "And today? What's on your agenda?"

Darren squinted. "I, err, have group counseling in the afternoon."

"With Gallagher?"

"I guess so."

Who the hell is Gallagher?

Darren made a mental note to recheck his welcome packet.

Jay marked that down too. Once finished, he placed his pen down and glared at Darren. "I'm only going to say this once." Darren shifted uncomfortably in his chair. "You have two choices. One, you follow the rules, do your time, get yourself situated and have a nice life, or two, you screw it up, in which case, I'll send you back inside where you can rot until your sentence is up. With a limited amount of time here, I suggest you choose wisely."

Full sentences. This was serious.

With pursed lips, Darren dipped his head and glared. "We done?"

"Go."

Darren didn't need to be told twice and bolted for the door.

"Halt," shouted Jay. "Confirm again. Where are you staying after here?"

"Whadda you mean?"

Shit. He knows.

"I mean, is the address on your submission form still current?" Jay asked, flicking through his notes.

Unsure whether Jay posed a rhetorical question or a set-up, Darren got ready to tell his second lie of the day. "Same address. Nothing's changed." He held his breath.

Jay slapped the desk with his palms. "Good enough." He slid the paper into the folder, presumably Darren's file. "Then have a good day, Mr. Crane. Shut the door behind you."

Dismissed.

***

Back in high school, Darren aspired to open a repair shop—"Crane's Automotive Repair Shop." He had always been handy with his hands, gifted with mechanical intuition, and a real natural with tools. While he may not have known the difference between an adjective and an adverb, he sure could take apart and put together a carburetor with his eyes closed. His friends joked that Darren had the uncanny ability to give beat-up old engines ready for the graveyard a second, if not a third, life.

Then he started hanging out with the wrong crowd. Started to drink and use drugs to fit in. Began stealing prescription drugs from his mother's medicine cabinet finding them easy to conceal, consume, and sell.

Darren hit the rave scene running and got heavy into it. As a cheap designer drug, Ecstasy's only job was to keep the user high; however, because it was also a stimulant, it kept Darren awake for days experiencing hallucinations. His vision became distorted and blurred, he often saw shadows where shadows didn't exist, and he swore items were shifting despite being entirely still. All in good fun until his occasional drug use morphed into a severe and addictive habit.

Darren and Olivia had met back in high school. Two sweet, regular kids under intense social pressure to conform and fit in. Two ordinary, sweet teens saddled with family problems and unable to cope. Childhood sweethearts who found safety in the arms of one another.

Olivia had been a better student than Darren, but not by much. She struggled to make good grades while he chose to ignore his studies and get high. Olivia knew Darren used, but most of the kids she hung out with in high school either drank, smoked, popped pills, or experimented with something. She didn't come from a life of intoxication, so for her, his drug use hadn't seemed like a big deal, comprehending too late how her boyfriend's occasional use had turned into full-blown abuse.

Olivia's mother had never liked Darren. She'd

seen trouble from day one and had repeatedly warned her daughter to stay away, but the more she had pressured or threatened Olivia to drop Darren, the harder he'd worked to convince Olivia to screw whatever her mother thought.

Darren leaned on the wall behind the school where all the potheads hung out. "I know she's your mom's and all, but fuck her, Liv."

"You don't understand, she's really mad this time," Olivia explained. "I mean, like, the maddest I've ever seen her. This morning she threatened to send me away to some military boarding school or something if I keep seeing you."

"She's bullshitting. You're sixteen. You could legally drop out if you wanted to."

"No, I think it's seventeen to drop out in Pennsylvania."

"Whatever." Darren opened his palm. "Take this and chill already."

"I can't. I have a test, third period, and if I fail, she'll really kill me."

Darren popped the Ecstasy in his mouth. "Suit yourself."

Olivia kicked a pebble at the wall with the bottom of her sneaker. "It wouldn't kill you to do better in school too, you know."

"What for?"

Olivia shrugged. "For your future."

Darren laughed. "My future, huh. That's a joke, right?"

By his last year, Darren had slipped so deep into

drugs he could no longer keep up with his studies. As soon as he turned seventeen, he dropped out. And without immediate family for support or guidance, he dove into a loop of dysfunction, spiraling from Ecstasy to crack to heroin in no time flat. However, funding his demanding habit soon took precedence in such a way that he wound up doing anything to score. Behaviors that, if sober, would have appalled him. Such as when he asked around to find out what his drug dealer's girlfriend wanted for her birthday and then stole that specific item to his dealer to trade for drugs. Or that time he attended a church service just to abscond with the money from the offering plate. As a drug addict, his moral depravity knew no boundaries, no obstacles. His cravings to satisfy his compulsion took priority over any genuine feelings he may have had. Nobody around Darren was safe, not even his daughter.

One day, while Olivia had been out shopping, Darren, desperate for a fix, sold Harper's crib, the one Olivia's mom had bought when she'd come over one day unannounced and found her grandbaby sleeping on the cold floor. When Olivia returned home and found out what Darren had done, she went berserk. Threatened to leave him until he pulled out of his pocket their next hit. Then all was forgotten. Washed away in a fog.

Together the pair existed in a state of limbo, a never-ending, vicious cycle. Stealing, lying, manipulating to get high, only to crash. Up-down-up-down, and all along. After a while, nothing but addicts and dealers comprised his inner circle. For him, Harper barely existed. Often left to fend for herself. Neglected. Not even her safety could compete with her parent's drug habit.

But like all drug abusers, Darren's biggest delusion had been in convincing himself that nobody knew what he was up to. That he felt, appeared, and sounded just fine. Completely unaware of how to everyone else, his speech and thought patterns seemed grossly disorganized, schizophrenic-like. How his body had started to appear emaciated from loss of appetite, his face tired and gaunt. Dark circles under his eyes only served to accentuate his pale complexion. But the biggest giveaway was in that drug-fiend way he walked around, always scratching and slumped over in the strangest positions. Often mistaken for older than his mere twenty-plus years.

For Darren, every choice, every decision, every action centered on acquiring the next high, the next hit. Nothing else mattered. Not his dream of opening his own business, rapidly blowing up in a puff of smoke. Not his dwindling circle of drug-free friends, who, after catching him pilfering through their personal belongings for anything to steal or hock, eventually gave up trying to get through to him. And not Olivia or even the child he had on the way. Darren risked it all for the promise of that next high, adamantly refusing to get help, blinded to his irrational and destructive behavior. The rest of the world had the problem, not him. So deluded…so convinced that he controlled his destiny, when in fact, his thought patterns remained muddled, self-serving, and trapped in a heroin cloud of chaos.

***

Darren headed down the hall and upstairs to his room. He needed to be away from everybody to rethink his plan of action. Come up with another way to convince Olivia to take him back, to give him another chance. He hadn't meant to lose his temper the way he did, but she could make him so mad.

Why had he assumed Olivia would be easy to win back over, considering all that transpired the night he had abandoned her over six years ago? Maybe because of how pliable and easy to manipulate she had been when they were both younger...dumber...and needed each other. But he didn't see any of that in her now. More of a determination and willpower, and that scared him.

He thought for sure when he chucked her mother's vase, Olivia would have given in. Instead, she gave him lip. Then, when he lunged, she kept mouthing off. Staring straight at him with hate. Yes, most discernibly, hate.

She despises me.

Darren shook his head, utterly confused. This new stubbornness wasn't at all expected. Coupled with Harper's lack of respect, he was in for a real ride.

Before Darren had a chance to close his door, he heard his name being called.

"Crane! You got a visitor," yelled the unfamiliar voice.

Darren shut his door, confused as to who would be coming to see him. At the bottom of the steps, he stopped short and groaned. "Oh. It's you."

CHAPTER 10

Irwin

"I'm sorry, ma'am, but we are a library. We loan out books. We do not sell postage stamps," said Irwin to the elderly woman stooped before him, holding out her change purse. "Is there anything else I can do for you?"

The woman mumbled a few colorful obscenities in response, which Irwin preferred not to bother decoding. She flipped him the bird before hobbling away.

"Next!"

"Hi," greeted an attractively dressed woman about Irwin's age.

"Can I help you?"

"I need to return these." The woman placed a stack of five thick books on the desk, all nonfiction history novels.

Irwin opened the first book and scanned the date. Then the next. As he made his way through the pile, a document from the fourth book slipped out. An

131

old, turn-of-the-century birth certificate. At least over a hundred years old, by his humble estimation. "Is this yours?" he asked.

"Oh, wow! Thank you. I forgot I put that in there." She took the document and hugged it tightly to her chest. "What was I thinking?" She had a lovely smile. "This belonged to my great-grandmother. I've been doing a bit of research lately, family-tree stuff. I'm trying to learn a bit more about how and when she came to this country and what she must have gone through to get here."

Irwin nodded. "While we have an extensive shelf of books about this period upstairs, you may find the e-books and film footage more helpful. The film cannot be removed from the library, but you could read through old newspaper clippings, birth records, that sort of thing. It may prove useful in your search."

"Oh, terrific. You're wonderful. Upstairs?"

Irwin blushed and pointed. "Anything else?"

"No, but thank you, again. I would have hated to lose this," she said, waving the birth certificate. "Well, bye."

Irwin reddened. "Next!" he called.

From across the room, Harper was watching him, evidently amused.

When did she get here?

He hadn't seen her slip in.

How much of that last interaction did she catch?

By the know-it-all smirk spread across her selfie-snapping-teen-blog-posting-face, all of it. Irwin repaid the girl's grin with a sneer.

Undaunted, Harper apparently took Irwin's

reaction as an invitation and ambled up to the side of the reception desk.

The next person in line, an elderly gentleman, decked out in hunting gear, a camouflage cap, and an orange vest, moved forward. Harper leaned her elbows on the desk to rest her chin on her palms. "Hi, Irwin."

"Mr. Abernathy to you," he quipped back without looking at her. "Can I help you, sir?" he asked the patron.

"Yep," answered the gruff man, scratching a trail of stubble on his neck so thick and coarse, it looked as if it could suffocate his neck. "Where do you keep the e-books?" he bellowed loudly.

Irwin cocked a brow. "I'm sorry…what did you say?" He leaned in closer. He couldn't have heard correctly.

"He wants to know where you keep the e-books," Harper replied piercingly, a smirk tugging at her mouth, clearly enjoying herself.

Irwin ignored Harper giving the man his full attention. "E-books are online, sir," he explained. "They are electronic books in digital form. We don't *keep* them; we have them on file, on computers. You can download them and watch or read them on your computer or any other electronic device."

"Oh," grumbled the man, seeming disheartened and still somewhat confused. "Well, I don't have a computer," he complained. "Now what do I do?"

Irwin's jaw tensed. Before executing one of his infamous sharp retorts, Harper interjected and came to his rescue.

"No problem. The library has a bunch of computers," said Harper cheerfully. "Do you have a library card?" she asked the man.

"Of course I do." The man whipped out a bulky, well-used wallet from his back pocket. With shaky fingers, he slowly thumbed through his collection of cards until he found it. "There you go," he said slapping the card on the desk as if playing poker with a full-house. "Now what?"

"Do you want me to set him up at one of the empty computers, *Mr. A-ber-na-thy*?" asked Harper, giddy with smiles.

Unfazed, Irwin answered the patron, "You have thirty minutes," and slid back his card.

As the man busied himself returning his card to his wallet, Harper leaned over and whispered to Irwin, "You're such a colossal snob, you know that?"

Roger, standing nearby, laughed, then quickly pretended to cough.

"Go," replied Irwin. "Next," he called out.

Harper slipped her arm through the gentleman's and gently guided him to the computer station by the children's section.

"I like her," said Roger over Irwin's shoulder. "She's got spunk."

"Next!"

A few minutes later, Harper returned to her chair. Funny how Irwin had designated that chair as hers in his mind.

For all Harper's prior giggles, Irwin thought the kid looked tired. And a bit sad. He chalked it up to last night's fiasco. However, he didn't have long to ponder before Regan soared from the children's room to the front desk. Her purple glasses bounced on the bridge of her nose as she stomped towards him in full combative mode.

"Who the heck let *that guy* on the computer?" she roared.

"Irwin," answered Roger without looking up from his computer screen.

Irwin side-eyed him. "Is there a problem, Regan?"

"Is there a problem?" she repeated. "Oh, there's a problem all right. Do you know what he's doing over there?"

Irwin shook his head. "No, Regan. I do not have a single clue what he's doing, but I'm sure that any minute now, you'll enlighten me."

"He's watching porn!" she announced loudly. "Hardcore boobs and all, right there near my children's section!" she shrieked.

"What's a hardcore boob?" interjected Roger.

"Lower your voices, both of you!" snapped Irwin, shooting Harper a glare.

Harper shrugged helplessly and mouthed, "Sorry."

"Roger," ordered Irwin, "man the desk while I'm gone. Regan, be quiet and come with me."

"Is there a problem?" asked Janice, turning the corner, pushing a cart full of books.

Regan and Irwin stopped short and shook their heads no in unison. "No. No problem."

"Ah-huh." Janice squinted. "I see. Well, okay then…" she mumbled, not believing either one of them. "I'll be in the back room should you require my assistance."

The last person either of them needed was Janice.

As soon as Janice closed the door, Irwin hightailed it over to where the old man sat entranced. A cacophony of loud moaning and humans gyrating in various contortions filled the computer screen. For once, Regan hadn't been exaggerating.

"Sir," said Irwin, appalled. "You cannot watch that…that…*stuff* in the public library. I'm going to have to ask you to shut it off and leave immediately."

"I still got fifteen minutes," was the old reprobate's only defense.

"For goodness sake." Irwin leaned over, pushed a few buttons, and closed the page down. "Now, leave, before I call security."

"It's the human body," protested the man.

"Pervert," snarled Regan.

After a few more grumbles and complaints, the old man left, but not before snapping to attention and bestowing upon Harper an exaggerated Bronx salute.

Harper cringed. "Gross."

Irwin shook his head in disgust.

I need a shower.

Since that option was out of the question, he settled on a cup of strong coffee from the café. On his way, he pointed at Harper. "Follow me," he ordered, not waiting for a reply.

Harper trailed after him. "You aren't mad at me about that pervy old guy debacle, are you?"

Irwin ignored her question. "Coffee, tea, or juice?" he asked her, once in front of the café counter.

"I'll take a coffee."

"One coffee, light, no sugar. One apple juice," he said to the young barista. "And add two Danish rolls to that, please."

"You got it."

While Irwin paid, Harper sat at the edge of her chair, nervous.

Roger appeared holding the girl's backpack. "Is this yours?" he asked.

"Shit. Oh, I mean, thanks." Harper reached for her pack.

Roger gave Harper a slight nod and winked at Irwin.

Irwin ignored Roger and placed a cup of apple juice and a small paper plate with a Danish in front of Harper. "Eat. Drink."

"I, um, said coffee."

"I know." Irwin sat down. He flipped the plastic lid open and took a cautious swig. "Ahhh, much better."

Harper sipped her juice. Its coolness slid down her parched throat. "Thanks," she said, glad he had ignored her request.

"So, how did you make out last night?"

Harper squirmed in her chair. "All right, I guess."

Irwin took another nip of coffee and a bite of his Danish. "Hmmm, not bad."

Famished, Harper dove into her food. "Pretty good," she agreed, greedily taking another bite.

137

Just as Irwin had suspected. The girl was hungry. He could already hear Cornelia's harping in his head. *"What is wrong with you? Can't you see the child is hungry? Get her another one."* He mumbled something incoherent.

"Did you just say something?" asked Harper.

"What? Oh, no," answered Irwin, flustered. For the next five minutes, the two sat and ate in companionable silence. Irwin sipped his coffee and ate his Danish while scrutinizing Harper as she swallowed and gulped her way through her snack, formulating his next move.

"I better get back to work," he said, dabbing his mouth with a napkin.

"Thanks for the Danish and juice," said Harper brightly.

"You're welcome." Irwin started walking back to his desk.

"And for last night," Harper added.

Irwin heard Harper and threw a half, dismissive wave up in the air. Afterward, he'd regret rushing away instead of talking more.

"I'm back," Irwin informed Roger. "Thanks for covering for me."

"No problemo."

"Did you do as I instructed?"

"All taken care of, *Capitan*."

"Next," yelled Irwin.

***

"Are you kidding me right now?" yelled Cornelia, sitting in Irwin's kitchen. "You never even asked her?" Cornelia slapped the kitchen table, incensed. "I don't understand you sometimes, Irwin. I truly don't. You had the perfect opportunity to get into her head, and you said nothing."

Irwin hated when Cornelia got all worked up, carrying on as if she had all the answers and he was nothing more than some lowly nincompoop. "She didn't want to talk about it," he tried to explain, somewhat contrite.

Cornelia rolled her eyes and groaned. "Teenagers never want to talk about anything. You've got to be smarter than them. Sometimes you have to lead them to the water while their guard is down. Slowly, methodically…make them feel safe before sneaking in a few well-placed questions. I can't believe I have to tell you this."

"I don't think it works like that."

"Oh, it most certainly does."

"I wanted to give her space." Irwin twisted the napkin in his hand.

"Nonsense. You just didn't want to prod, mostly because you hate when people do that to you. Plus, if Harper told you anything of consequence or expected something from you more than a grunt, then you'd feel obligated to do something to help her. And right now, you don't want that responsibility, do you?" Cornelia shook her head. "I get it. I don't agree with it, but I get it."

Cornelia knew him better than he gave her credit for. "Okay, so now what?"

"As in, what do you do now?"

Irwin nodded.

"Nothing. You do absolutely nothing. You

139

should be good at that." Cornelia wasn't holding back but paused to control her temper. "There's nothing for you to do but wait her out until she reaches out to you. If she reaches out to you again."

"You think I blew it?"

"Of course, you blew it." Cornelia leaned in and tapped her finger on the kitchen table. "Answer me this. How can someone so well-read be such a big dummy?" She clasped her hands in front of her. "The next time Harper talks to you, don't slink away and hide. Be there for her. Listen to what she tells you, but most of all, pay close attention to what she's not saying."

"And how am I supposed to listen to what she's not saying?"

"The same way you've been listening to Dakota not say a damn word for the past four years."

"Ouch."

Cornelia flung her arms melodramatically in the air. "I'm sorry, Irwin, if the truth hurts. But it's time you pulled your act together." Cornelia pushed her hair back from her eyes. "You can't stay locked up in your little protected bubble for the rest of your life, pretending that what happens to other people doesn't bother you."

"Why don't you tell me how you really feel?"

"Look, all I'm saying is that you finally had a chance to help somebody who really needs a break, and for whatever reason, this person picked you. Don't you get that? Harper picked you because she sees something in you worth her trust." Cornelia glowered. "I mean it, Irwin. We've been neighbors *and friends* for a long time. I've watched you go from being a whole, happy, human being to an empty, dotty shell of one. I understand Gilly's death devastated you and what happened to Dakota isn't fair, but Harper's here, very much alive and, from what you've described, in some serious trouble."

"I don't know what I can do for her, Cornelia. I am a librarian. I go to work. I come home. I've never been married, and I don't know the first thing about children, and certainly not teenagers. And let's not forget that Harper's got a mother—and a father, for what he's worth. Me? I'm a total stranger."

"A stranger who she's gravitated to—"

"A stranger who has no business messing around in her life."

"No. Nope. Not this time." Cornelia had all but lost her patience.

"What do you mean, *not this time*?"

"I mean I usually stay out of your business, but not this time."

This was news. Cornelia rarely if ever stayed out of his business, but Irwin didn't think mentioning that detail would help him a whole lot right now. "And why not?"

Cornelia looked about to cry but sniffled it back. "Honestly?"

"No, lie to me."

"Because, Irwin, dear, I think your life depends on it."

"Slightly overly dramatic."

Cornelia snorted. "This coming from a man obsessed with mourning his fiancé's death for four solid years, not to mention her comatose daughter."

"That's different, and you know it."

"No, it's safe. Gilly's gone, and Dakota can't complain. Neither one had expectations of you, but Harper is alive, in your face, and could use a helping hand."

"And what if I wind up hurting her more than helping? Then what?"

"You won't."

"You don't know that, Cornelia. I tried to be there for Gilly. She's gone. I tried to be there for Dakota, and now she's leaving me too. I'm just not good with stuff like this."

"Then get good at it," Cornelia stammered, slamming her fist on the table. "Harper needs you," she repeated. "And soon, perhaps you'll realize that you need her too."

"Maybe if I had more time," he mumbled, spent.

"If?" Cornelia found herself again wishing she could turn back time. "Make the time, Irwin. And while you're at it, find yourself again, because frankly, I really miss that guy."

CHAPTER 11

Harper

Harper unlocked the front door, bracing herself, wary a new set of surprises would greet her. Except, thankfully, tonight there were none. All the shards of broken glass were swept up. The pillows on the couch fluffed. The table cleared of junk and cups. Although sparse, the room looked tidy and clean, but she kept her boots on, just in case.

"Mom? Are you home?" she called out, peeking around in the different rooms, but no response.

"Mom? I'm home." Harper flicked on the kitchen light. A note in the middle of the table read:

Harper,
I'm working an extra shift tonight. Will be back late. Dinner's in the fridge, red plastic container. Just warm up in the microwave. Make sure to lock up the house. I'll be

home as soon as I can.
Love, Mom.

Harper placed her mother's note back on the table, dashed to the refrigerator, and tugged. On the middle shelf, as promised, her mother had left her a container filled with what appeared to be pasta and tomato sauce. As dull and as unappealing as it looked, she was starving and wishing she could have indulged in a second helping of that delicious Danish from hours before. But for now, the pasta would suffice.

While waiting for the food to warm up in the microwave, Harper dumped her backpack on the table and pulled out the book Irwin gifted to her, saved for such an occasion. The monitor on the microwave beeped. She left the novel on the table while she went to retrieve her hopefully hot food. One could never be sure with this old model, ready for the trash pile years ago. After placing her food on the table, grabbing a fork, and filling a glass with cold water, she finally felt ready to plop down to a good read.

Harper shifted and scooted around in her chair, rubbed her hands together in anticipation, opened the book to Chapter One.

"What the heck?" A plastic card in a cardboard casing, the size and look of a credit card, slipped out and landed on the kitchen table.

Who? How?

She flipped it over. The front of the gift card displayed the name of the grocery store near the library. Harper's name appeared on the cardboard envelope printed in the precise handwriting she had begun to recognize. Well, not exactly her name, but close enough.

TO: Juvenile Delinquent.
In the amount of $100
From: Mr. Grumpy
PS: Chew with your mouth closed.

How did Irwin pull this off?
Then she remembered. Harper laughed.
When I forgot my bag. And I suppose that librarian dude is in on this too?

This had to be one of the coolest things anybody had ever done for her, that and the book Irwin bought her. She'd never forget the book.

With one hand, Harper held the card, refusing to put it down, lest it disappear. With the other hand, she stabbed cheerfully away at her noodles with a newfound vigor and vitality, shoving mounds-full into her mouth, giddy with excitement and the promise of a much needed, well-stocked refrigerator.

She squeezed her eyes closed and kissed the card. "Thank you, Mr. Abernathy, sir!" Then she paused. Why would Irwin be so generous? A hundred dollars was a lot of money to go giving away to a complete stranger. And while admittedly she didn't qualify any longer as a complete stranger, she sure was close enough. Harper frowned. Would Irwin expect something in return?

Part of her wanted to hit the store tonight. Blow

the entire amount. Every last penny. Buy the snacks and goodies she hadn't indulged in for the longest, and keep it hidden upstairs, her little personal stash.

Selfishness aside, a hundred dollars would buy a nice haul of smart, healthy food—food she and her mother could both enjoy. She remembered the holidays were coming. They'd be running a whole bunch of sales. She'd stop by there on the way to the library tomorrow and pick up their circulars. See where to get the most bang for her dollar. Perhaps clip a few coupons the way she had watched her mother do a thousand times to stretch her less than ample paycheck.

Damn it, what do I do?

Harper wished she could ask her mother, but knowing her, she'd automatically turn negative and think the worst. Always suspicious of anybody being this nice. And, more than likely, her mother would make Harper return it. No matter what Harper decided to do, she'd have to either give the money back or spend it without her mother's knowledge.

A bit of caution couldn't hurt. She'd hold onto the card, just in case the gift came with strings attached. Harper moaned. She hated thinking anything negative about Irwin, him of all people, but she couldn't help it. Her mother's negativity had already washed off on her. Then again, she saw the dark side of people way too many times to just casually kick caution to the curb. Besides, it felt weird accepting such a significant gift.

I'll keep this for a bit. See what happens.

And though Harper didn't want to return it, she

would, if she had to.

Before she changed her mind, Harper bolted upstairs and into her bedroom to hide her delicious secret inside a box kept at the far back bottom of her closet.

I'll give it three days.

Once downstairs, Harper finished the last few bites of her dinner and straightened up. She turned off the lights, checked the locks as per her mother's reminder, and headed up to bed, her mind consumed with visions of heaping plates filled with baked ziti, topped with fresh grated Parmesan cheese, and thick slices of Italian garlic bread slathered in real butter.

***

Three days later

With food store circulars in hand, Harper worked up the courage to march to the front reception desk where she found Irwin keeping himself busy doing nothing in particular, except skillfully avoiding her.

"Thank you," she said, heart pounding. Waiting for the other shoe to drop and possibly break a toe…or her heart.

Irwin didn't glance up from his paper. "You're welcome."

That's it?

"Well, I appreciate it," she said.

Irwin nodded and bowed his head.

Wait, was that shyness she just detected?

"I just need to know why?" she asked him.

Irwin shrugged. "What's to know?"

"That's a lot of money. How am I supposed to repay you?"

"By using it." Irwin bent his head, continuing to avoid making eye contact.

"That's not what I meant."

Irwin froze and stared at Harper wide-eyed. "I know exactly what you meant. Now please excuse me," he said in a gruff whisper and then disappeared into the back office area.

Harper felt awful. Terrible. Dreadful. There was no mistaking the hurt in Irwin's eyes.

What a complete and utter shit I am. Damn it. How could I have misjudged him like that?

Just as Harper turned to leave, Irwin returned gripping a pair of scissors. He marched towards her looking like Edward Scissorhands's doppelganger.

"You're not planning to stab me with those, are you?" she asked, quick to take a slight step backward.

"Regrettably, not today," he answered, tone flat, not missing a beat. Irwin slammed the scissors on the table. "You're going to need these to clip coupons."

Harper tipped her head. Was that a slight grin tugging at the corner of Irwin's mouth? On second thought, she could have imagined it.

"I need to ask you for a favor?" She hoped she wasn't pushing her luck.

"Speak."

"Well, if I go food shopping, I'll have too many packages to carry. I'll need a ride home."

Irwin busied himself with a stack of books. "Fine. Get your shopping completed by the time the library closes. I get off at eight. I will pick you up at eight-ten sharp."

"Thanks."

"Halt." Irwin put a finger in the air. "I'm not done. If you should not be outside waiting when I pull up, you're out of luck and on your own. Am I making myself clear?"

"Irrefutably. I will be ready, sir!" Gruff or not, Irwin didn't seem mad, or at least not angry enough to hate her yet. A sense of relief swept over Harper that she hadn't permanently ruined their friendship if one could describe what they had as a friendship.

Harper jetted off to her seat. With pen and paper, she busied herself compiling a food list, circling items on the circular, and cutting out coupons, calculating a running tab. Halfway through, she peered up in time to catch Irwin staring at her, wearing a genuine smile on his face, and this time, he hadn't bothered to hide it.

***

Harper zipped through the food aisles, conferring back and forth with her list and watching the clock like a hawk. She selected boxes of healthy cereal along with a variety of pasta and jars of various flavored sauces. Harper lifted a ten-pound bag of rice like a baby and shoved it lovingly under the cart's rack. She chose fresh produce, a five-pound bag of apples, bananas, two-dozen eggs and a quart of milk. Her coupons covered most of the paper products. Lastly, she bought a box of tea, a few kinds of cheeses, a jar of real-fruit jam, and the water crackers her mother enjoyed.

Harper had less than fifteen minutes left. Time to check out. Irwin was not the type to bluff. He'd just as soon leave her to prove a point than wait an extra two seconds.

"Excuse me, Miss," said a cute, young man, not much older than Harper. "Aisle four is open if you want to bring your cart around."

"Oh, cool." She tried not to blush.

"Coupons?" asked the cashier, whose name tag read "Kevin."

Harper handed the collection over.

"Do you have a preferred shopper card with us?"

"No."

Kevin smiled.

Harper liked his smile and the rest of his face too.

"No problem," he said and scanned a card from his keychain. "It might save you a few bucks."

"Thanks." Harper continued to pile her items on the belt in record time while Kevin rang her up and scanned her coupons into the system. Together they bagged the items.

"That'll be eighty-four, thirty-seven."

Harper swiped her gift card, pleased she'd come in under budget and with a few dollars to spare.

Kevin handed Harper the receipt. "You saved fourteen dollars and six cents."

"Thanks to you."

This time Kevin reddened. "And your coupons. They helped a lot."

Harper smiled back, sure it was his shopper card that did most of the heavy lifting.

"Have a good night," said Kevin, calling after Harper, already making a mad dash to the front of the store.

"You too," she shouted and half waved, excited to surprise her mom with the groceries and giddy from the cute guy's attention.

Not a bad night for once.

As promised, she found Irwin parked in front of the store, engine on. As soon as he saw her, he got out of the car, popped the trunk, and helped her load.

"Did you find everything you needed?" he asked.

"I did. Thank you. This was really nice of you to do."

Irwin slammed the trunk closed. "Let's go."

Harper opened the front passenger door.

"Uh-uh." Irwin shook his head. "In the backseat," he ordered, offering no further explanation.

"You're kidding, right?"

Irwin's face said not kidding. Harper poked out her jaw, rolled her eyes, and closed the front door. Then she slid into the backseat.

"Seatbelt."

Harper complied.

"Where am I going?"

"Make the next left and take Main Street down for about a quarter of a mile. Then make the right after the light onto Smith Lane."

The pair rode in silence.

"Slow down," said Harper. "The turn is coming up."

"Now what?"

"Go slow. My house is number one-twenty-one. The grey one on the left."

Irwin pulled into an open space directly in front of the house. He turned off the engine and popped the trunk to start unloading the packages, bringing them only as far as the bottom of the stoop. Within less than a minute, they had the bags unpacked. Irwin turned to leave when the front door burst wide open.

"What in the hell is all this?" yelled Olivia. She stood at the top of the steps with her hands planted on her hips. She stared first at Harper, then at Irwin accusingly.

"I can explain, Ma. Just go inside."

"No. You'll explain right now," Olivia countered, none too happy. "Is this your doing?" she asked Irwin. "You think we need your charity?"

"Ma!" Harper shrieked.

Olivia ignored her daughter. "Well, do you?"

Irwin calmly folded his hands and looked Olivia in the eye. "It isn't charity," he said, voice composed. "Your daughter helps out at the library a few times a week. Some of our older patrons don't understand how to properly use the computers and Harper helps them. The gift card came from the staff to show your daughter our appreciation."

What a lie.

Harper was impressed but squashed the laugh.

"I am merely the taxi service for the delivery," he added, straight-faced.

Olivia squinted at Irwin as if trying to gauge his bullshit barometer. Then she turned her attention to Harper. "Is this true?" she asked. "Is that what

152

happened?"

Harper nodded yes.

The porch standoff lasted for a few more moments before Olivia moved out of the way to allow Harper to bring the shopping bags inside.

"I owe you an apology, Mr.—"

"Abernathy," groaned Harper as she lifted two heavy loads.

"Mr. Abernathy. Thank you for driving my daughter home."

"My pleasure, ma'am." Irwin turned, got into his car, and pulled away. No rush, no muss, no nothing. Not even a wave goodbye.

Harper grabbed the last bag and followed her mother inside, steamed. "I could use a hand putting this stuff away," she said, saddened that her surprise had turned into yet another mother-daughter battle.

But Olivia wasn't done. Harper saw her mother's lips pursed in disapproval. Instead of being happy or appreciative, the woman looked heated, pissing Harper off even more.

"This is a lot of food. How much were you gifted?" asked Olivia.

"One hundred dollars."

"And you were able to get all of this?"

"I used coupons and shopped the sales like you do."

Olivia merely nodded.

No "good job." No "thank you, honey, for thinking of me." Nothing.

"Stupid me. I thought you'd be happy."

"I do appreciate what you did," said Olivia. "It's just that, well, I got caught off-guard. I wasn't expecting to see Mr. Librarian standing on my stoop."

"Mr. Abernathy, and he's a nice person, Ma."

"Uh-huh."

"I mean it. He's not like what you're thinking."

"And how do you know what I think?"

"Because it's written all over your face." Harper shoved the paper towels under the sink. "You're just mad because somebody is nice to me," she grumbled loud enough for her mother to hear.

"That's not true."

"Yes, it is."

"Harper!"

"You always ruin everything."

"Harper Leigh! That guy's older than me! What business does he have hanging around with you? You're just a kid!"

"I knew it." Harper sneered. "I knew you'd think the worst of him." Harper leaned on one hip and pointed at her mother. "Well, I got news for you. He's not like that. He's always polite to me, and as a matter of fact, he made me ride in the backseat on the way home!"

Olivia groaned. "That doesn't mean he's not a child molester."

"Oh! Like now all of a sudden, you're the resident expert on perverts, right?" Harper turned. "A bit late," she mumbled.

"What's that supposed to mean?"

"Forget it."

"No. You said it. Tell me what you meant."

"I said forget it!" Harper stormed upstairs. She turned the lock behind her. Pressing the small of her back against the wood frame, she cried. Angry tears spilled down flushed cheeks. Harper thumped the back of her head against the door, incensed that she couldn't follow her own advice. But some things in life couldn't go unseen. Nor could they be forgotten.

CHAPTER 12

Irwin

Irwin tolerated Bones and Bones used Irwin, but tonight, the sound of the impertinent cat's purring elicited in Irwin a sense of comfort. At least somebody, albeit a cat, seemed glad to have him home. Happy to see him, if only to secure the next free meal.

Irwin flicked on the kitchen light, hung up his hat and coat, and locked the side door. Bones purred louder, circling his legs and making it difficult for Irwin to move without tripping. "Give me a minute," he complained halfheartedly, careful not to misstep.

Rough week and rougher night, but nothing on God's green earth could have prepared him for Mrs. Crane's surprise attack. The way she glowered at him as if he were some dirty old man.

Irwin cringed. With one look, she had him feeling guilty. Dirty. Foul. Embarrassed that he had told a lie. A shoddy, bald-faced lie of epic proportions. Not even a smart lie, but one easily disproven. And not only did he tell this appalling untruth, but he drew Harper—a kid—into his subterfuge. A lie turned sham, with him as the chief instigator and Harper as his trusty sidekick. What a mess. And no matter how many different ways Irwin played back the conversation in his head, nothing offered a better alternative.

What should I have done? What choice did I have?

Admit to the assistance? Get my ass tossed off the property? Have the mother haul off and punish Harper for the criminal offense of food shopping? Mrs. Crane looked mad enough to do almost anything, including preventing Harper from ever stepping one more foot into the library, and admittedly, while a month ago Irwin wouldn't have noticed or cared, he did now. Quite the telling revelation.

Irwin refreshed the water in the cat's bowl and filled the other with dry food. Then he put the kettle on, threw another frozen chicken pot pie in the toaster oven, and sat down to sift through his mail. Besides junk, a circular, and a few bills, there was nothing of interest.

Oh, wait.

Another letter from his attorney somehow got stuck behind one of the bills. Irwin anxiously slid his finger under the lip and opened it. Enclosed, a single sheet of paper containing the news he had been waiting to hear.

Dear Mr. Abernathy...We are pleased to

*inform you...should you have any further
questions or concerns...please call to make an
appointment at your earliest convenience...and
warmest regards...*

Much better news than the letter he received last
week. The one Cornelia saw fit to wave in his face.
Irwin returned the missive safely to its envelope.

Ah, Cornelia.

While she could be a royal shrew in the butt
sometimes, she sure nailed his duplicity royally. As
pledged, he'd given all he could to Dakota, but now
his attention would no longer be required. And for
whatever reason, still undetermined, Harper sought
him out for help. His help. Irwin had begun to
genuinely care about this whacky child's welfare
and safety. He wanted to see her embrace a future
without being stifled by the dysfunction that seemed
to shroud her. That realization not only scared the
shit out of him but clearly revealed to what lengths
he'd go to see it through—including being a
lowdown, lying son of a bitch.

Enough.

He'd call the attorney tomorrow to make an
appointment. It was time to stop procrastinating and
get his affairs in order, start the process he had put
off for much too long.

***

The Witching Hour

The call came at three in the morning, startling

him awake from a sound sleep.

"I'm sorry to disturb you, Mr. Abernathy. This is Doctor Rollins, Dakota's physician."

Irwin rubbed his eyes. "Yes, Dr. Rollins," he mumbled groggily, fumbling for the light switch. "It's fine," he said, his voice flat, hiding the terror set to pounce a mere second away. "What's happened?"

"I need you to come to the hospital immediately," she said, her voice urgent but kind. "I can meet you in the ICU. Just have reception page me when you get here."

Irwin sat up, now fully awake. Heart pounding. "I, I'll have to get dressed, but I can be there shortly."

"Is there somebody close by that can drive you?" she asked.

Irwin thought about phoning Cornelia but then decided against it. "I'll be there shortly, Dr. Rollins. Thank you again for calling."

"See you soon then."

***

The hospital had a comfortably furnished room near the ICU available for Irwin to wait while they paged Dr. Rollins. The doctor arrived within minutes.

"Mr. Abernathy?" Dr. Rollins entered the room, still wearing scrubs. Irwin stood to greet her. "No, please, stay seated," she said.

Irwin removed his hat and sat back down on the small, well-worn couch. The doctor joined him, taking the adjacent seat.

"I am sorry, but I have bad news," she began. "I know you are aware of Dakota's ongoing treatment, but Dakota has been struggling. She went into cardiac arrest this morning. We tried to resuscitate, but we were unsuccessful. She died shortly before I phoned you."

There was the word he had been in fear of.

Died. She died. She's dead.

"Did she feel any pain?" he asked. The question seemed to spill out of nowhere, but he had to know.

"No. I don't think so. I think Dakota's heart simply got tired and stopped."

"I should have been here," he mumbled.

"You were here, Mr. Abernathy. Dakota knew that. You have shown no shortage of love and devotion to her." She paused. "You have supported Dakota every step of the way over these past four years."

"Has her father been called?"

"Yes. He has been notified as well."

Irwin dreaded hearing this kind of news for four years, and yet now that it had arrived, he had no words to express the grief overpowering him. "May I see her?"

"Of course. Just let me go speak with the nurses for a moment and then I'll come back to walk you over."

"Thank you."

Dr. Rollins reached over and softly squeezed Irwin's hand. "I'm deeply sorry for your loss."

***

All life supports were disconnected by the time Irwin entered Dakota's room. The ventilator, endotracheal tube, and the cardiac monitors were gone as well. Her body now lay covered with proper bedclothes, her face wiped clean. No traces of blood or jelly used for the DC shock remained. She looked at peace, if that were possible.

He had witnessed her health gradually decline, but watching her slip away had been cruel. The anticipated finality and the awareness that the end beckoned left him feeling empty. All the fabricated hopes Irwin had built up in his head for Dakota now dissolved. No more birthdays, no more visits or long hours spent reading. No more flowers.

Irwin stood at the foot of her bed, a respectful distance away. In all the years he'd come to visit, he never once touched Dakota. She was Gilly's baby, someone else's daughter. And although he loved her as if she were his own, he would mourn Dakota from afar. Sequestered to the griever's ledge, near but never near enough to entirely matter.

As he paid his silent homage, Irwin thought about all the hours and days he spent watching over his sleeping princess, never once feeling resentful as some people do when they dedicate their life and time as the primary caregiver. As he stood, frozen in place, he felt no relief that she was gone, no longer here or that his responsibilities, however self-anointed, were now complete. Only the overriding guilt that he hadn't done enough dared to linger and torment.

Irwin retrieved the photo kept in his wallet. A stunning picture of Gilly and Dakota during happier times. He walked to the side of her bed and leaned it against an already existing photo frame.

Irwin cleared his throat. He folded his hands and bowed his head. "Safe travels, sweet princess," he whispered, his voice choked up. "Tell your mother how much I love and miss her." His shoulders trembled. "Thank her for letting me take care of you."

The nurse had kindly explained to Irwin that Dakota would remain at the hospital until her father gave them permission to transfer her to the funeral home. She was not permitted to say more than that. He understood.

Irwin bid the nurses and doctor a solemn, final farewell. He thanked them for all they had done to keep Dakota comfortable and safe. As he rode down the elevator to the main floor, his shoulders sagged under the weight of hopelessness and a brooding sorrow, knowing he'd never see Dakota again. She was gone. Just like Gilly. And now, so was a big piece of his heart.

***

Irwin hadn't been home a full minute before he heard a barrage of insistent knocks hammering against the side door.

"Irwin? It's me." Cornelia banged again. "Open up," she demanded.

Irwin unlatched the lock. Cornelia pushed forward and barreled in before he even had a chance to pull the door closed.

"I saw you leave early this morning," she said. "I

couldn't sleep. My insomnia's been driving me crazy." Cornelia appeared frazzled. Worried. An unexpected three a.m. departure for Irwin usually only meant one thing. She stopped talking and stared. "Why do you look like shit?"

"Because I feel like shit."

"Sit. Let me make you some tea." Cornelia bounced around the familiar kitchen. "Dakota, right?" The name hung heavy in the air.

"This morning. Doctor Rollins called. Said they tried to save her, but Dakota had no more fight left in her."

A wide-eyed Cornelia merely nodded. "I'm so sorry, Irwin." Incapable of standing still, she bustled back and forth, then into the living room, and returned holding a handmade quilt. She wrapped the warm blanket gently around Irwin's shoulders and resumed preparing his tea. When she glanced over, she spotted Irwin's hands trembling as he readjusted the blanket over his slumped shoulder.

Cornelia slipped three heaping teaspoons of sugar into the hot water. "You're in shock. You need this." She popped open the cookie tin. "Here, eat these too," she said and proceeded to drop three cookies on the side of his plate.

Irwin rubbed the nape of his stiff neck. His movements decelerated, drained of energy. His mouth twisted in a scowl more egregious than his usual frown face. He had so much to say, and nothing at all. How does one go about recounting the loss of a daughter he never had?

The air felt stale. Even Bones sensed sorrow, burrowing his body protectively by Irwin's feet.

"What can I do to help?" asked Cornelia, situated in the chair across from him.

Irwin shrugged. "There's nothing to do. They notified her father. More than that, I don't know."

Cornelia nodded at her friend before her, swathed in grief. As a widow, she understood grief. Knew anguish. Detested loneliness. "You made her journey better, Irwin. I'm not just throwing out empty platitudes. You know me better than that."

Irwin stared into space. His fingers tinkered with his spoon, stirring distractedly. "Another chapter is over," he finally said.

"Yes. It is."

"This one didn't end well."

"No. No, it didn't."

"I used to tell myself that one day if I just kept reading to her, she'd hear my voice and awaken."

"I know."

"She was so young."

"Too young."

"She fought hard."

"Like a warrior."

"I'm not sure if I can do this again."

Cornelia frowned. "What do you mean? With Harper?"

Irwin nodded.

"Too late."

"No, it's not. I didn't get a chance to tell you, but her mother confronted me last night after I gave her daughter a ride home. Not so much in what she said, but you should have seen the way she stared at me. Her eyes practically accused me of—" Irwin shuddered, his face scrunched in disdain. "You know what I mean."

"Why, that's ridiculous."

"Not really. Not considering all the terrible things you read or hear about happening to young girls these days. I can't say I blame her."

"True enough, but that has nothing to do with you. Once Harper's mother gets to know you better—"

"That's not going to happen."

"What you mean?"

"I mean, I'm done. I feel bad for Harper, but I need to bow out."

"And then what, Irwin? What's Harper supposed to do?"

"She's young. Smart. Let's not forget, the girl has parents, or at least a functioning mother, Cornelia."

"And look where that got her."

"Please. Stop pushing. I can't do this right now." Irwin stood. "I have to call the job and let them know I won't be coming in today."

Cornelia began clearing the dishes.

"Leave them. I'll get to it later."

"I can stay. Let me cook you a nice meal."

"No. I think I need to be alone. But thank you."

Cornelia pressed her lips together. "Then I guess Bones and I will take off and leave you to it."

As if on cue, Bones bolted into the next room.

Cornelia stomped her foot. "That darn cat!"

Irwin peered into the living room and found Bones curled up on his favorite reading chair. One big furry hairball. "I found him."

The phone rang.

"I'll get it," called Cornelia.

Irwin entered the kitchen holding Bones.

"Hello? Abernathy residence."

Irwin rolled his eyes at his friend's flair for the dramatic.

"Yes. I see. No, no trouble at all. One moment, please." Cornelia paled, visibly flustered. "Um, Irwin. I think you better take this."

"Tell whoever it is I'll call them back. I'm not in the mood to talk right now."

"Too bad, Irwin," hissed Cornelia, thrusting the phone in his face. "This can't wait. Now, here. Take it."

Irwin growled, shoved the cat in her arms, and grabbed the phone, all while giving Cornelia the Death Glare.

"Hello? This is Irwin Abernathy."

"Mr. Abernathy? It's me, Olivia Crane...Harper's mom."

"Yes?"

"I'm sorry to bother you."

Irwin flinched. He'd heard that same ominous phrase spoken only a few hours ago—and the news then had been catastrophic. He braced for the worst.

Cornelia stood close by watching and waving her hands to grab his attention, mouthing, "What? What happened?"

"Yes, Mrs. Crane, what I can do for you?" he asked, shooing Cornelia away.

"It's Harper. She's missing."

"What do you mean missing?"

"I mean missing, as in not here!" screeched the hysterical mother in the phone, causing Irwin to

166

wince.

"Since when?"

"Not sure. After you dropped her off last night, we put the food away." Olivia's voice lowered, sounding guilt-ridden. "We got into a disagreement. About you, as a matter of fact."

Irwin gnawed his bottom lip.

"Anyway, she ran to her room all upset. I assumed that's where she was, but when I went to wake Harper up for school, the room was empty. Her bed wasn't slept in all night. Mr. Abernathy, I don't know what to do."

Irwin didn't either, but he took solace at not having been accused of kidnapping.

"Is she with you? Did you take her?"

And there it was.

"Did I what!"

"I'm sorry. I know how that sounds, but I had to ask." She began to sob. "Harper's never run away before."

"Have you phoned the police?" he asked.

"I did, but they said she hasn't been missing long enough. Isn't that the stupidest thing you ever heard? They claim that most of the time the kid will turn up."

"That's it?"

"They told me to call around. See if she's gone to any friends' homes. The only problem is, Harper doesn't have any." Olivia took a deep breath. "Oh wait, they did ask me for her description, like what she was wearing, hair color, stuff like that, but I'm not sure what they plan to do about it if anything! Oh my God! Where is my child?" The sobbing grew louder.

"Mrs. Crane," Irwin announced loudly. "Did Harper happen to take her backpack with her?"

"Her backpack?" She sniffled. "Um, I don't know. Hold on. I'll go check."

Irwin heard the phone wobble and shake; then the pounding sound of footsteps climbing up wooden steps.

"Yes, she took it," puffed Olivia into the phone, out of breath. "Why?"

Irwin had an idea. Not many. Just this one but he hoped it was the right one.

"Listen. Get ready. I'll be there to pick you up in less than five minutes. We'll search for your daughter together."

"Thank you, Mr. Abernathy. I'll be ready." Olivia clicked off.

Irwin hung up the phone. He leaned forward on the counter, head bowed. "I can't believe this is happening," he muttered, then slowly turned around towards Cornelia, his eyes wet and bloodshot.

Cornelia already had her coat on. She tossed Irwin his hat and coat and grabbed his keys. "I'll drive."

CHAPTER 13

Harper

In an attempt to appear more community friendly, the library had placed benches directly in front of the building near cement planters. And despite the fact they faced a parking lot, the seats were a welcomed respite for tired legs. Harper sat, fighting off a bit of a chill. She'd spent most of the night out walking. Walking and thinking and trying to decide what to do next. She hadn't initially planned on being out for as long as she was, but one hour turned to the next, and before Harper realized it, she'd stupidly fallen asleep by the side of the library, blocked from onlookers by bushes planted near the narrow cement pathway. Fortunately for her, the temperatures had remained relatively mild, but now, as the sun rose and the sky turned a menacing bright, it was a stark reminder that going home meant certain punishment.

Harper sipped her juice purchased with the extra money left on her gift card. Luckily, the food store

Irwin got her the card for stayed open around the clock. By her calculations, she had more than enough left over to buy herself something to eat while she waited for the library to open and her mother to leave for work before heading home to take a long, hot shower. Harper stretched. Her body ached from sleeping against the cold, cement wall.

With nothing left but to wait, Harper retrieved her book from out of her bag, ready to indulge in some reading, when a car came careening into the parking out of nowhere, driving like a bat out of hell.

Shit.

Harper recognized the car pulling up to the curb, screeching to halt right in front of where she sat.

Double shit.

Harper cringed at the angry, fuming face sitting in the back seat.

Within a second, her mother leaped from out of the backseat screaming and limping towards her, arms outstretched and hands flapping. Cornered, Harper slunk down, holding the book near her face, not sure if her mother planned to hug or wring her neck.

"Don't you hide from me, Harper Leigh Crane."

Harper winced. The use of her middle name meant big trouble.

"How dare you pull this stunt!" shouted her mother, loud enough to wake the dead. "Where the hell have you been all night? Do you know how worried I've been? My God, Harper, what the hell were you thinking?" Olivia threw her hands in the air and slapped her thighs, beyond exasperated. "Do you know how many girls your age get killed for doing the same stupid damn thing you just pulled? I have a good mind to punish you for the rest of your breathing days."

Harper glanced sideways at Irwin as she sat in the passenger seat. He was wearing that ridiculous hat again, staring straight ahead, stone-faced. Next to him in the driver's seat sat an older woman Harper didn't recognize, but unlike Irwin, she appeared absorbed by the drama, intently watching the show.

"Let's go," demanded Olivia. "Grab your stuff and get your narrow, tiny ass in the car. Now."

Harper scrambled to collect her stuff, chucked the unfinished juice container in the garbage can, and tossed her backpack over her shoulder, too scared to do anything to agitate her already irate, distraught mother.

Irwin stepped out of the car, his face a mixture of irritation and relief. He opened the back door and glared directly at Harper. "Well?" he said. "Get in."

And she did.

"Move over," snapped Olivia, still seething, apparently not ready to make nice. Harper rested her backpack on her lap and scooted over as far as she could, directly behind the driver's seat.

"I can't believe you did this, Harper," griped her mother. "I really can't."

"Seatbelts," ordered Irwin.

The older woman in the front turned around to face Harper, extending her small but firm hand for a shake. "You must be Harper. I'm Cornelia, Irwin's neighbor and self-anointed caretaker," she said, wearing the biggest smile. "So nice to finally meet you."

Harper swore she heard Irwin groan.

"I can't thank you both enough," said Olivia, flustered but calming down.

"Our pleasure," answered Cornelia.

Irwin squeezed his eyes shut. "Can we please go—"

"You bet," chimed Cornelia. "Oh, but I'm afraid we're going to have to make a pit stop back at your house, Irwin. I have to pee something fierce."

Harper squelched a giggle. Olivia, still upset, merely nodded. Irwin banged the back of his head against the headrest.

"And off we go." Cornelia revved the engine and tore out of the parking lot like Evil Knievel. "Sorry about that, folks. Hold on. This might be a bumpy ride."

Cornelia glanced in the rearview mirror, caught Harper's eye, and winked. This time Harper couldn't hide the grin, as much trouble as she was in. And boy was she in a heap! She felt strangely content. Happy to be stuck in a car with three grownups who cared enough to drive around looking for her. Harper hugged her backpack tight, curious as to how this triad of crazy came about, but she wouldn't inquire until the dust settled.

Irwin lived close to the library. Certainly within walking distance. Harper didn't get a chance to fully see the entire front of the house with how fast Miss Cornelia peeled into his driveway, but from what she caught, it looked elegant. No sagging porch or peeling paint. The front yard, though small, well kept. But it was the beautiful willow tree with a hanging birdfeeder that held center stage. Unquestionably an older home with architectural history and design. Harper looked forward to seeing the inside.

Cornelia parked and bolted out of the vehicle, leg shaking. "Come on. Come on. Hurry up, Irwin. My bladder's ready to explode."

Irwin slammed his door shut. "Don't you have a bathroom in your house?" he asked, unlocking the door.

"Move out of my way."

As soon as the door opened, Bones dashed out, loudly meowing in utter discontent.

"Pipe down, Bones. We have guests," said Cornelia, shooing him away with the tip of her shoe. "Momma's on a mission. Go bother Irwin." Without another second to waste, Cornelia darted down the hall in a blur.

Irwin tossed his keys on the table, opened up the refrigerator, and pulled out a carton of juice. He started to pour himself a cup when Cornelia returned, brow arched, confused.

"Where's Harper and Olivia?" she asked, palms up in the air.

Irwin shrugged and took a long, exaggerated swig from his cup. Apparently, Harper and Olivia had remained in the car.

"Oh, Irwin!" Cornelia marched to the back door, stood on the stoop, and waved them inside. "Come, come. Don't be shy."

Irwin ignored it all.

"Sorry about that. We thought you were behind

us," said Cornelia, holding the door wide open.

"No, we didn't," corrected Irwin.

"Ignore him," said Cornelia louder. "Come on in. Would you like some tea? I could also make coffee."

Harper followed her mother into the warm and inviting kitchen. Bones purred, circling and rubbing his body on her leg. "He's beautiful," said Harper, leaning down to pet him.

"He's yours," said Irwin.

All three looked at Irwin, not sure if he was joking.

"I don't know about you ladies, but I sure am famished. How about I whip something up?" asked Cornelia.

"We don't want to put you both out more than we already have," said Olivia, much calmer than before. "Honestly, we can walk the rest of the way home from here. It's not far."

"Don't be silly, dear." Cornelia winked. "After the morning we all had, a hearty breakfast, now brunch, will do the trick. Anybody up for pancakes? I saw a box of mix in Irwin's pantry." Cornelia opened the cabinet. "See! What did I tell you?" she said, triumphantly shaking the box. "Almost full." She read the front. "Would you look at this, all I need to do is add water. What will they think of next?"

Harper giggled.

Cornelia smiled. "I'm serious. Irwin never buys the real stuff. To tell you the truth, I'm never sure what he eats besides condiments. Totally worthless in a food store."

174

Now both Olivia and Harper laughed. Irwin did not.

"Harper, help Irwin set the table," said Cornelia. "Olivia, you just sit and catch your breath. Just relax. You've had a hard morning. I'll have us eating in no time."

Harper helped Irwin, but as soon as she sat back down in her seat, Bones jumped on her lap, purring and stretching, nudging Harper's hand to scratch under his neck.

As Cornelia chattered and cooked, Olivia sipped her tea, Harper nursed a glass of juice, and Irwin sat slumped in his chair, drained.

"Thank you again, Mr. Abernathy. I didn't know what to do or where to go."

Irwin took a sip of his tea and nodded.

"What's with all the formality?" asked Cornelia, walking toward them carrying a serving tray filled with mounds of fluffy pancakes. "Just call him Irwin. Everyone does, except Regan. She calls him a bunch of names. Now, dig in, everybody."

Cornelia had been right. The pancakes hit the spot. Nobody talked for the next ten minutes except to ask for this or pass that. After much chewing, swallowing, and clanking of silverware, Harper cleared her throat.

"Um, I just want to say I'm sorry. For everything. I didn't mean to scare you, Mom." Cornelia and Irwin stopped eating. Olivia lips pursed and put her fork down. Harper wasn't sure if it was safe to continue.

Olivia wiped her mouth. Voice tempered, she stared directly into her daughter's face. "Don't ever pull a stunt like that again. I mean it. If you get mad, stay mad at home. Pout as much as you like from the confines of your bedroom. I won't bother you, but don't ever leave the house without letting me know again. Is that clear?"

Harper nodded.

"No, Harper," repeated Olivia. "I mean it. Is that clear?"

"Yes, Ma. Clear."

Cornelia winked at Harper. The sad kind of wink that says: *Let's make peace, but today you scared me half to death. I almost had a heart attack thanks to you. Please never break my heart. I can't bear to lose you. I love you too much.*

Irwin continued eating.

"I'm sorry to the both of you too," said Harper, eyes watery.

"Oh, poo," said Cornelia. "That's life. Things like this happen. Right, Irwin?"

Irwin grunted.

"Ignore him. We were more than happy to help," Cornelia added, reaching across the table to give Olivia's hand a gentle squeeze.

Irwin took a final swig from his cup and started to clear his spot.

"Leave that, Irwin. We'll take care of everything," said Cornelia. "Why don't you try to grab some rest?"

Harper tilted her head, remembering today was Friday—his Gilly-Dakota visit day—but kept it to herself.

Irwin pushed his chair in, gave a slight nod to all, and headed into his den.

"We should really be going soon too," said Olivia. "Harper. Let's help Miss Cornelia clean up."

Harper stood and gathered the plates and silverware. "Do you have work today?" she asked her mom.

"No, I called in sick. I didn't know when you'd turn up."

Harper flinched.

Olivia snapped her fingers. "Shoot. I better call the police and tell them we found you."

"The school too," reminded Harper meekly.

Exasperated, Olivia merely nodded. "That too. Excuse me for a moment," she said to Cornelia, stepping outside on the stoop to make her calls.

Harper felt terrible for all the inconvenience she had caused everybody, not to mention her mom losing out on part of her paycheck. Money they depended on.

"Harper," Cornelia whispered, leaning in. "Sit for a minute," she said, tapping the chair next to her. "I want to ask for a favor."

Harper sat down and leaned in to hear Cornelia better.

"If you and your mom wouldn't mind staying a bit longer, I'd really appreciate it. Irwin's gotten some terrible news today, and I don't want him left alone."

Harper's mind went straight to Dakota, but before she asked, her mother returned.

"Ready?" asked Olivia to Harper.

"Ma, uh, Miss Cornelia was just asking if we could stay a little longer. She needs our help."

"Of course." Olivia sat back down. "What can

we do?"

"Well," said Cornelia, "I was just telling Harper that Irwin's got some awful news today. Heartbreaking, actually. Somebody he cared strongly for passed away this morning."

"Oh, no," chorused Olivia and Harper.

"Yes. Irwin's pretty heartbroken about it."

"That's so sad," said Olivia softly. "I'm sorry."

"Thank you."

Harper looked pleadingly at her mother.

"If you're sure we're not in the way," said Olivia.

"In the way? Oh, no, darlin'. You and Harper are just what the doctor ordered," insisted Cornelia. "I'd like to pop out for a bit and do some shopping. Fill his pantry up, so he doesn't have to go out if he's not up to it for a while."

"Of course," agreed Olivia.

"But doesn't Irwin need to go to the cemetery later?" asked Harper.

Oops.

Cornelia nodded. "Ah, so you know about that, do you?"

"About what?" whispered Olivia, now leaning in closer to the conspiring pair, looking back and forth between the two.

Cornelia lifted a finger indicating she needed a sec, then she tiptoed into the next room to check on Irwin. "He's fast asleep," she whispered, taking her seat. She crooked her finger for Harper and Olivia to lean in again and began to tell Irwin's story.

"So, here's the thing…"

An hour and a half later, there wasn't a dry eye

in the house, including Irwin's, who overheard every word from the next room.

***

Irwin

Irwin suspected the Three Musketeers would take his absence as an opportunity to yak about him. Cornelia thought she was so slick. Little did she realize what a heavy footstep she had or how her operatic voice carried. Great for the stage, not so much when playing snoop.

However, Irwin must have drifted off for at least a short time because when he awoke, he found Harper curled up on the sofa, reading. Bones nestled by her feet, licking his paws. A delicious aroma emanated from the kitchen. If he had to guess, he'd put his money down on a stew.

Irwin stretched to lower his feet from the recliner when he realized somebody had placed a blanket over his lap.

Harper glanced up and smiled.

"You're still here?" he said. "Don't you have a home?"

"Did you have a good nap?"

"What time is it?"

"Are we playing one hundred questions?"

Irwin smiled. She was quick. He admired that.

Harper closed her book and slipped her feet from underneath Bones. "Can I use your phone?"

"What for?"

She stood. "Cornelia said to let her know when

179

you woke up."

"Pardon me?"

"That's what she said."

Irwin grimaced. He hated when Cornelia played babysitter. "Where is Cornelia now?"

"With Mom."

Irwin closed his eyes and drew in a long, tortured breath. "And where is your mom?"

Harper hesitated. "I'm not allowed to say."

Irwin opened his eyes.

"And why not?"

Harper shrugged. "I don't know."

"Liar."

"They threatened me."

"I'm threatening you now."

"No offense, Irwin, but I'm more afraid of them than you."

Just then, the door in the kitchen thankfully opened and the sound of two chatty women emerged. "We're home," piped Cornelia behind a rustle of bags.

Harper whizzed past Irwin. "I didn't tell him anything," she told the two women.

"Here, grab this while I help empty the trunk," instructed Olivia, handing Harper two bags.

"What is all of this?" Irwin asked in vain. He leaned on the counter, too drained to protest. Bones, a creature of comfort, sashayed near his feet. With outstretched paws, he then demandingly nudged Irwin with his head, rubbed his pant leg, then arched his furry, slick back.

"What could you possibly want now?" Irwin asked the feline albatross.

"I'll feed him," said Harper cheerily. "Come, Bones. Auntie Harper's gotcha."

Auntie Harper?

Everything was moving too fast for Irwin to keep up.

Olivia and Cornelia reappeared a moment later carrying a few more bags, a box from the bakery, and a large, elegant wreath and stand.

"What is all this?" asked Irwin.

"Rose sends her condolences," said Cornelia.

There was another knock at the side door and a head popped in. "Hey, anybody here?" called out the head. Roger's head. "Hey, Cornelia, where do you want me to put the table?"

"The table?" asked Irwin. "What table?"

"Hey, Irwin," said Regan, trailing after Roger. "Where should I put this?" she asked Irwin, referring to the two trays of food in her arms.

"I have no idea what *this* even is!" he snapped. "Cornelia!"

"Stop all that shouting," Cornelia chastised Irwin. "I'll take that, dear," she said sweetly to Regan.

Irwin stood frozen in place, watching his home fill with more people, lots more flowers, and tons of food. He eventually managed to corner Cornelia and drag her to the side.

"What the hell is going on?" he asked, apparently unable to process. "Why are all these people in my house?"

"I thought that would have been obvious," she said. "For such a smart man, you can be such a dunce sometimes, you know that?" She gently rubbed his arm. "Now, please, don't be difficult for once in your ornery life and go upstairs and get ready."

"Get ready for what?"

Cornelia rolled her eyes and puffed out her cheeks. "Dakota's memorial service, you big dope."

"But how? Her father—"

"Forget him. Dakota is with us in spirit, and that's all that counts."

Irwin shook his head. "I'm not sure we should be doing this," he protested.

"Oh, nonsense. Of course we should, and we are." Cornelia clasped both of Irwin's shaky hands in hers. "Listen, Irwin," she said softly. "Dakota was as much your daughter as Stupid Stanley's. In my opinion, more yours. And as her father, you need, no, scratch that. We all need to give her a proper send off. Then, when we're done, we'll head to the cemetery to lay Dakota's wreath next to Gilly where it belongs." She paused, his hands still gripped in hers. "Now please, Irwin, go get yourself ready. Your dark suit is hanging up on the back of your door."

"Which one?"

"The dark navy blue one. Gilly always liked that one on you."

Irwin glanced at everyone doing this and that in the kitchen. What before had been overwhelming noise now reached his ears as merely sound. He climbed the stairs to his bedroom, not entirely sure what just happened, but somehow, in all its confusion and perplexity, everything felt perfectly imperfect.

***

News of Dakota's passing quickly made the rounds. For the next few hours, Irwin's home filled and filtered more people than he'd ever imagined possible, all coming to share stories of Dakota and to pay their last respects. A large procession of Dakota's school friends, teammates, coaches, and teachers also came to say goodbye. They presented Irwin with Dakota's team shirt and signed yearbook.

Most of the library staff showed up in shifts, including Janice, who brought with her a large tray of deli and bagels along with a stack of books, all on mourning and grief. One book dealt explicitly with the importance of maintaining hope to cope during the loss of a child.

Dr. Rollins and a few of Dakota's nurses also managed to make it in time for the service. It touched Irwin how they held on to one another, shoulder to shoulder, as if the moment one moved, the rest, like dominos, would scatter. At other times, he noticed they would hold one another in warm and supportive embraces, their hands interlocked. These weren't just Dakota's doctors and nurses, but extended family…her protective angels.

The table Roger brought, now covered in a baroque tablecloth, held a lovely collection of framed photos of a smiling, beautiful, and full of life Dakota. Irwin recognized most of the pictures, but a couple were new. A small wicker basket at the end of the table overflowed with condolence cards, while flowers of soft pink with hints of white hue filled every vase and glass container Irwin owned.

Cornelia, Olivia, and Harper had organized and hosted the memorial to perfection, each exceptionally lovely in their dark dresses. However, much to Irwin's mortification, Harper had insisted on wearing her work boots underneath hers. Supposedly, that was the style. Irwin cringed.

On what planet?

The following day, a small blurb appeared in the local paper recounting not only Dakota's passing but Gilly's as well. A short but thoughtful article concisely highlighted their much too short lives, expounding on the enormous impact each had made on those left behind.

By week's end, word eventually trickled back to Irwin that Dakota's father had come to claim his daughter's body. And, as assumed, the selfish bastard instructed the hospital to release Dakota's body only to the funeral home he chose instead of letting her rest at peace next to her mother for eternity. Irwin mourned for Gilly. He had held out hope against hope that Stanley would eventually do the right thing for once. He should have known better.

Nevertheless, that evening, as Irwin laid in the dark, he felt calm…finally at peace knowing that those who had truly loved Gilly and Dakota in life had sought fit to celebrate them instead of lamenting. Voice after voice spoke of the many ways they had each touched hearts.

Perhaps, wondered Irwin, his eyes heavy, ready to sleep, *that's all anyone can honestly ask for.*

CHAPTER 14

Darren

York's visit had come as a complete shock. Darren couldn't imagine why or how his old celly found him, but he didn't care.

"York! I can't believe it! You're still an ugly bastard! How are you?" laughed Darren. "What the hell are you doing here?" he shouted, rushing down the stairs to give the big man a bear hug. "You look great," he said, clapping York on the arm and vigorously pumping his hand.

York did, in fact, look mighty sharp. He stood tall, decked out in a pricey three-piece suit, fresh buzz cut, and carrying an expensive-looking leather briefcase.

"Thanks, man," cheesed York.

"How the hell did you find me?" asked Darren, mouth agape.

"Grapevine." York shrugged. "You know how it is. Don't let anyone tell you different, the biggest gossipers are inside. Can't keep nothing a secret."

185

The two men shared a knowing laugh.

"So, what can I do for you?" asked Darren, a bit self-consciously, dressed in his drab attire.

"Actually, I'm here to do something for you. That is, if you're interested."

"For me?" Darren pointed to his chest. "Like what?"

"Like a J-O-B."

Darren tilted his head to the side. "You're offering me a job?" he asked, somewhat stupefied. Inside he'd heard York talk about going into business for himself but, at the time, didn't put stock in it. Inmates were forever talking about their grandiose plans. Follow through? Not so much. "Doing what?"

"Why you look all shocked? I told you I was going to open a restaurant over two years ago. Thought I was joking?" York laughed. "Me and my brother-in-law went into business together."

Smiling, Darren shook his head. "That's incredible, man. I'm proud of you."

"Yeah, well, that's why I'm here. We're looking for kitchen help."

Darren threw back his head and laughed. "A chef? I can't cook, man."

York shook his head. "No, not a chef. I'm the chef," he said, thumping his chest. "With food prep and clean-up. We'll pay minimum wage to start, and then once your sorry ass passes a probationary period, we'll adjust your income."

"You're serious?"

"Do I look like I do stand-up?"

"He'll take it," bellowed Jay, emerging from of

his office. "When does he start?"

"York, this is Jay," said Darren. "He runs the place. Jay, this is York, my former, um—"

York reached out to shake Jay's hand. "Clifton York. Darren's former cellmate."

"Former, huh? Still on probation?" asked Jay. Although state-specific, general conditions usually prohibited a parolee from fraternizing with anyone previously convicted of a crime. Most of the time, however, the final decision was left to the discretion of individual Parole Officers.

"No, sir. Free and clear. All legit." York handed Jay his business card.

"Oh, The Insider, on eighth and Main? Great name. I get the reference."

"We like to hire guys trying to do right on the outside."

"I'll keep that in mind," said Jay, pocketing the card. "I hear the food's great."

"You heard correctly. Best seafood in the Poconos," spouted York. "Why don't you stop by for lunch one of these days? My treat."

Jay pumped York's hand. "Sounds great. I think I'll take you up on that." Jay glanced at Darren. "When do you want this guy to start?" he asked York.

"Tomorrow works. We typically open at one, but we prefer our support staff by eleven."

"Eleven it is," said Jay. "Got that, Crane?"

"Got it," said Darren, grateful for the job.

***

The first week at the new job had been rougher than Darren anticipated. It had been a long time since he'd held a full-time job, and he felt nervous. Worried he wouldn't be able to handle the pressure, troubled his old yearnings and past haunts would pull him back into the drug life again.

In more ways than one, life outside the prison had been a culture shock. At least inside, behind bars, he knew how things worked and what to expect. From the time Darren woke until lights out, all decisions were made for him. And while the food sucked, at least he ate. Even the cement roof over his head was guaranteed. Now, that burden fell on his not-so-ready shoulders. With Olivia not answering her phone, and the days of his stay at the halfway house winding down, the pressure to do something magnified.

Unlike York, who had been a chef before going to prison, Darren had no previous skills to lean on. Had it not been for York stepping up, his work prospects looked bleak. As Darren strolled to work, he reflected on the long list of poor choices he'd made. A fresh start was all he needed to get grounded again, he told himself, and perhaps if he worked hard enough, he could prove to Olivia that he changed. Show her that he could contribute to the household. Be a father to Harper. Darren shook his head. He was getting ahead of himself. For now, the most he could hope for from Olivia was for her to let him come back home. The rest, hopefully, would come in time.

Everyone in the restaurant gave it their all. Darren watched them with curiosity. He respected their dedication. The way everyone seemed to move seamlessly through their responsibilities and tasks, often joking around, but getting the job done right. On the other hand, he spent most of his long shift nervous, hyper-vigilant, quiet. Never quite sure of himself. At times embarrassed by his lack of basic experience. He listened to them talk politics, compare histories, and discuss music. He often wondered what lives they led at home. If they had families, children, a wife, or a lover waiting for them to return at night. Somebody to confide in. Some time to remind them that everything was going to be okay. Maybe they were that person, the okay person. The one to make things right. Darren wanted to be that person for somebody.

The prison had offered Darren entrepreneurship and business training before release, but he had turned it down. In hindsight, another one of his big mistakes. Without a doubt, it would have helped him to prepare better and move forward, acquiring the necessary skills to get and keep a job, but most of all, teach him to hold the insecurity that plagued him at arm's length.

Now, after working at the restaurant and seeing everything that went into running a successful business, Darren admired York more than ever. The man worked hard—harder than anybody Darren had ever seen. He also took pride in his work, making sure each plated dinner left the kitchen designed to perfection. He individually hand-selected every vegetable or fruit, ensuring the right amount of crispness and color. Darren also marveled at how York, without complaint, got up at the butt-crack of dawn every day to make the two-hour drive to New York to purchase fresh meat and fish. The man was a machine.

Darren's route to and from work led him directly past the library. He still needed to speak with Harper alone. Get her to listen to reason, get her on his side. Help him convince her mother to give him another shot. But with the way things stood now, he'd find himself released without a home to go to, and the prospect of sleeping on the street scared him to death.

Over the past two weeks, desperation had begun to set in. More than once Darren felt tempted to go inside the library in search of Harper, but the one time he got close, the sliding doors opened and revealed the old librarian guy at the front desk, casually chatting with his trio of crazy.

Darren changed his mind and chickened out. He couldn't afford to screw up and get into another argument, not now when finally things were going so smooth. Jay had stopped busting his chops, York seemed happy enough with his work, and he finally had a few dollars in his pocket. Not too terrible. Even the counseling keeping him from using again seemed to be working—not that he didn't want to. Every stress led back to him wanting to, but for now, Darren thought he had the monster contained.

His walks to and from work gave Darren time to think. He had mixed feelings about Olivia that kept interjecting themselves into his mind uninvited. Many of which he could barely unpack without turning bitter and angry all over again. For all his tough talk, he could not equate his sense of

190

abandonment against the callousness of his actions. Nor was Darren near ready to take responsibility for what decisions he had already made, driving Olivia to bolt in the first place. Ownership of those behaviors required humility, and that emotion still stymied him. Not so with York, who at one point felt compelled to call Darren out on his hypocrisy one night when they were alone after work.

"Have you decided on what you plan to do after you finish at the halfway house?" York asked while busy prepping vegetables.

"I plan to go home." Darren wiped down one of the counters. "Be a family again."

"Ah huh." York nodded and sliced through an onion. "So I take it Olivia's good with that?"

Darren pursed his lips and turned his head away. "I don't care if she is or isn't."

York stopping dicing and shook his head. "Crane, Crane, Crane."

"What?"

"Will you never learn? You're still playing the tough guy as if you're in a position to call all the shots. You know what?" York asked sardonically. "You're hardheaded."

Darren shook the rag out over the sink to let the crumbs drop. "I'm not hardheaded. I just don't have a lot of choices right now, and Olivia's being a bitch and standing in my way."

York stopped, flummoxed. "Not from where I stand."

"Oh?" Darren jutted out his chin.

"Nope. Looks to me like Olivia is leaving you alone. That's a whole lot different than being a bitch standing in your way. Uh-huh. No, I think what's got your panties in a twist is that she doesn't want or need you like she used to. So you're hurt. Or maybe I should say your ego hurts." York slid the cuttings into the garbage pail. "I like you, Crane. We go way back, and I consider you a friend, but you know me. I'll call bullshit when I see it."

Darren sneered. "Fair enough," he agreed, rinsing off his hands in the sink. "But you don't know her." Unwilling to meet York's stare, Darren took his time drying his hands off.

York put his knife down and wiped off his fingers on his apron and turned. He leaned his massive frame on the counter and crossed his muscular, tatted arms over his chest. "You're right. I don't know her. Never laid eyes on the woman, but I sure as shit know you. I've known you for years, Crane. I've listened to you talk and moan and complain. Shit, I've even listened to you cry yourself to sleep when you thought nobody else could hear you. But there's one thing I never heard you say in all the time I've known you. Can you guess what that is?"

Darren side-eyed him. "Pffh, nope."

"I know you can't, and here's why." York leaned over the edge of the table and clutched the counter. "Because you only think of yourself."

Shift over, Darren grabbed his coat from his locker. "Yeah, well, we all can't be you."

York clapped his hands. "And there it is. I've hit a nerve." York's face turned deadly serious. "Deflect all you want, my friend, but you know I'm speaking the truth. You can stand there and tell

192

yourself whatever lies you want to believe, but at the end of the day, it doesn't make it true." York marched over to the fridge and pulled out a head of lettuce. "Olivia made it clear to you when you were inside. She's done, man. Finished. You need to be too." He slammed the head of lettuce and snapped it in half with his bare hands. "Move on. Close the door and cut your losses before you find yourself knee-deep into something you can't climb out of."

Darren didn't want to hear it. "I gotta go."

York shrugged. He picked up his knife and began slicing again. "I need you here early tomorrow…by ten."

Darren zipped up his jacket. "Later."

"Mmhm."

Darren stomped down the hall and out the door to begin his late-night walk back to the halfway house. Most of the time he enjoyed the time spent alone. The roads were still and there were fewer people, but not tonight. Tonight, despite the nippy temperatures, people seemed to be out and about. Luckily, York fueled Darren's irritation enough to keep him toasty warm.

Who does York think he is lecturing me like that? Because he gave me a job? Shit, last time I checked, employment didn't grant anybody license to hound a person on their personal life.

Darren crossed the street, straight past the block he'd turn down if heading to Olivia's.

Don't stop.

Darren kept walking.

That guy doesn't know the first thing about Olivia or our relationship except what I might have told him inside, and even that's not the whole story.

Darren thought about York's comment, that supposed one thing he never heard Darren say, but he couldn't figure out what the hell he was talking about. But then again, York always spoke in riddles, still basking in his past role as his prison guru. But instead of sitting high up on some throne or mountain, York preferred to pontificate to the disadvantaged from his kitchen, hiding behind a damn apron.

Darren sucked his teeth. He didn't appreciate anybody looking down on him, thinking they were smarter or better than him. Much like how Harper's librarian did the other week; another condescending stuck-up guy who thinks his education and job status entitles him to judge others or interfere in their life.

He strode past the library's parking lot, now empty having closed hours earlier. Darren recalled how as a kid, he'd spend time in the library reading. He preferred keeping a distance from the noise of the street and the troublesome pull of his friends. Away from his doped-up mother and her crowd, forever dropping by and stinking up the house with their foul, unclean bodies and drugged-up stench. It had never occurred to Darren before now, but perhaps Harper used the library for the same reason. He wondered if the temptation of drugs also beckoned her to stray and indulge much as they had done with him and Olivia.

Olivia.

Damn! I've done her wrong so many times.

Dragged her down into the gutter with him when

the bottom fell out. But hadn't she gone willingly? Didn't she bear any responsibility for what she did? Harper didn't seem to think so, but it was a question Darren contemplated over six, long miserable hard years. It was a question he wished he could ask Olivia—and now Harper—if either one ever decided to talk to him again.

What was I thinking?

Showing up at the house the way he did, like some badass.

Showing off...asserting my way into places I'm not wanted and then losing my temper when I don't get my way.

He felt terrible for smashing Olivia's mother's vase. Darren felt terrible about a lot of things he did and said.

Ten more minutes to go, but tonight Darren didn't linger about or take his time walking back. His body ached. His head pounded. And he felt lonely. He was ripe to slide, desperate to numb the pain away. Get high and forget everything and everyone. To hell with them all.

Just keep walking.

He hurried past old haunts. The bar. The alley behind the food mart...past places he used to cop.

The familiar aroma of alcohol strained this reserve, luring him to succumb. He kept stepping, pounding the pavement. Faster. Faster. Straight past the apartment building where he spent many a night lost in a drug-induced fog, plastered out of his mind. Waking up half the time pissed, pissed on, and pissed off. Worst part, it never stopped him from doing the same thing the next night, and the night after that, and all the nights soon after.

Darren swiped a bead of sweat from his forehead but made sure to keep his head down and eyes diverted. Inside, his heart raced. The vicious craving cycles his counselor warned him about had arrived, yanking him into a downward spiral. Darren wished he could eliminate the urges, quiet the temptation to go back to using. The cravings were strong. Almost too strong.

One, two, three, four, he mumbled, counting each step forward. *Twenty, thirty, forty...*

He thought about what his counselor had told him.

"To recover and maintain sobriety won't be easy, Darren. This process is going to take a conscious effort on your part. It won't disappear on its own."

Think of something. Anything else.

Darren fixated all his thoughts on the warm bed waiting for him. He concentrated on the goals he wanted to reach. He imagined one day sitting in Olivia's kitchen enjoying a meal, trading stories with her and Harper. The deflection almost worked until another surge of old sordid memories crept its way in.

Alcohol. He fondly remembered the tinkling sound of ice hitting against the side of a glass. The cooling sensation of a cold beer coating his parched throat.

Darren lowered his gaze as he strode past three teenagers hanging out behind the Shop Smart Mart. The sweet aromatic fragrance of marijuana assaulted his shaky senses, feeding into his ever-growing craving.

He pushed harder. Walked brisker. Anything to thrust the thoughts of escape or numbing out of his head.

Resist.

Although dead quiet, Darren checked for oncoming cars before crossing the road.

Almost there.

Once across Main Street, he headed straight down the shadowy block.

Keep going.

Darren's struggles were rewarded soon enough when his eyes latched onto the soft glow coming from the front porch at the halfway house. A welcomed respite from a grueling, arduous journey through temptation.

Relief.

Fighting the panic, Darren briskly pressed the bell three times. He was about to push it a fourth when someone inside released the lock.

Darren tugged the door open and practically jumped inside, winded but temporarily safe. He nodded to the guy staffing the front desk and headed straight upstairs to his room, determined to make the haunting particulars of his crumbling life wait for introspection at another time. For tonight, his only plan was to sleep his anxieties away.

***

In the morning, a light knocking on the door awakened a slumbering Darren.

"Crane?" said the voice. "Crane! Open up."

Jay.

197

Darren threw his covers off and trudged to the door wearing nothing but a pair of boxers.

"Yeah?" he said through the closed door.

"Get dressed and meet me downstairs in ten. We need to talk."

"About?" he shouted in reply, but by then, Jay had already left, halfway down the tiled, bland hall.

What now?

CHAPTER 15

Olivia

Olivia read the document over again until the words bled into her brain. This time, there were no mystical rabbits to pull out of the bag, no quick fixes, barely any options left.

She stared, transfixed on the court eviction notice. The official document declaring her unworthy of this home. It stated in bold print that she had one week before her hearing, and by the way things stood, she had no legal leg to stand on.

Truth be told, this latest kick to the gut hadn't come as a total shock, just a miserable one. Olivia had repeatedly been late with paying the rent, short a few times and remiss once over the past four months. She suspected the stories she told to the landlord, while all true, had worn out the last of his patience, and by the look of these court papers, he was all too ready to kick them to the curb.

Most places expected at least one month's rent and one month's deposit before handing over the keys. With money tighter than ever, it had been impossible for Olivia to save.

Eyes glazed, she folded and unfolded the letter, while her fried brain tried to figure out what to do, but whatever she decided, she'd have to do it soon. Housing availability in the Poconos for the working poor—a hot topic of debate in the local papers—had expounded on the lack of anything affordable or available in the area. Added to that the pressure of finding a decent place in the same school district so Harper could graduate with her friends next year.

With less than nineteen days before the sheriff showed up, Olivia had to either convince the landlord to drop the case against her or come up with the extra money to move. Both options looked as unlikely as Olivia letting Darren move back in. Or maybe not. Darren's income combined with hers…they could afford a way nicer place than this one…and in the same district.

"Damn it," Olivia groaned, slamming her fist on the table. "What the heck is wrong with me?" She shook her head, disgusted. "Harper will kill me if I do something *that* stupid."

***

"Thanks!" Harper's chipper voice carried from outside.

Since the memorial service, Irwin had been giving Harper regular lifts home from the library with Olivia's blessings, although according to Harper, he insisted she remain seated in the backseat. But Harper said she didn't mind. Even teased him that he was "Driving Miss Daisy," but Irwin pretended not to get the reference. Cornelia, on the other hand, explained to Harper in comical detail Irwin's propensity for decorum. She said that to others, his behavior may appear old-fashioned or even archaic when, in fact, he merely acted out of a strong sense of decency. Harper said she found Irwin's idiosyncrasies charming.

Olivia heard Harper open the front door.

"I'm home," Harper shouted.

"In the kitchen," answered Olivia, pocketing the notice in her sweater pocket.

Harper raced in to join her, all smiles and carrying a hefty-sized take-out bag. "I come bearing gifts, otherwise known as dinner," she said, pulling out two large containers of shrimp lo mein and rice. "And before you lose your mind and yell, Irwin insisted." Harper tugged off her jacket and tossed it on the back of the chair. "I'm starving," she said as she zoomed past her mother to grab plates and forks. On the return trip, she placed a kiss on the top of her mother's head before joining her.

"Smells good," said Olivia, ignoring the lump growing in her throat.

Harper reached down into the bag and produced two cans of soda and a small bag containing two shrimp rolls. "One for you and one for me," she said playfully, doling out the goods. "And one for you and one for me."

"This is too much food," said Olivia.

"I know. I told him the same thing, but Irwin never listens to me." Harper bit into the shrimp roll. "Mmhm," she moaned. "I love these things."

"You should have invited Irwin to eat with us."

"I did, but he already ordered food for him and Cornelia." Harper stuck her finger in the air to indicate her mouth was too full to talk. "Get this. Cornelia made him pick up a container of sweet and sour shrimp for Bones."

"For the cat?"

"Yep." Harper giggled. "Irwin grumbled and complained, but he did it."

"That's hilarious," said Olivia, masking her anxiety. Harper looked so happy these days, she didn't have the heart to crush her daughter's spirit with a new set of problems that, frankly, weren't hers to solve.

"Oh, before I forget." Harper twisted around and retrieved an envelope out of her jacket pocket. "Here."

"For me?" asked Olivia. "From who?"

"Cornelia."

"Is she okay?"

"Yeah. Why wouldn't she be?"

"No reason." Olivia shrugged. She recalled Cornelia's strange, empty, glazed stare at the store when they were picking stuff up for the memorial, struggling to remember why they were there. Cornelia had snapped out of it quick enough, and at the time, Olivia contributed the odd response to grief. But still…

"Anyway, Irwin told me to give it to you."

"What's it about?"

"Again, no idea. Believe me, I was itching to read it, but Irwin told me to stop minding your business." Harper bit into her roll and side-eyed her mother's. "Are you going to eat yours?"

Olivia swiped it playfully away. "You bet I am," she teased, snatching it out of Harper's reach, but then slid it back. "Kidding. You can have it."

"Are you sure?"

Olivia nodded. "Go ahead," she said, her appetite crushed by the looming bad news currently sequestered to her sweater pocket. Olivia read the note.

"Well? Spill the beans. What does it say?" Harper leaned forward, trying to peer over the top. "Is it about me?"

"No, Miss Nosey. Hate to break the news, but not everything is about you." Olivia smiled, fanning her face with the card.

"Ma!"

"Oh, fine. It's an invitation for us to come for dinner."

"At Cornelia's?"

"No. Not exactly. Apparently, Cornelia is inviting us over to Irwin's."

"When?"

"This Saturday."

"Can she do that? I mean, invite us to Irwin's?"

Olivia waved the card in Harper's face, and they both laughed.

"We're going, right?"

"I can't see why not." Olivia plastered a fake smile on her face. "It'll be fun."

Harper bit into the next shrimp roll, beaming. Reaching out with greasy fingers, she asked, "Can I see it now?"

"Wipe your hands first." Then Olivia handed

Harper the card.

"Wow, pretty fancy, but why send a card just to ask us for dinner?"

"I don't know, but I kind of like it."

"I guess." Harper leaned back in her chair. "I wonder if we'll need to dress up?"

"I don't think so." Olivia shrugged, then re-read the invitation. "It doesn't say anything about dress code." Olivia frowned. "You know what? Ask Irwin tomorrow, just in case. I'd hate to go and feel out of place."

Harper nodded and swallowed. "I'll make brownies for dessert," she said, remembering the two boxes of mix she'd purchased on sale the last time she'd gone shopping.

"Sounds good." Olivia glanced towards three bananas on the counter. "I'll whip up a loaf of banana bread."

"Can you add the walnuts to it?"

Olivia laughed. "Do we have walnuts?"

"I'll go check." Harper sprinted to the cabinet. She pulled out a small plastic bag and shook it. "Not much left." She frowned.

"Let me see." Olivia held the bag up to the light. "It's enough for a crumb topping. I'll make it work."

"I wonder what she's up to now?"

"Who? Cornelia?" asked Olivia. "Why?" She peered at the card in Harper's hand. "It's only a dinner invitation."

Harper sniffed the paper. "If you say so, but don't you get the feeling that Cornelia never does anything *just because*?"

"Hmmm." Olivia grinned. "You know, you may be right."

When did my daughter become so intuitive?

Harper handed Cornelia's card back to her mother. "Here."

"Thanks." Olivia returned it to the envelope, folded it in half, and stuck it in her sweater's other pocket. "What's today? Wednesday?"

"Thursday."

"Ah, well…we will find out soon enough."

Harper leaned back in her chair and rubbed her palms together. "Showtime in two days. I can't wait."

***

That evening, with thoughts of eviction bombarding her awake, Olivia tossed and turned, too wound up trying to figure out her next move and frustrated that nothing seemed remotely feasible. She dreaded breaking more lousy news to Harper, but she didn't have long. Perhaps Sunday—after dinner at Irwin's. Olivia didn't have the heart to ruin that for Harper too.

Olivia punched her pillow and flipped it over a few times searching for a comfortable spot to lay her face down. Squeezing her eyes closed, she did her best to prevent another round of tears from falling, but once one renegade escaped, the rest of the water squad soon followed.

No. This is my problem. Not Harper's.

Olivia buried her face in the pillow to muffle her sobs.

I have to fix this.

***

Harper

The next morning came too soon. Feeling lazy, Harper wished school would end already. It had been a stressful week of tests and projects. She especially looked forward to tomorrow night's dinner at Irwin's.

The card?

She didn't want to forget to ask Irwin about the dress code.

Where'd Mom put it?

She wanted to bring it with her.

Harper, barely awake, padded her way into the kitchen for a cup of water when she spotted her mother's sweater still hanging from the back of the chair. Remembering that her mother had stuffed the card into the pocket, Harper slipped her hand inside to retrieve it, but instead of the invitation, she held a long, official-looking envelope in her fist, all scrunched up.

What's this?

Before attempting to open it, she listened for any movement or footsteps coming from upstairs, but the house remained perfectly still. As quietly as she could, Harper slipped the letter out, unfolded the crumpled paper, and began to read.

"Oh, no," she whispered.

No, no. Damn it. No! This can't happen.

Moments later, the sound of footsteps and doors

opening upstairs alerted Harper that her mother was awake and on the move. Harper quickly stuffed the letter in the envelope and back into the sweater pocket, completely forgetting to grab Cornelia's card. She zipped back to her bedroom and closed the door. A confused mixture of anger and fear bubbled up within her as she leaned on the door, panting, out of breath, and furious.

How could she do this? Evicted?

Harper wanted to toss everything within her reach.

How could she hide this from me?

"Harper!" yelled her mother from the kitchen. "Hurry up. You're going to be late."

There's always something with her.

"Harper!"

"I know!" she screamed back.

When did she plan on springing this latest fuck-up on me?

"Harper!"

"Stop yelling at me." Harper so wanted to add, "you lying bitch," but didn't.

On autopilot, Harper readied herself for school. Unable to control her tongue, she wanted to avoid crossing paths with her mother, so she washed, dressed, and hightailed it out of the house in record time, slamming the front door behind her.

Ditching school again was out of the question, but nobody said she couldn't be late. Harper jogged straight past the bus stop and down a lane behind a row of older houses and then back out onto the Main Street. She kept walking, taking long, determined strides one after the next. Her eyes darted back and forth as if being followed, but she just kept going, weaving through parked cars, snaking around slow walkers, and crossing the road at the light.

Overnight, the air had turned much brisker, but Harper, wearing nothing but a light jacket and no hat, didn't feel a thing, nor did she notice the people passing her all bundled up in heavy coats, some already wearing winter hats and scarves. She just kept walking faster, in an angry daze, building up a sweat underneath her shirt with every determined step she took closer towards her destination. Without giving it any thought, Harper turned down one side street and ran the last of the way, leaping up the porch steps two at a time as if her life depended on it. Out of breath and legs trembling, she banged on the door. "It's me, Harper," she sobbed and pounded again.

"Harper?" called the voice through the door, followed by sounds of bolts promptly unlatching. "What's the matter, honey?" asked Cornelia, appearing shocked to see the sobbing child standing on her stoop. "What happened?" she asked as she shooed her inside. "Come in, come in." Cornelia guided Harper by the elbow inside. "Are you hurt? Did somebody hurt you?"

Harper dropped her backpack on the floor and threw her arms around Cornelia's neck, crying. "I'm going to be homeless," she barely choked out.

"What?" Cornelia barely understood. "What are you saying?"

"The let-ter," wept Harper, choking back air. "She didn't pay, and now we're going to be *homeless.*"

"Oh, honey," soothed Cornelia, rubbing Harper's back. She locked the front door. "Follow me."

Harper rubbed her wet face with the back of her hand and followed Cornelia into a large, warm space filled from floor to ceiling with books of every conceivable size. Piles of papers covered a heavily ornate wooden desk. Gold-trimmed paintings depicting seasonal landscapes christened the walls, and a big round clock hung over the mantle.

"Sit," instructed Cornelia, tenderly. "I'll get you some water."

Harper sniffled and plucked a tissue from the box on Cornelia's desk then sat down on the couch. As she leaned back, she caught movement from the corner of her eye and gasped. She froze, eyes darting, ready to bolt until she realized what, or rather, who, just came in to join her.

"Bones!" Harper exclaimed, patting her chest with her palm. "You little creeper. You scared me half to death."

Unaffected, Bones sashayed over to the couch. He stretched his furry neck and nuzzled his cheek against Harper's calf before leaping onto her lap to claim his rightful space.

"You're so bad, Bones," teased Harper, more than happy to accommodate. Something about the vibrations emitted from Bones's purring soothed Harper so much that by the time Cornelia returned, Harper no longer had tears running down her cheeks.

"Ah ha! There you are, Bones," teased Cornelia.

"You bad kitty." Cornelia handed Harper a bottle of water. "I must apologize for my furry friend's lack of manners."

Harper smiled. "I don't mind," she said, scratching the cat's belly. "He's got such a beautiful coat."

Cornelia grinned. "That's thanks to the double meal plan he's on between my place and Irwin's."

Harper continued to massage the cat's back. "Is Bones your cat or Irwin's?"

Cornelia lowered herself on the couch next to Harper and gave the girl a half-smile. "This insufferable but quite lovable animal happened to have been Gilly's companion," she said, giving Bones a gentle scratch behind his ear.

"Oh," Harper said, lowering her gaze, embarrassed. "I'm sorry. I should learn to mind my business."

"Don't be silly. You've got nothing to be sorry about. Besides, to tell you the truth, Irwin and I belong to Bones more than the other way around."

"I think he's sweet."

"Well, he sure has taken a liking to you."

Harper beamed, caressing the cat's exposed belly. "The feeling is mutual."

Cornelia propped a couch pillow behind her back. "So. What's all this about being homeless?"

Harper frowned. "This morning I found a letter hidden in her sweater from the court saying that because we didn't pay the rent, they're going to kick us out. They worded it differently, but you know what I mean."

"I see." Cornelia clasped her hands on her lap.

210

"Did they give you a specific date?"

"Yeah, but I can't remember what it was now, but it's definitely this month. I remember seeing that."

Cornelia nodded, her face drawn into a frown.

"I know money's been tight, and my mom does what she can, but I thought she was at least paying the rent."

"She probably has been, but rent is outrageously high in this area. It's hard for most people to keep up these days." While Cornelia had paid her mortgage off years ago, she still found herself struggling to make ends meet.

"I guess." Harper shrugged, not entirely convinced.

"What did your mother say?"

"She didn't," Harper sighed. "We've been arguing about everything lately. I was too angry when I found it and didn't want to get into it with her about this too, so I put the letter back and left."

"I can understand that." Cornelia's lips remained pursed in a grimace.

Bones slid off Harper's lap. "I should go. This isn't even your problem."

"I'm not upset at all," said Cornelia. "This is my thinking face. Irwin says I look constipated."

Harper giggled. "Irwin's funny."

"Yes. He's a regular riot."

"Still, I better get going. My mom's gonna lose it bigtime if she finds out I skipped out on school again."

Cornelia nodded. "Well, here's where your mother and I are in total agreement. This skipping

211

school thing needs to stop."

Harper glanced around the room. "You sure have a lot of books. Have you read them all?"

"Most of them cover to cover."

"I love reading."

"Do you? Well, feel free to borrow whatever piques your interest."

Harper walked over to the bookcase, bent over, and slid a book from the bottom shelf. Her eyes lit up when she realized whose name was plastered on the cover.

"Hold up. You're a writer?" she asked, waving the paperback in the air. "I mean an author?"

"I am. Mysteries. Cozy mysteries to be exact. I write some of my books under a *nom de plume*. That series is called—"

"Wait, don't tell me." Harper wandered over to another small shelf nearer to Cornelia's desk. "Hmm," she purred before choosing a book with a drawing of a furry cat, who could have easily been mistaken as Bone's evil twin displayed on the cover. "Yours?"

"Very good. You found it. I'm impressed."

"*The Cornelia Bones Mystery Series*. I should have known." Harper turned the book over. "I've always wanted to be a writer."

"Which is why we need to get you back to school straightaway. Speaking of which, how late are you?"

Harper glanced at the clock. "Is that accurate?" she asked, pointing.

"Give or take five minutes."

"Then I'd say second period will end in about

fifteen minutes or so."

"Oh gosh, we better hurry up. I'll get my keys, but before we take off, I need you to listen to me for a minute."

Harper put Cornelia's book down. "Okay. I'm listening."

"First off, do you trust me?" asked Cornelia, stone-faced serious.

"I do," answered Harper with no hint of a waver in her voice.

Cornelia stared into Harper's eyes for a good five seconds. "Good. I believe you."

"Can I ask why?"

"You can ask, but I won't tell. Not yet, but let's just say I've got an idea that could possibly, not promising, but possibly, settle this whole sordid mess out once and for all, but for now, no questions. Can you live with that?"

"I can."

"Good. And I need you not to worry. What I can promise you is this—you will not be homeless."

Harper gave Cornelia the biggest, warmest, happiest smile then threw her arms around Cornelia's shoulders, hugging her tightly.

"Remember," whispered Cornelia. "Not a single word about this to anybody else."

"My lips are sealed," pledged Harper, pressing her finger to her lips.

"Not your mother, not Irwin, nobody."

"I promise."

"I'll take you at your word." Cornelia turned the knob and waved Harper through the front door. "Hold down the fort while I'm gone, Bones," she hollered over her shoulder at the purring feline actively kneading his front claws on her couch cushion.

"I don't think he's paying attention," said Harper.

"Who? Bones? Sheesh, don't let that old cat fool you. He sees and understands everything."

CHAPTER 16

Olivia

Olivia grabbed her keys, her wallet, but most importantly, the letter from the court, and stuffed everything in her handbag. Then she slipped on her sneakers and groaned. Her ankle felt tender. Although the swelling had gone down quite a bit, it still felt slightly inflamed. With little time to lament, she grabbed her coat and pulled open the front door.

"Ah! What the—" she screeched, leaping back. She pressed her fingers on her throat, gasping. "What the *hell* are you doing here?"

Darren lowered the hand he was about to knock with. "Sorry, Liv. Didn't mean to scare you."

"Argh, well, you did!" Olivia grumbled, shoving her second arm into her jacket.

"I wondered if I could talk to you for a minute?" he asked.

Darren's lack of haughty demeanor didn't go unnoticed.

What knocked the wind out of his sails?

215

"About what?"

"Us. You and me. Harper. All of it."

"Oh." Olivia tugged the front door shut, zipped her jacket closed, and talked while she walked. Darren trailed behind. "Well, today's your lucky day because this is going to be the quickest conversation you ever had, so pay attention. One, there is no 'us' or 'you and me.' Secondly, Harper is no longer your concern, not like she ever was. And thirdly, but just as importantly, I'm late for work, so any soul-searching tête-à-tête you want to have now is about, hmmm, I'd say six years too little, too late." Olivia pushed forward.

Darren had little difficulty keeping pace next to Olivia's long, angry strides. "Granted, you have no reason to trust me, Liv. I get that. I haven't exactly given you much of a reason, but that's in the past. I'm clean now and trying to get my life together. I'm working hard to make something of myself."

What "us" is this guy talking about?

Olivia side-eyed him, measuring her response in her head as he spoke. She and Darren were fire and water together. Nothing more than former drug buddies. Casual sex partners. Maybe at one time she would have said she loved him, but now? "What does any of this have to do with me?"

Darren sniffled.

"Are you crying?" Olivia couldn't help but glower. In all the years she'd known this man, not once had she seen him cry. Throw temper tantrums—too many to recount. Toss seedy motel rooms—a standard. Land the occasional cutting remark—most assuredly. But a tear? Never.

216

"No, runny nose," he lied. "My allergies. Do you have a tissue?"

Olivia dug in her bag. "Here," she said, offering him a small travel packet.

Darren plucked a single tissue and handed it back. "Thanks."

Olivia stuffed the packet in her bag, continuing to walk while she talked.

"Listen, Darren. I don't mean to blow you off." She distinctly heard Darren humph. "Okay, maybe I do, but I get that you had it hard inside. I even understand that it must be difficult to get acclimated to life outside prison, but me and Harper, we're not your welcoming committee or safety net. Shit, trust and believe, I'm barely our own safety net no less anyone else's, and I don't need you dragging us further down."

"But…" Darren looked ready to interrupt.

"No, don't interrupt me. You listen for once. I've got a lot on my plate right now," continued Olivia, her hands wigwagging wildly. She tended to use her hands to talk. Gesticulating, snapping her fingers, the occasional clap. When the two had first begun hanging out, Darren had once compared her way of expressing herself to that of a plastered music composer. She'd also clearly remembered him stinking of alcohol and sweat, eyes bugged out and desolate, threatening to break her finger the next time she dared point it in his face.

"I can't babysit you," she said emphatically. "You're going to have to figure your life out on your own. Or better yet, find somebody else to save you, but I'm not the same person you left for dead six years ago."

Just leave us alone.

Darren reached for Olivia's arm. "Liv, stop walking. Just for a minute."

Olivia's chin jutted. She hated how casually he used his pet name for her. *Liv.* As if no time or disaster had jimmied between them. "Make it quick. I'm not getting fired over you."

"Okay, fine. Quick you want—quick it is." He positioned himself in front of her, blocking her from continuing to walk. "For the record, I know I haven't been around, but I have a job now, and it pays well. I could help. That's if you let me." Darren stared into Olivia's eyes, much in the same way he did when he would try to persuade her to score for him. It worked then, not so much now.

Olivia checked her watch and looped her hand in the air, gesturing for Darren to hurry and wrap his pitch up.

"I won't bullshit you."

That'll be a first.

"Bottom line, I need to find a place to live. My parole officer has a stick up his ass and has made it clear that my time at the halfway house is coming to a swift close. If you let me stay with you, I could—"

"I knew it," groaned Olivia.

"No. Stop. I mean, please wait. Just hear me out."

"You must be joking."

"Liv, come on, I'm not asking for you to take care of me. I'm not even asking for a handout. I can contribute to the rent, help pay the bills, buy the food. Whatever you want."

Olivia pinched the bridge of her nose, weighing her almost non-existent options. She thought about the court letter tucked in her bag, about the back rent owed, the pending eviction if the court didn't decide in her favor.

"I can't," she mumbled.

"I'll sleep on the couch," Darren interjected, apparently reading her face. "I swear, you won't even know I'm there."

She sneered. "Right."

"No, I mean it. And if I do anything to piss you off, I'll leave, no questions asked."

How many times had she heard that one before?

The temptation to take Darren up on his offer pulled at Olivia's heartstrings, not for him, but for what staying at the house would mean to Harper. Darren offered a way out or, at least, a temporary reprieve. On the other hand, she knew full well her daughter would lose her mind if Darren came back home to stay with them, despite whatever monetary contributions he could offer.

Darren shifted his stance and took a step back, giving Olivia room to move. "You know what? Just think about what I said. That's all I ask." He dug in his pocket and handed her a small folded paper. "Take this," he said, pointing, with nails trimmed and clean. Another surprise. At the height of their drug-induced escapades, dirt-encrusted nails were a commonality. Living in filth, the norm. How many dirty beds had she woken up in, slept in, sold her body for a hit in?

"These are my two phone numbers. My job's the

first one, and where I'm staying is the other. You can reach me at either one." Without affording Olivia a chance to respond, Darren gave a slight nod and took off in the opposite direction. "Call me," he shouted, his hand cupped to his ear like a phone.

Olivia stood frozen in place. She clutched the slip of paper like a lifeline as she watched Darren cross the road and disappear down a side street.

What the hell just happened?

***

"Olivia? When you have a minute," suggested Olivia's manager, Ralph Findley, his lips concealed by a bushy white beard and lopsided mustache. Built low to the ground and stocky, his usual attire consisted mainly of over-sized, plaid flannel shirts. Long sleeve, short sleeve, didn't matter. As long as they were large enough to conceal his paunch belly adequately. Olivia knew he married his childhood sweetheart. She often envisioned the pair holed up in some mushroom-shaped cottage at the edge of a forest instead of living in the small coop he owned next to the food mart. However, despite Ralph's dreary disposition and gnome-like appearance, he'd always treated Olivia fairly.

"Sure thing." Olivia finished ringing up the next customer. She positioned her CLOSED stand after the last of the items. Since her shift was almost over, Olivia removed her cash tray and brought it upfront before tracking down Ralph.

"Thanks, Olivia," said Harriet, accepting the tray. "You done for the day?"

"Sure am." Olivia winked. "Do you know where Ralph went off to?"

"I think he's in his office. If not, you might want to check the meat department. I think a delivery pulled in a short while ago."

"Great, thanks." Olivia checked the office. No Ralph. She then followed Harriet's suggestion and headed towards the meat department, bumping into him halfway.

"Ah, Olivia. Good. I was just coming to get you," said Ralph. "Follow me." He kept walking in the direction of his office.

Despite her swollen ankle, Olivia did her best to keep up. She followed Ralph to his office.

"Take a seat," he said as he closed the door.

"Is there a problem?" asked Olivia, worried. She'd only been to Ralph's office a handful of times over the years.

Ralph sat on the edge of his desk cupping his one knee with his hands while the other leg remained on the floor. "I was about to ask you the same thing."

"Really?" Olivia squinted. "Why's that?"

"For starters, you've been calling out more than usual. Secondly, you look distracted, not your usual friendly self. And most noticeably, you're limping. Why are you limping?"

Olivia couldn't afford to lose her job. She tried to stay as calm as possible, but it was hard, especially knowing she'd already lost the house.

"Olivia?"

"I stubbed my toe the other night," she blurted out. "Right on the corner of the coffee table. Stupidest thing." Her gazed lowered. "It's still swollen."

Ralph made a noncommittal nod. "If you're having any problems at home, anything you want to talk about, you know you can talk to me," he offered.

"Everything's fine," she assured him, speaking louder and with more oomph than called for. "Really. Everything's great." She shrugged. "Minus my stupid toe." Olivia plastered the biggest cheesy smile across her face, or at least, her lips did.

Ralph stared a moment before replying. "All right. I'll let it go for now, but consider yourself warned. You've used up all your call-out time for the month. I suggest you soak that toe over the weekend and heal up." Ralph rose and walked to the back of his desk to take a seat. "I'll see you Monday morning," he said, no longer looking Olivia in the eye.

Shit. He knows I'm lyin' and he's mad.

"You got it, boss," said Olivia as she headed for the door. "Monday, bright and early." Her heartbeat raced as she hastily left the office.

"Have a good weekend, Olivia," called Harriet from behind the cash register. "Give my best to Harper."

"Will do." Olivia fake-smiled while returning the wave, careful to conceal her gimp. She didn't look forward to the hike home. She dreaded, even more, telling Harper about the eviction notice. Most of all, she despised herself for contemplating Darren's self-serving offer. Then again, desperate times called for drastic measures, and if she wasn't desperate, then damn it, who was?

222

***

Olivia limped up the steps and immediately noticed something—a piece of paper wedged between the front door and the doorknob. White. An envelope most likely. What now? Olivia snatched the envelope, half expecting another official notice of something terrible, but instead, she saw her name scribbled across the front in a lovely, measured script.

"Hmm?" Olivia flipped the sealed envelope over. The handwriting looked strangely familiar. She unlocked the door, stepped inside, and bolted it shut before taking a deep breath in preparation for the next wave of disappointment.

Dearest Olivia,

Sorry to have missed you.

Excuse my popping over uninvited, but I wanted to see if you were up to having tea. There's a nice little tea shop that opened in town, and I've been dying to try it. Perhaps next time.

I look forward to seeing you and Harper tomorrow for dinner at Irwin's. Dress comfy and bring your appetites.

Hugs, Cornelia

Olivia smiled, relieved. She liked Cornelia a lot.

Irwin also. In a short period of time, the two had brought such joy into her and Harper's life. If only she could reciprocate.

Olivia took a magnet out of the drawer and used it to stick the note on the fridge. She'd have to remember to let Harper know not to worry about dressing up. Then again, it might be nice to see Harper out of her usual drab attire and into something more agreeable.

Olivia limped into the kitchen. The bananas sat on the counter, ripening. Tomorrow she'd get up early to bake the bread.

***

Harper

Harper had a difficult time concentrating in class. Every once in a while, she'd notice how her classmates kidded around, their only concerns centered around their studies and social life, oblivious to the kind of real-world problems she seemed to attract.

Being an introvert, she hadn't made a lot of close friends, but she hadn't made any enemies, either. The thought of having to leave her school and change school districts, flaws and all, saddened her. With one year left before graduation, Harper didn't feel much like traversing her way through a new set of school politics and social expectations.

More than that, the realization that she could lose her home scared her. Moreover, although she trusted Cornelia, Harper didn't know what could be done to stop an eviction, short of a wad of cash falling from the sky into their laps, and even then, what was to prevent the same thing from happening again?

Harper considered the scholarship paperwork, languishing in her drawer. The guidance counselor had made it her life mission to harass Harper on a daily basis about getting it filled out and handed in early to increase her chance of getting financial aid. Harper had wanted to go over it with her mother over the weekend to discuss college options. However, now, with everything else going on…

Harper sighed.

Why bother?

The change of class bell echoed throughout the building. The rest of the other students ran for the door, laughing, joking around, pushing their way through, and partnering on the way out. Without making eye contact with anybody else, Harper lingered, taking her time to stuff her textbook and notes into her bag.

She needed to speak to someone. Somebody she could trust and who would never reveal her secrets. Somebody who wouldn't judge her. Harper swung her bag over her shoulder and bolted for the door. She knew just where to go.

***

Darren

His time at the halfway house was running out, and as much as Darren disliked going back on his word, he found himself headed straight in Olivia's direction to see if she'd made up her mind yet. He had little choice. And if not, well, at least he'd know where he stood.

Before knocking, Darren peeked through the front window of the kitchen. Through the flimsy curtain, he could make out Olivia sitting at the round kitchen table. She had her head bowed on the surface, enclosed by her arms. On closer inspection, he noticed her shoulders bob up and down. Olivia was crying. Scattered across the table in front of her were a bunch of papers. Darren wondered what they could contain to make her so upset.

Darren inched slightly away from the window, careful not to let Olivia catch him snooping.

He returned to the front door, contemplating whether to leave. He lifted his fist to knock but stopped. Darren thought back to the last time he saw Olivia crying like that. He'd done something to hurt her. He couldn't recall about what now. That list seemed endless. How many nights had he left her sobbing to feed his habit, while she remained home not knowing where their next meal would come from or how they'd pay for another month's rent? Darren didn't leave only Olivia, though. His neglect extended to Harper as well. The baby he never wanted or cared for. The infant he never washed or fed or protected. The vulnerable, beautiful child his actions exposed to the underbelly of life, including the danger strangers brought with them, flitting in and out of their lives, taking whatever they wanted, including…

Darren practically choked on his shame. He

226

should have killed that guy when he had the chance. He should have beaten the shit out of him as soon as he walked in and found him standing over Harper's crib as she slept, his fingers lingering over her skin, touching his baby girl, and he too blasted out of mind to stop it. Head stuck in a fog and more concerned about finding his next high.

A car alarm blared further down the block, giving Darren a jolt. He bent over and picked a weather-worn leather bracelet off the grass, assuming it belonged to his daughter. It seemed like something she'd wear. He played with it, flipping it over a few times. He noticed how small and worn the leather was: soft and supple. He'd personally return it to her later if she decided to talk to him again.

Darren thought about Harper's vulnerability, her pent-up anger, her distrust. He often wondered if she had any memory of that night. She couldn't have been older than two at the time. A baby, so vulnerable. How many times did he want to write and ask her over the years, see how much she recalled? But each time he tore the pages up, too terrified to learn the truth.

God, what if she does remember? What if she blames me for what happened?

Darren couldn't blame Harper if she did. He'd been a coward.

Darren's overriding guilt never prevented those images from haunting his sleep.

That's probably why she hates me so much.

Behind bars, Darren tried to make amends, in his own dysfunctional way. Instead of writing more letters to Olivia, he redirected his rage on others, especially anyone suspected of child molestation. It became a quest of sorts. A recompense. Darren made it his business to taunt his prey, creep up behind them when they least expected it, and then whisper a few threats for them to take back to their cell. Something to mull over behind bars, in the dark. He'd lay it on heavy, in full technicolor sordid detail outlining for these bastards all the unthinkable things he planned to inflict upon them if he ever caught them alone. Most were empty threats. A measured way to pass the time as quickly as possible, but not always.

One afternoon, Darren caught a known pervert alone in the showers. Refusing to let this window of opportunity disappear, Darren dove in blaring, fists first, beating the bastard within an inch of his miserable life. Minutes later, sirens deafened the air while teams of correctional officers swarmed the unit. The guards threw Darren into solitary confinement. The inmate, too scared to talk, remained silent on the matter, and eventually, the prison dropped the charges and released Darren back into general population with a stern warning. From that point moving forward, Darren had made a name for himself on the tier, nicknamed Crusher for the way he smashed his victim's face in, crushing bone. The title served him well.

Darren glanced over towards Olivia's house, ashamed. The old house's dilapidated exterior stood as a clear testament to his long list of shortcomings. Instead of being a real man and fixing the issue, his ex and daughter lived in squalor, by the looks of things. But here he stood, ready to maneuver himself back into their already struggling lives—as if he had the right to do so.

His shoulders sank under the weightiness of understanding. Darren knew he had no business coming back into their lives, making demands no less. He could see that now. It was only his absolute selfishness that kept him expecting fixes from everyone else for the problems he alone created. Shame turned the tips of his ears a burnished red, and his culpability made him sick.

The old neighborhood began to stir awake. Slowly, doors opened and lives resumed. A couple of cars passed by, but nobody bothered to glance in his direction.

Absentmindedly, Darren reached out to hold the railing and, "Shit!" He grumbled behind gritted teeth when he almost took a spill as a piece of the railing gave way.

Hands a bit unsteady, Darren struggled to light a cigarette. He puffed as he walked farther and farther away, never once turning to look back. He had come searching for answers, and now he had them. Just not the ones he had hoped for.

CHAPTER 17

Irwin

Friday. Time to visit Gilly. In the days since the memorial service for Dakota, Irwin had felt less anxious about his self-imposed timetable. Although he left the library at the same time, he had begun arriving when he did instead of the tense push of the recent past. At first, Irwin thought his laid-back attitude was because he didn't need to stop at the hospital to sit with Dakota, but after some contemplation, Irwin decided it had more to do with an overriding peacefulness. Today, almost as an afterthought, he added a stop after the florist to pick up a bag of candy. A variety of sweets to keep in his pocket.

By the time Irwin arrived at the cemetery, he was a good forty-five minutes later than usual, but the sun was shining, the winds of the past week had calmed down, and the warm air felt great against his face. Leaves of every hue sprinkled down from the sky like raindrops.

Instead of his customary march, Irwin took his time walking the cement path toward Gilly. It wasn't until he saw the same young man from the last time, solemnly standing by his lost one's grave, did Irwin pick up the pace. He was excited to fill Gilly, and now Dakota, in on all the latest happenings, especially the long-awaited news he'd received from the lawyer about—

Irwin stopped dead in his tracks. Then, without much thought, he just as quickly skirted off to the side to hide behind a terribly thin tree trunk. He looked rather comical poking his head out just enough to get a better look while trying not to be detected. Too late. The young man saw Irwin. He was about to say something when Irwin lifted his finger to his lips pleading for him to shush. The young man shrugged but complied.

Irwin went back to spying, but it didn't take x-ray vision to realize that it was Harper standing by Gilly's headstone, and from the looks of it, she was having a full-blown conversation. Irwin wasn't sure if he was shocked, angry, or just plain jealous. Irwin tiptoed closer and crouched behind a large headstone, close enough to eavesdrop.

"Everyone who knew you and Dakota keep telling me how close you two were," said Harper, her backpack hiked on her shoulder, a small collection of wildflowers in her hand. "My mom and I used to be close like that too, but recently, things aren't so good between us. We argue all the time about anything. It's almost as if she doesn't trust me enough to tell me the entire truth...just pieces, until it blows up in her face. Then she freaks out, loses her shit, and dumps it all on me. Somehow, I'm expected to listen without having any say. I mean, is that even fair?" Harper bent over and leaned the bouquet carefully against the stone. "These aren't as fancy as Irwin's, but I thought they were pretty. They grow wild by the side of the highway."

Irwin cringed at the thought of Harper walking on the side of a busy highway while cars sped past.

She could have gotten herself killed. I have a good mind to—

"Lately, I've mostly been talking to Cornelia and Irwin about my problems, but I feel like a burden on them. It's like every time I talk to them, there's some new major crisis I need help with." She wiped a lone tear from her cheek. "They must hate me."

Far from it.

Irwin stretched his neck so as not to miss a single word.

"The thing is I need advice, and I know how much Irwin trusted…trusts you. I hope it's okay that I came." Harper hugged herself. "So, I guess I better start, right?" She dug her hands into her pocket and swayed. "I found out this morning that we're getting evicted."

Irwin gasped and almost gave himself away. *Evicted?*

"My mom's been having a hard time making ends meet. She has problems with her feet and had to take a few days off, and I guess we kind of got behind on the rent. Of course, she never said anything. Always plays like everything's all right, so like usual, I had to find out on my own." Harper dug her boot heel into the soft earth and wiped her eyes. Her voice cracked slightly when she began to speak again. "I—I don't know what do? Is it so bad to want a normal life like other kids? Go to school, graduate, go to college—if I can get in—graduate, and get a job. Then I'll be able to take care of my mom," she mumbled. "But nothing can ever go smoothly for us, I swear. As soon as one problem gets solved, another one shows up, and I'm sick of it. Ju-just sick of it," she whimpered in a ragged, breathless sob.

Irwin leaned forward and mistakenly stepped on a pile of dry leaves. He froze, teeth gritted, and half expecting Harper to turn around any second. Thankfully, she was too preoccupied to notice. Irwin blew out a silent, grateful breath.

"And now I probably won't even be able to graduate from the same high school—unless my mother can find a place in the area, but who knows if that'll happen?" Harper subconsciously brushed the top of Gilly's headstone. "You know, Irwin really misses you still, but I guess you know that already with him coming to talk to you all the time." Harper suddenly jolted. "Oh shit, Irwin!" Her head spun all around as if caught shoplifting. "Today's Friday."

Irwin pressed his body as hard as he could against the tree trunk, attempting to make himself invisible, but as he did, he caught the young guy nearby grinning, obviously finding Irwin's plight entertaining. Irwin shot him *the look,* the one he saved for all unruly or intractable humans.

Unfettered by Irwin's annoyance, the young man

233

merely shrugged, a slight smirk never leaving his lips.

"I better get going. Irwin should be rolling up here any minute, and I don't want him to know we chatted." Harper hiked her backpack over her shoulder and placed a small flower on the edge of Gilly's headstone. "Thanks for listening, Gilly. I wish I could have met you in person," she said before taking her leave.

Irwin, doing his best impersonation of a fledging ghost, lurked around the trunk a little at a time as Harper walked past, but he needn't have worried. She was too upset to look up, and she strode straight past him, none the wiser.

As soon as the coast was clear, Irwin straightened himself out, fixed his coat, and adjusted his hat. Anything to salvage what dwindling dignity he had left. Irwin headed over to Gilly, ignoring the chuckle coming from behind him.

"Slick moves, old man," said the young man, standing with his arms crossed playfully over his chest. "I thought for a minute you were toast."

Irwin muttered something unrepeatable under his breath.

"Is she your daughter?"

Irwin halted and stared at the handsome young man with squinted, beady eyes. "Yes. My wife and I couldn't decide what to call her, so we named her Jailbait."

"Whoa," said the young man, almost stumbling backward, his hands held high in the air in mock surrender. "I'm not on it like that. I was only asking because she left something over there," he said, pointing.

Irwin looked. The young man was right. There, crumpled in a small bundle, was one of Harper's scarves.

"Oh. Right." Irwin walked over and picked it up. He shook it out and reluctantly stuffed it in his pocket. "Thank you," he muttered.

"No problem."

Finally alone, Irwin faced Gilly's headstone, unable to speak, uncertain about where to start. After what he just overheard Harper saying, his news, by comparison, seemed anticlimactic.

"Well, I see you and Harper have met." Irwin bent over on one knee and laid his flowers in their customary spot and removed the older ones, careful not to disturb the wildflowers brought by Harper. "I never knew you two were conversing," he said, slightly tilting his head. "But at least now you have a face and voice to go with the stories I've been telling you." Irwin tugged his coat sleeve, more out of habit. "She's a good kid, Gilly. Just over stressed with adult problems. But clearly, you already know that." Irwin brushed off his one knee and stood. "Listen, hon, I came to tell you that I got approved for the building." Irwin took a deep breath and exhaled, on the one hand glad to start the long-awaited process, but on the other torn that Gilly wouldn't be there to see it through. It had been more their dream than just his. "I should be signing the final paperwork sometime tomorrow." Irwin shrugged and shifted his weight to his other leg. "The lawyer finagled me a good price on the building. Not the one we first looked at that had the steep steps in the back, but the one around the corner with the good parking in the back. You know the building I'm talking about, near the donut shop, walking distance from the house."

Irwin had the strangest sensation of being watched. He peeked over his shoulder and saw the young man staring in his direction.

Irwin grumbled at the intrusion, but more out of embarrassment. His last surly comment had left him feeling oddly horrible, a sensation he was not accustomed to. "Who do you come to visit?" Irwin called out, feigning interest.

The young man rubbed the headstone. "My mother. You?"

Irwin never referred to Gilly as his fiancé when speaking to strangers. The label fell flat on his ears, especially because she'd been so much more than that. "My heart," he answered uncharacteristically.

The young man nodded. "I hear you, man," he commiserated and began walking in Irwin's direction.

No. Stop walking.

Irwin squeezed his fists tightly.

What is he doing?

He dreaded further discourse.

"I'm Christopher." The young man reached out to shake Irwin's hand.

Irwin reluctantly reciprocated. "Irwin."

"Nice meeting you, Irwin. I mean, despite our..." Christopher tilted his chin towards the graves. "You know what I mean."

Irwin fought down the sharp quip burning at the

back of his throat. "Indubitably," he mumbled instead. The two men stood shoulder to shoulder until Christopher spoke again.

"It's none of my business, but your daughter seemed pretty upset."

Irwin stared straight ahead.

"Yeah. I saw her crying pretty hard before you showed up."

Irwin turned his head to stare. "Was she?"

"Hell yeah. But I can't blame her, though. I mean, I still can't believe my mother's gone."

Irwin cleared his throat. "'For life and death are one, even as the river and the sea are one,'" he recited.

"Ah, Khalil Gibran," said Christopher.

"You're a reader," said Irwin, pleasantly surprised.

"Fourth-year, Pre-law, eventually law school. At the local college, or at least I did. Tuition's pretty high, but it's the room and board that's killing me. Unless I can find a job that works around my weird schedule, I'll have to put this last semester off." Christopher stuck his hands in his pockets. "Want to know something kind of weird?"

"Not really."

"The first time I came here alone, the words of Norman Cousins sprang to mind," said Christopher.

Irwin stretched his neck to the sky. "And what, pray tell, were those oracular words?"

Christopher lifted his eyes to meet Irwin's. "'Death is not the greatest loss in life. The greatest loss is what dies inside of us while we live.'"

Irwin lowered his head as if in prayer. "This is

true."

"Indubitably," muttered Christopher, staring off into space.

Irwin grinned.

This kid's all right.

***

Cornelia

Cornelia struggled to balance a massive tray of baked ziti on her knee while using her chin to clamp hold of a loaf of Italian bread. With the heel of her shoe, she hit the side of Irwin's door.

"I could use a hand out here," she hollered, annoyed with Bones, who thought now was an appropriate time to thread his furry body between Cornelia's legs. "Like today, Irwin."

Irwin opened the door. "What's all this?"

"The makings of an android," snipped Cornelia, shoving her way forward and trying not to trip. "It's dinner, ya big buffoon. Now grab this already. It's heavy," she said, shoving it into Irwin's chest. "Bones!" she hollered at the cat wafting back and forth. "I swear this dastardly feline is determined to make me fall on my ass."

Irwin rescued the tray from Cornelia's death grip while Bones, tail curled in the shape of a question mark, trotted straight past him to his water dish.

"That cat will be the death of me one of these days." Cornelia grabbed the loaf of bread and swung it in the air like a scepter. "Throw the tray in the oven to stay warm while I slice this bread."

Irwin set the heat and timer on the stove. "I have salad. It's in the salad drawer."

"Not one of those pre-made things, I hope."

Irwin opened the fridge, raised the small bag in the air, and shook.

Cornelia rolled her eyes. "I guess it'll have to do. Grab a bowl and dump it in," she grumbled. "You have anything to drink that's not past its expiration date? I'm parched." Not bothering to wait on Irwin's reply, Cornelia yanked the refrigerator door open. "Ah, geez, Irwin," she grumbled. "Do you not believe in food shopping or what?"

"I didn't have time."

"Didn't have time? Oh please."

"I'm serious."

"What utter nonsense. You act like you're some big-wig executive." She shook her head, mumbling. "You don't have time. Give me a break already."

"I've been busy."

"Oh, stop it " Cornelia reached in the drawer and grabbed a bread knife. She stood motionless for a moment, trying to remember why.

Irwin handed the folder from the attorney to Cornelia. "I need you to read this."

"Huh? Oh, yes. After I'm done."

"I need you to read this now."

Cornelia stomped her foot. "I said after I'm done," she snapped and immediately regretted it. She'd been losing her temper more and more recently. "Sorry. I didn't mean to do that." Cornelia gripped the counter top to steady herself. She wiped her hands on a towel. "Hand it to me." Irwin obliged. "That looks awfully official. Another letter from your attorney?"

"Yes."

"Please tell me you're not in trouble."

"Don't be ridiculous," Irwin bristled. "Why do you always think the worst of me?"

Cornelia's brows arched. "Let's leave that one alone for now." She snatched the envelope from Irwin and peeked inside. Realizing Irwin was looming over her, Cornelia tentatively slid the packet of papers out. "Pretty thick stack you got going on over here."

"It's a contract."

"A contract. For what?"

"Read it, and then I'll answer all your questions." Irwin stepped back to give her some room. He leaned back on the kitchen counter, head bowed and fidgeting with his fingers.

Cornelia read the first three sentences and peered up at Irwin. "You can't be serious right now?"

"I am."

"This is—" Cornelia's eyes widened. "Well, it's life changing, Irwin."

"It could be, or it could be an absolutely unmitigated disaster."

"No, don't say that. I mean, sure, this is one hell of a big step, but not in a bad way. It's just, well, I guess I just assumed you weren't still contemplating doing this since Gilly passed."

Cornelia's mind raced past thoughts of her earlier conversation with Harper. She needed to speak to Irwin tonight about so many things, but now with this news, she wasn't sure it was the right time. Still, Harper's situation was urgent. Cornelia continued to read.

"Is this the two-story building on Gold Street? The one near the donut shop?" she asked.

"That's the one."

"Uh-huh. And will you have use of the entire building?"

"The whole kit and caboodle."

Cornelia nodded, her eyes affixed to the page, skimming the fine print. "You wouldn't happen to have any plans for the downstairs?"

"I'm still planning on opening a bookstore."

"Right. Of course. The bookstore." Cornelia took a seat. "Correct me if I'm wrong, but doesn't the building contain two or three floors?"

"Two, with a working basement for storage."

Cornelia nodded again, taking the information in. "And upstairs? What are you doing with that space?"

"The upstairs has apartments. Two, actually. One's a nice sized studio—single occupancy—and the other is a two bedroom. Both aren't excessively large, but they're in fairly good shape. Nothing a can of paint and a few updated fixtures can't fix."

"I see."

"And depending on the closing costs, I might put in a few new appliances. At least a stove in the bigger apartment. Maybe a microwave in the studio, but I'm not sure yet."

Cornelia clearly heard the excited lilt rise in Irwin's voice. She tapped her nail on the table.

Apartments…

"Hmmm. And when exactly do you plan on making this official?"

241

"Well, as far as I'm concerned," said Irwin, grabbing a seat and joining her. "The sooner, the better. I sign the papers tomorrow. Then it's up to me when I open."

"Really?" Cornelia read further along. Her thoughts raced with the possibilities.

Irwin watched but remained quiet.

Cornelia appreciated his patience. After a good ten minutes, she finally looked up and smiled.

"Well?" he asked. "Tell me the truth. Am I insane for doing this? I can still back out. I have until tomorrow to decide."

"Insane?" Cornelia chuckled. "You passed that mood marker a long time ago, but *this*?" Cornelia laid the contract reverently down on the table. "*This*, my friend, is brilliant."

Irwin stared in relieved disbelief. "You think so? I mean, you don't think I'm biting off more than I can chew?"

Cornelia smiled. "Don't be silly. Nobody loves or knows books better than you. What better way to spend your time? Besides, what do you have to lose?"

"My savings."

"Yeah, okay, there's that."

"There's also my pride."

"Irwin…"

"Not to mention my self-worth if this thing goes belly up."

"Enough. Nobody likes a Debbie-downer. This sleepy town desperately needs a nice bookshop, and I bet, with the right marketing and—" Cornelia froze. Her brows furrowed in consternation.

"What is it?" Irwin leaned in, apparently alarmed. "Why'd you stop talking?"

Cornelia pursed her lips. "Irwin," she said softly. "You do understand that people come to bookstores?"

"Yes, Cornelia. I realize that."

"Young people, old people, nice people, not-so-nice people…"

Irwin tilted his head and crossed his arms over his chest.

"But the common denominator is they are people."

"Cornelia."

"Wait, hear me out. Unlike the library, where you're practically a fixture, as a business owner, you won't be able to insult, offend, or curse at your customers. I mean, you could, but it won't end well. You do comprehend this concept, don't you?"

"I'm not an idiot, Cornelia."

"Certainly not, but you are a bit of a…"

Irwin, with a twinkle in his eye, leaned forward again. "A what?" he goaded.

Cornelia grinned. "A bit of a curmudgeon."

Irwin nodded. "A bit."

"And a killjoy."

"A killjoy as well?" he teased.

"And one hell of a sourpuss. Admit it, Irwin, you do tend to get a bit standoffish at times."

Irwin snorted.

"See? That's exactly what I mean. You can't act like that around potential customers."

Irwin stood. "Although I find your description of me wanting, I do concede to the fact that human

243

interaction isn't one of my stronger suits."

This time, Cornelia snorted. "You can say that again."

"And because of this slight imperfection—"

"Slight imperfection my arse."

"—I have come up with a plan," said Irwin louder.

"A plan?" Now Cornelia crossed her arms over her chest. "This should be good."

"More of a solution, actually. And one I hope will help solve a few other outstanding issues as well."

"Ah, yes. Other outstanding issues," agreed Cornelia. "I know them well."

"What do you mean by that?"

"What do you mean by that?" countered Cornelia.

"Cornelia!"

"Irwin!"

The two stared at one another, marking their territory.

Cornelia squinted at Irwin. "It means we need to talk about something important and it can't wait."

Irwin's face grew taut with trepidation. "Go ahead," he said, returning to his seat.

Cornelia drew a deep breath before her thoughts tumbled forth in a torrent. "Harper came to see me this morning. Crying." Cornelia glared pleadingly into Irwin's eyes, enunciating each of her words. "She told me that she and her mom are getting evicted. She only found out this morning when she saw the notice sticking out of her mother's sweater. In my opinion, Olivia was probably trying to protect

Harper until she could find the right time to tell her, but of course, Harper being a typical teenager automatically jumped to the conclusion that her mother must be hiding something."

Irwin lifted a finger as if to say something.

"Wait, there's more," said Cornelia. "Not only that, but Harper's convinced they'll wind up in some homeless shelter."

"And that's why—"

"Hold on, let me finish. If they have to move, Harper won't be able to graduate from her high school if her mom can't find them an affordable apartment in the same district." Cornelia rested her hand on the table. "She's terrified, Irwin."

Irwin laid his hand gently over Cornelia's. "I already know," he murmured softly.

"You already know what? Which part?" complained Cornelia, ready to pounce. "And you said nothing to me?"

"I just found out myself."

"Likely story." Cornelia winced, more because she hadn't come clean with her news. Here she was accusing Irwin of the same thing she was guilty of doing, but finding the time to tell him hadn't been easy.

"But in this case, a true one. I saw Harper at the cemetery this afternoon."

"At the cemetery? You took her with you?"

"No. She was already there when I arrived. I found her talking to Gilly."

"Go on."

"And I kind of overheard what she said."

Cornelia's eyes widened. "You were spying on

her?"

"No…okay, maybe, yes…a little, but the point is, I know."

Cornelia leaned back in her chair, gaping at Irwin with newfound admiration. "You sneaky old reprobate—"

Irwin grinned.

"Always the first one to act as if you couldn't care about anybody, but all along…" Cornelia playfully wagged her finger in his face.

Irwin pretended offense, but Cornelia caught a slight jiggle of his brow. "But don't say anything yet," he warned.

"Oh, no worries. Your ill-gotten secret's safe with me."

I probably won't remember it anyway.

For the longest time, Cornelia opted to ignore the symptoms. She chalked up her wonky memory lapses and growing impatience to getting old. But soon the increased forgetfulness, the lack of recollection, the loss of taste and smell, and most recently, her personality changes had turned profuse. On top of that, never before had she been so easily aggravated.

But what really convinced her to seek help was when she woke up in her car early one morning fully dressed in her clothes from the day before. That's when she panicked and made an appointment with her general practitioner.

The doctor ordered a slew of tests. As Cornelia waited anxiously for the results, her emotions collided, spilling out over here and there. Everything from fear to denial, anger to grief. When the diagnosis finally came, she thought she'd be prepared. But who the hell is ever prepared for Alzheimer's?

Like so many who heard the devastating news for the first time, Cornelia left the doctor's office clutching her bag, now filled with a prescription, a few brochures, and her appointment card for her next follow-up. She had sat in her car paralyzed with fear, too scared to turn it on. Too frightened to know what to do next.

In a hazy daze, she had somehow driven home. Once parked, she had stumbled over to Irwin's in desperate need of a shoulder to cry on, but her timing couldn't have been worse since that had also been the day Dakota died. Cornelia didn't have the heart to dump one more mega-sized burden on Irwin's already crumbling shoulders.

Overwhelmed by how her life had already started to change, she clung to what she knew. Denial. For Cornelia, who had been highly independent all her life, denial seemed like a good choice since it seemed impossible to comprehend the enormity of what she would inevitably face.

Coming to terms and moving forward with her newly disclosed diagnosis had been difficult, especially as her symptoms began to reveal themselves in more visible and insidious ways. It was only a matter of time before Irwin figured it out, time she didn't control nor have much left of. She feared how this would affect Irwin. There was a sense of loss, an overriding resentment that this monster had selected her brain to attack.

Eventually, she had come to accept her

diagnosis. With Irwin, Harper, and Olivia, Cornelia was determined to live her life in a positive and fulfilling way, but there was no denying how much everything would drastically change as a result. But despite feeling overcome by the roller coaster of emotions, she held it together in the only way she knew how—in helping others. And it worked. For a bit. But since then, she had cried herself to sleep every night.

CHAPTER 18

Irwin

Irwin twitched in his seat, feeling inexplicably nervous under the barrage of inquisitive glares coming from the men who passed him as he waited, sitting on a hall bench. A few offered him an indifferent quipped "hello," while most barely acknowledged his existence.

The halfway house seemed brighter inside, more inviting than Irwin had assumed. However, the air transmitted an institutional odor. Or perhaps he was just smelling somebody's overzealous use of bleach.

Irwin sat erect, his hat resting on his lap. He shifted and stretched his foot, which had begun to fall asleep. The unease of seeing this cockamamie plan of his through had made sound sleep nearly impossible. For the last few nights, he'd toss and turn until eventually dozing off about three hours before having to wake back up.

Irwin heard the echo of a set of heavy footsteps

pummeling down the stairs.

As soon as Darren turned the corner and saw Irwin, he groaned.

"Ugh, not you again," Darren grumbled. "What's with you and coming here? You know, this could be construed as a form of stalking."

Irwin stood, refusing to swap banalities. "Have you thought about what we discussed at our last meeting?" he asked, voice resolute.

"Yeah." Darren locked eyes on Irwin. "I gave it some consideration."

Irwin's eyes remained fixed on Darren's face. "And what have you decided?"

Darren leaned back on the wall. He crossed his arms over his puffed chest. "Before I say anything, I need to know why you're doing this." He lowered his voice and leaned in. "What's in it for you?"

Impervious, Irwin stepped closer, his weary eyes locked ominously onto Darren's.

"Mr. Crane, I am not here to debate my motivations. As I explained to you before, if you intend on being a positive influence in Harper's life, then you are welcome. And I will do everything in my power to help make that happen. However, should you decide to leave, I will not stop you, but either way, you decide. Harper has the right to know where you stand."

"Yeah. I'm not an idiot. That part I get, but you haven't told me what's in it for you. What's with all the super protective stuff towards my kid?"

"Fair enough." Irwin clasped his hands in front of his body. His shoulders remained stiff. "I have never had children of my own, but I've seen what happens when they've been neglected and abandoned. I've seen promising young lives dissolve under the angst of believing they are unwanted. I watched families torn apart and forever impaired because of one person's self-centeredness. Mr. Crane, Harper is smart, talented. She has succeeded in becoming an exceptionally good person despite the less than affable hand she's been dealt. I, for one, will not sit idly by and watch you unravel your daughter's questionable stability more than you have already." Irwin narrowed his eyes. "Be in her life, Mr. Crane. She needs a father. But if you can't and decide to disappear, then do it now before you cause further irreparable damage and heartbreak."

Darren glared, ready to bolt. "And let's say I decide to stick around. Are you really going to help me out or was that all talk? I mean, you're not pulling my chain, right? Because if I find out you are…"

Irwin took a step closer. "Don't threaten me, Mr. Crane. I am a man of my word. You, on the other hand, have a dubious relationship with the truth. Which begs the question…it's not whether I will follow through, but will you?"

***

Darren

Darren found York bent over in the back room, sifting through boxes, handling inventory.

"Well, it's about time you showed up," York

said.

"Sorry." Darren washed his hands and changed into his apron. He lifted a cardboard box of tomatoes and brought them over to York.

"Just put it down over there," directed York, counting. Darren dropped the box.

"Hey! Careful with that," reprimanded York. "That's food."

"Sorry."

"What the hell is wrong with you, anyway?"

"What do you mean?"

"We're playing that now?"

Darren shrugged. "I'm not playing anything. I just have a lot my mind is all."

York tilted his head. "Your parole babysitter called me," said York, unprompted. "Said he wanted an update on your progress."

Darren waited. "And what did you tell him?"

"I told him the truth. That you've been, for the most part, pretty unremarkable."

Darren blanched.

York glanced up and caught Darren's dire expression. "Chill, man. I'm only messing with you," he said and winked

Darren's shoulders relaxed. "You had me going there for a minute." Darren gripped his waist, bowed his head. "Don't do that. I got enough shit to contend with without you busting my balls."

York lifted a small crate of onions and handed them off to Darren. "Speaking of ball busting, how's Olivia doing these days?"

"Man…I went to her house to, you know, see if she's changed her mind."

"And?"

"And nothing. She wasn't home when I got there," said Darren, glossing over the truth.

York began jotting down numbers on his clipboard. "Then what do you intend on doing about your living arrangement? Jay said you didn't have much more time to figure it out."

"He told you that, did he? What a guy."

Finished, York stood and dusted off his knees. "If you need to take time off to look for a place, all you had to do was ask."

Darren considered Irwin's offer. He'd been thinking of nothing else for weeks since the first time Irwin came to speak to him. Darren had hoped that, by now, Olivia would have changed her mind, but seeing as that didn't look likely, Irwin's proposal seemed the most promising direction to take. If the offer was for real.

"I actually wanted to run something by you," he told York.

"Go for it."

"Do you remember me telling you about that librarian guy? The one hanging around my kid?"

York nodded. "Yeah. What about him?"

"Well, he swung by to speak to me today and made me an offer."

York turned his head, his jaw tight. "What kind of offer are we talking about?"

Darren didn't appreciate York's accusatory tone. "No, no, nothing like that. Relax. Totally legit, I think anyways."

"You think? Stop talkin' in circles, Crane. What exactly did he propose?"

"He started off hounding me about whether or not I intend to be in Harper's life like he's got some right to do that."

"What did you tell him?"

"I told him it was none of his business. I don't have to answer to him or anybody else."

York tilted his head. "You said that to him?"

"I damn well did. I don't need to answer to that old guy."

York shook his head.

"What?"

"Nothing."

"No. I want to know," demanded Darren, tired of everybody treating him like he was stupid or something.

"All right. I'll tell you. I'm looking at you this way because I'm always in awe of what a malignant liar you are."

Darren almost fell back. "What did you call me?"

"A malignant liar. A person who can't tell the truth to save his life."

"I know what it is."

"Then you also know why I'm calling you that."

Darren squinted. York was holding something back, and he aimed to figure out why. "So what are you saying?"

Not easily intimidated, York rose to the challenge. "I'm calling you a liar, Crane. I spoke to Mr. Abernathy after he came to see you. He phoned me and told me what he proposed. I highly doubt you blew him off. As a matter of fact, I think the old guy was right in putting you on the spot. It's time for you to step up or step off, for everyone's sake, but especially Harper's."

Darren's face grew hot and red. "You can't talk to me like that," Darren shouted.

"I can, and I will. Somebody has to," York roared. "You're out of that hell hole, and you've been given a chance to succeed. I like you, man. You know that, but I won't lie to you or for you. You have to take care of your business and stop making excuses. The only way you are going to stay out of prison is to take responsibility for your choices. Take this opportunity to rise to the occasion and be somebody. Make things right."

Darren paced the room. Half of him wanted to book, run far away, while the other part of him—the part that had become whole again—knew he had to stop running.

"Don't walk away from this. Face it. Head on," encouraged York. "I'm here for you, man, but you gotta be here for yourself as well."

With sunken shoulders, Darren nodded and rubbed his tired eyes.

"Are you hearing me?"

"I hear you," Darren said, letting out a deep exhale.

"Do you? Cause it's now or never. You're at the twenty-yard line. You can either fumble, run the ball, punt, or call it quits. The choice, my friend, is up to you."

"You and your football analogies."

"The best kind."

Darren grinned. "Okay. Using your analogy, what if I decide to run the ball myself, go for the touchdown?"

York smiled. "I was hoping you'd say that," he said, giving Darren a congratulatory slap on the shoulder.

CHAPTER 19

Cornelia

Cornelia scurried around the kitchen, prepping this, stirring that while Irwin sat alone in his study lost in his thoughts and busy making copies of his paperwork.

"They're gonna be here any minute, Irwin," shouted Cornelia from the kitchen. "Are you ready?"

Irwin slid the last batch of clipped papers into a large envelope.

"Irwin! Did you hear me? They're gonna be here any minute." She plopped down in a chair to rest. "Are you even listening to me?"

Damn obstinate man.

Cornelia shut her eyes, counting off what she had left to do, repeating in order her tasks, a trick she had incorporated since the forgetting had begun.

Irwin wedged the envelope under his armpit and pulled shut his office door. "Smells good," he

257

announced, walking into the kitchen.

"Oh!" Cornelia grabbed her neck. "You startled me."

"I scare you in my own house."

"Mere details."

The kitchen table had been set for six. Cornelia adjusted one of the forks to line up straighter.

"Listen," muttered Irwin, "can that stay warm for a bit? I'd like to get this over with."

"What?" Cornelia's brow furrowed. She glanced around the kitchen.

"The meeting with everyone?" Irwin stared at his friend, who looked lost in thought. "I'd like to get it over with and then come back to the house to eat."

"That should be fine." Cornelia tucked a piece of loose hair behind her ear. "How long do you think it will take?"

"An hour, if it all goes according to plan, but just in case, let's shut it off."

"You do it. I need to sit down for a minute."

"Are you all right?" Irwin helped lower Cornelia to the seat. "You look a little disoriented."

"Just tired is all. I didn't sleep well last night." In reality, Cornelia hadn't slept a wink. Instead, she wandered around her house, tenderly touching different mementos on her shelves, forcing her mind to recall their history, while desperate to protect the memories she still clung to before having them savagely ripped away. Cornelia glanced up at Irwin. His face was ashen with worry. She knew that the longer she kept him guessing, the madder he'd be, but finding the right time to disclose kept evading her. "Are you nervous?" she asked, wishing to change the subject. "Because I'm nervous."

Irwin shrugged. "I would describe myself as apprehensive more than nervous."

Cornelia laughed. "That's fundamentally the same thing."

"*That's* fundamentally a matter of opinion."

Before they could continue trading barbs, Bones skittered to a sliding stop. Once regaining his footing, the cat leisurely arched his back and nuzzled his face into Irwin's leg, purring.

"All that purring. Glad somebody's happy," mumbled Irwin, bending over to scratch the spoiled cat behind the ear.

"Are you nervous?" asked Cornelia again.

Irwin paused. "You just asked me that."

"Did I?" Cornelia lowered her gaze.

Irwin shut off the burner and took a seat across from Cornelia.

"What aren't you telling me?"

Irwin's grim expression and sad, pleading eyes made Cornelia want to spill the entire jar of beans, but she couldn't. Not yet. *Especially* not today. She laid her hand gently on his. "Listen. I do have something I want to discuss with you, and I will. I promise, but just not today."

Irwin stared steadily into his friend's eyes. "Then when?"

"Tomorrow. After we're all done with this," she said, her hands circling the room. "We'll talk, and I'll fill you in on everything, but give me today not to have to think about it. Deal?"

Irwin gently squeezed Cornelia's hand. "I'm your friend to the end."

"I know that." Cornelia squeezed Irwin's hand back.

"You can tell me anything. I'm here for you."

"I know that too." She blinked back a river of tears ready to slide down her cheek. "Believe me, I know."

Irwin leaned over and hugged Cornelia.

After an awkward moment, she pulled away. "Okay. Enough of this mushy stuff. Let's get this show on the road, shall we?" Cornelia swiped her keys off the table. "I'll drive."

"Are you sure? You're not looking too well."

"Don't be silly. I'm fine. Mildly starving, but more than capable of driving a car. Let's go so we can come back and gorge."

"You cooked enough for a small army."

While Cornelia played it off that she was doing okay with whatever news she had to share, Irwin moved with obvious trepidation. He turned away before Cornelia could see him cry. "Yes," he rumbled, having to cough and clear his throat. "Let's get this show on the road."

Irwin grabbed the folder, and the two old friends were on their way. The whole trip took less than four minutes, minus one extraordinary long light. Irwin made a mental note to put in a complaint with the township.

Although late in the afternoon, the streets remained packed. Most on-road parking was filled to capacity. While they waited for the light to turn, they saw Harper and Olivia already waiting in front of the building. Christopher, approximately half a block up, looked close to crossing at the light.

The light changed, and Cornelia pulled in front of the building and put her hazards on. "Get out. I'll find parking," said Cornelia.

"I'll do it. You go inside."

"Don't be ridiculous. I'm already driving. Besides, everyone's waiting for you, not me. Now go on. Scoot."

"Are you sure?"

"Of course, I'm sure. Oh! Look, a parking space is opening up across the street," she said, pointing. "Would you hurry up and get out so I can grab it? Come on, move it. Shake a leg."

Irwin disembarked quickly from the ride and closed the door. He stepped towards the three and waved the thick envelope as a greeting. The three waved back, wearing mutually confused expressions.

"Greeting to all," Irwin said. "I'm sure you're all anxious to find out why I have called this impromptu meeting. But before we start, does everyone know one another?"

Olivia gazed at Christopher and smiled. Christopher smiled back and nodded hello, while Harper blurted out the obvious.

"No," she said to Irwin, then not one to stand on protocol, exuberantly reached out her hand for a shake. "Hi, I'm Harper. This is my mother, Olivia. We're friends of Irwin's."

"Nice to meet you both. I'm Christopher. I'm, err, well, Irwin and I met—"

"Christopher is also a friend of mine," interrupted Irwin. "How about you all follow me?" As he walked, the keys jiggled in his hand. "There's something I want you all to see."

"Where's Cornelia?" asked Olivia.

"Parking the car." Irwin pointed across the street where Cornelia had her hazards blinking, indicating she was waiting for the driver to pull out to claim the spot.

"Maybe we should wait for her?" asked Harper.

Irwin thought about it but shook his head. "Cornelia knows where to go. She's already instructed me to get a move on so we can all go back to my place to eat." Everyone laughed. "Follow me, troops," instructed Irwin.

The march lasted about fifteen steps. Irwin stopped, took a deep breath, and proceeded to unlock the front door. The quartet trailed inside after him. The clean but large empty store area gleamed with high-polished floors, high wood empty bookshelves, and a desk with a cash register. A long sign leaned face forward against one of the walls.

Harper spoke first. "This is really nice, but I don't know what we're looking at exactly."

Irwin walked to the middle of the room and let the packet drop to the floor by his feet. Arms extended out wide, he twirled around and announced, "My friends, I stand before you the proud new owner of the Burg's newest and hopefully finest bookstore."

"What!" exclaimed Olivia.

"No way!" cheered Harper.

Christopher, all smiles, clapped. "Congratulations!"

"What are you calling it?" asked Harper,

pointing to the sign.

"All in good time," said Irwin. "First, I want you three to walk around. Take it all in. Get a feel for the place."

Harper didn't need to be told twice. She ran her hands across the wood shelves, moved the cushioned chair catty-corner to make a nook, and peeked through the back to where the storage and kitchenette was.

Olivia went straight to the desk, marveling at the old-fashioned cash register. "Would you just look at this old thing? I used to work on one as a kid when I worked for a cleaner. Loved the sounds the big keys made."

Christopher pointed to the envelope. "Is that the contract?" he asked.

Irwin nodded.

"Are you renting the space?"

Irwin shook his head no.

"Then this is all yours?" asked Harper, who had been listening.

"Correct. This entire building is mine."

Christopher whistled. "Nice."

"Lit," agreed Harper.

"Congratulations, Irwin! This is wonderful! I am so happy for you," exclaimed Olivia.

Irwin smiled.

So far, so good.

"Which brings me to my next point. As you all know, I am not the most personable human being."

Harper snorted. "Understatement of the century."

"Harper!" admonished Olivia.

"No, no, Olivia, Harper is absolutely correct.

Which is why I have asked the three of you to accompany me here today."

The three glanced at one another, apparently not catching on. Irwin continued.

"I will need three people to help me run this business. One full-time employee and two-part time." Irwin looked at Olivia. "I would like to hire you full-time, Olivia. Whatever you are earning at your current job, I will double it." Olivia gasped. "Christopher, I'd like to hire you part-time. Same goes as far as salary, and we will work around your college schedule." Christopher unable to respond, remained in place, his mouth agape.

"Harper?" said Irwin.

"Yeah?"

"I'd like you to be my other hire. Same goes for you regarding salary and schedule. However, there's one string attached."

Harper crossed her arms and stood as if waiting for the other shoe to drop. "Okay...which is?"

"You must keep a GPA of 3.5 or above and graduate with honors. Colleges are competitive, and if we are going to get you into a proper school, you'll need good grades."

Harper winced. "But how—"

Irwin stuck a finger to his lips. "Silence. I will answer all questions at the end of this tour. Follow me."

"There's more?" asked Olivia, her eyes wet and nose turning red.

"I think he's recreating a Willy Wonka experience," mumbled Harper.

"I can hear you," said Irwin as he led the way to

the back and opened a heavy door. "The staircase is well-lit, but still, watch your step." Irwin stopped and turned. "Olivia, will these steps be a problem?"

"No. I'm okay. My ankles aren't too bad today."

"Excellent. Then we shall proceed." Once the group got to the next floor, there were two doors at opposite ends of the hall. Irwin opened the door for the larger of the two and waved them all inside. "This is apartment number one. Olivia, Harper, this apartment, while not as big as your current house, has two bedrooms, a decent-sized eat-in kitchen, bathroom, living room, and a small room—possibly could be used as a study."

Olivia gripped Harper's hand and squeezed. "What are you saying, Irwin?"

Irwin stood erect. "I'm saying that I'd like you two to live here."

Olivia blanched. "But how? A two-bedroom in this area easily goes for $1,700.00 a month. I can't afford this."

"Yes, you can. This one is $500 a month, including utilities. Now, please, both of you, look around and make sure it's satisfactory. Let me know if anything is missing or that needs to get fixed."

Olivia's legs began to tremble. Still gripping Harper's hand, a stream of tears slid unabashedly down her cheeks.

"For real?" Harper stood frozen in place, stunned but deliriously happy.

"I wouldn't say it if I didn't mean it," barked Irwin, trying to keep his emotions in check. He didn't want them to know how desperate he felt for them to agree. Both he and Cornelia agreed that everyone had to be onboard for this to work as planned. "Christopher. Please follow me."

Christopher practically skipped behind Irwin, periodically glancing back at Harper, who could do nothing but shrug.

"This apartment is a one bedroom, and therefore your rent would be $250 a month, including utilities."

Christopher ran his hands through his hair. "Man, I don't know what to say. This is incredible."

"Then say yes," said Irwin encouragingly. "You can move in immediately or as soon as you wish."

Just then, from down the hall, Irwin and Christopher heard sobbing. Both men rushed to see what was going on. They found Harper and Olivia hugging and talking at the same time.

Irwin and Christopher remained to the side until both women finished.

"Well? What say you, Crane women?" bellowed Irwin with a lot more bravado than he felt. Even as the words left his mouth, he felt his heart skip a beat, only to lodge squarely in his throat, scared to death they wouldn't accept. Fortunately for him, his reservations didn't have long to wait.

"Yes! Yes! Yes," they chorused between fits of laughter, hugs, and a host of tears. The room soon filled with damp cheeks and bright smiles.

Irwin exhaled and rubbed his hands together. "Excellent." He turned his head. "And you, Christopher? What say you?"

Christopher, already beaming, glanced from face to face. "Are you kidding me? I second that emotion," he said, a smile spreading across his handsome face.

Harper strolled around the rooms with newfound exhilaration, touching every available surface with a transformed sense of spirit. "I love these walls and floors and especially all the light coming from these amazing tall windows." She leaned on the window ledge to peer out. "Everything is so bright and— holy shit!"

Just as Harper yelled, the group heard a barrage of honking horns and people screaming from the street below. Together the group rushed to the window to see why.

There, standing in the middle of one of the busiest roads on Main Street, stood Cornelia, face clutched and spinning helplessly in circles. Even from above, it was clear she was scared, not knowing where to turn or what to do next.

"Hey, lady! Get the hell out of the road," yelled one irate driver, half his body hanging out of his car window.

"Move it!"

Honk! Honk!

Both Irwin and Harper struggled to unlock the old heavy window and pull it up.

"Cornelia," shouted Irwin, but she never heard him.

"Cornelia, get out of the road," Harper screamed hysterically. "Oh my God. There's a truck coming!" she said, pointing frantically down the street.

Everyone started screaming Cornelia's name, anxiously trying to gain her attention, but Cornelia didn't register Harper's pleas, nor anyone else's for that matter. She appeared too consumed by

267

confusion to grasp the danger barreling down straight at her.

"What the heck is she doing?" wailed Olivia, half hanging out the window.

"Trying to kill herself, apparently," grumbled Irwin, banging his fist on the window pane. "Get out of the road, crazy old woman!"

A few shocked bystanders yelled for Cornelia to move, making her more frightened and disorientated.

"Wait! Over there. I think I see Darren." Olivia was correct. Darren had just turned onto the main road and could be seen waiting by the light to cross. "Darren!" hollered Olivia at the top of her lungs. Irwin, Harper, and Christopher joined in, waving their arms and chanting his name.

Irwin wedged two fingers in his lips and blew out the loudest whistle anyone had ever heard, causing Darren to look up. He saw the quartet and tentatively waved. Olivia, half hanging out of the window herself, pointed to Cornelia frantically. "Get her! Get her!" she shouted, half sobbing. Harper joined her. Christopher had already left, taking the stairs by twos to reach Cornelia before she got herself killed.

Darren peered down the road at a large moving truck in the distance coming towards them. "Shit," he mumbled. Without another word, Darren pushed through the crowd. "Move out of my way!" he shouted and darted out into the street. Using all his might, he tried to drag the sobbing Cornelia out of the way of the truck.

"Don't touch me," she wailed, swatting Darren's

hands away. "Leave me alone, or I'll call the police."

"I won't hurt you," pleaded Darren. "Let me get you to the side of the road, luv. Come on."

"Police!"

"Ah, shit. Don't do that, lady. I gotta enough problems with the boys in blue. Now come on. Stop fighting me."

Christopher met the pair halfway. "We've got to hurry," he said, helping Darren to drag the fighting but mortally terrified Cornelia to safety.

The trucker, driving way too fast and barreling down on the scene, realized far too late about the commotion taking place ahead of him. He tried in vain at the last possible minute to floor his brake. But that only caused his truck to skid and spin, clipping the exiting Darren in the hip and sending him flying face-first onto the cement curb. The crowd screamed as Darren landed with a thud.

Olivia shrieked, "Oh my God, Darren!" Ankles be damned. Olivia tore down the stairs at lightning speed with Harper trailing close behind. Irwin took up the rear.

Police sirens sounded, and somebody yelled, "Call an ambulance!"

By the time Olivia and Harper reached Darren, they found him unconscious, bloody, and bruised. A shopkeeper came out holding a blanket, while a woman claiming to be a nurse bent over Darren's body, taking his pulse.

"He's breathing on his own," she announced, more to herself than anyone else.

Olivia sobbed.

Harper removed her jacket and rolled it up in a ball.

The nurse supporting Darren's head and neck to keep him from twisting waved Harper away. "No, hon, we don't want to move his head." Then she spoke directly to Darren as if he could hear her. "You're going to be just fine," she said while checking to see that he was still breathing. To Harper, "Anybody know his name?"

"Darren," answered Harper and Olivia together.

"Okay, Darren. We're going to keep you warm. Okay, buddy?" She looked at Harper. "Can you cover him with your jacket? I'd like to keep him warm." Harper complied.

The veteran nurse had already checked for any major bleeding and life-threatening injuries but, as a true professional, kept those thoughts to herself.

Olivia bent down on her knees. "I'm his wife," she said.

The nurse glanced up at Harper.

"Daughter," confirmed Harper.

"His full name?"

"Darren Crane," said Olivia.

"Age?"

Olivia and Darren were a year apart. "Thirty-six."

"Any extenuating health issues or allergies I should know about?"

Olivia hesitated. "Not that I can remember."

"Good enough. Okay, Darren, the ambulance will be here any minute, and we'll get you right as rain. Don't you worry. Just hang in there for me, buddy." The nurse eyed Harper. "I need to keep him as still as possible."

A tearful Harper and sobbing Olivia nodded. The three waited until help arrived.

***

Irwin

Off to the side, Christopher struggled to comfort Cornelia.

"It'll be okay," he said soothingly, but Cornelia, still much too disorientated to understand, covered her ears.

"Don't touch me," she cried out, pulling her arm away. It wasn't until Irwin approached that she stopped curling into herself. "Irwin?" she sobbed. "Why am I here?"

Irwin gathered and held Cornelia in his arms.

"I—I don't understand," she whimpered, face plastered into his chest. "What did I do?"

Christopher stared solemnly at Irwin and mouthed, *I'm sorry.*

Irwin merely nodded.

I should have been paying closer attention.

The stark realization of what had just occurred laid heavy on his heart. The truth of what unforeseen calamity had befallen his friend crushed his already disquieted spirit. Irwin blamed himself for not picking up on the now-apparent signs from earlier.

Her repeating words, the forgetfulness, her irritability, the sudden loss of taste, all of it.

"What happened?" Cornelia stuttered, tugging on

Irwin's sleeve. "Tell me."

"It's all right," consoled Irwin.

"Why's everyone staring at me?" pressed Cornelia, her eyes beseeching Irwin's for answers. "What the hell did I do now?"

Irwin held Cornelia tighter. His hand pressed supportively against the small of her back. "It's okay now. Everything's going to be okay," he assured her, while his own eyes glistened with tears. "You don't have to be afraid."

"But, Irwin." Cornelia sniffled, her body chilled and trembling. "Did I hurt that man?" she said. Her words caught in her throat as she pointed to the unconscious Darren lying on the cement sidewalk, surrounded by a small crowd of onlookers.

"No, no. Don't be silly." Irwin glanced towards Harper and Olivia, still crouched on their knees next to the nurse. "Shush now."

Harper, her nose pink from crying, leaned over her dad and placed a soft kiss on his forehead. When she glanced up at Irwin hugging Cornelia, the two locked eyes and exchanged a look complete with a thousand and one conversations.

"It's okay. Everything's going to be okay," muttered Irwin, his head bent skyward up into the heavens. As gently as possible, he wrapped his jacket around Cornelia's shoulders and escorted her to a nearby bench. "Christopher, while I'm visiting with Cornelia, please keep an eye out on Harper and Olivia for me."

"Sure thing."

A small but growing crowd began to assemble around Darren, gawking. Eventually, the nurse ordered everyone to move back. Irwin glanced at Darren. "—and *him*."

"You got it."

Irwin gently ushered Cornelia to the bench. "Come, Cornelia. Sit. You've been through a lot." Irwin waited while Cornelia settled down before taking his place next to her. Placing a protective arm around her shoulder, he worked on controlling his breathing. The sheer trepidation of what promised to come threatened to smother him.

"Irwin?" Cornelia slurred. "I need to tell you something."

"Shush. I know."

"You probably do. And by the look of things, I'm kind of guessing you figured out most of it on your own."

"You could say that." Irwin handed Cornelia a tissue and kept one bunched up in his fist for himself.

"I'm sorry for not telling you sooner, but with Gilly, then Dakota's passing, and this whole stressful situation around Harper and her father, not to mention Olivia and the eviction fiasco, it just never seemed like the right time to dump this on you." She shifted in her seat. Her shoulders slumped.

"Cornelia. Listen to me," said Irwin, his voice slow and steady. "I don't want you to worry about any of that stuff right now."

"But, Irwin—"

"Please, Cornelia, you don't owe me any explanations." Irwin cupped Cornelia's soft hand in his. "As far as I'm concerned, nothing's changed.

Not between you and me, anyway," he corrected. "I'm here for you as you have always been here for me."

Cornelia squeezed Irwin's hand. Within a few minutes, her hazel eyes glazed over, and she began to mumble something incoherently. Irwin couldn't make out what.

As the rest of the happenings unfolded around them, the two old friends remained seated on the bench silently holding hands, each lost in a world of shifting memories and imposing grief.

CHAPTER 20

Darren

Two days later…

Darren grabbed his crutches. He placed the one crutch under the arm opposite of his busted foot, then positioned his other arm under the second crutch. Moving forward, he made sure to keep the support close to his body for balance, which now felt impossible.

It could have been worse.

When the truck swerved, it thankfully had missed careening into Cornelia, but Darren hadn't been as lucky. The rear fender wound up clipping him on his hip hard enough to send him flying sideways into the crowd. They told him he landed on the curb, smacking his head against the cement, leaving him unconscious with one hell of a severe contusion on his hip and a fractured fifth metatarsal in his foot.

"We typically treat these kinds of fractures

without surgery," explained the doctor to Darren, pointing to the x-rays. Olivia and Harper sat in the room intently listening.

"How long before I'm out of this Draconian boot, Doc?" questioned Darren.

"If all goes smoothly, six to eight weeks." The doctor smiled at Olivia and Harper. "Looks like you have a lot of support to help you out, which is great, because you're going to need it."

"Well, actually…" mumbled Darren.

"Yes, he is," interjected Olivia over Darren's protests. "Extremely lucky."

Darren glanced questioningly at Olivia.

"Anything else we should know?" asked Harper.

The doctor closed the file in his hand and handed Olivia a sheet of instructions. "Basically, put ice or a cold pack on his foot for about ten to twenty minutes every one to two hours for the next three days. You'll want to put a thin cloth between the ice and his skin. Prop the foot on a pillow when you ice it, or any time he's sitting or lying down for the next three days as well. I advise you to keep it above the level of his heart to help reduce the swelling."

"What about for the pain?" asked Darren. "I've had issues with pills in the past. I can't be trusted with them things again."

"There are a few over-the-counter anti-inflammatories you can take. That should get you through the roughest parts, but try to wean off those as fast as you can as well. Any headaches from the concussion?"

"No. I'm good," said Darren.

"Anything else? Any other questions or

concerns?" The doctor looked from face to face. "No? Okay then. The nurse will be in to make a follow-up appointment for you two weeks from today. I'm not in my office on Wednesdays, so make it for either Tuesday or the following Thursday."

"Sounds good. Thanks, Doc." Darren reached out to shake his hand.

"Take care of yourself," said the doctor, "and call me if you have any problems." He shook Darren's hand, then Olivia's and Harper's.

Harper left after the doctor, carrying her father's jacket. "I'll wait for you in the waiting room. I'm gonna text Irwin to pick us up."

Olivia hoisted her purse over her shoulder and reached out to help guide Darren out.

"Ack." Darren attempted to shift his leg but grimaced with each subsequent unbalanced clunky step forward on his crutches. "These things are terrible. I'll never get the knack of them."

Olivia collected Darren's things. "Oh, stop your pouting. You will too. Give it a few weeks, and you'll be up and about. Until then, you'll stay with us."

Darren's eyes grew big. "Are you sure, Liv?" asked Darren. "I mean, don't get me wrong, I appreciate what you are offering, but it's not like we've been on the best of terms lately."

"I know, but it's already decided. This is only temporary until you're back on your two feet again, but for now, you can't be left on your own."

Darren took a small step forward. He cheeks turned red. "And you're sure Harper's okay with this?"

"It was her idea."

***

Eight weeks later…

Surprisingly, organizing the bookshop into working order took less time and effort than either Irwin or Olivia anticipated originally. With Olivia preoccupied with setting up the accounting and computer files, Cornelia at the helm micromanaging the crew from her perch set up behind the front desk, and Harper and Christopher's boundless energy, the shop looked ready to welcome its first customers. Irwin occasionally had to pinch himself, unable to fully believe his vision was finally coming to fruition. After years of dreaming, squirreling away enough savings, and planning for every contingency known to mankind, the shop had become a breathing and inviting place. More beautiful and as close to perfection than Irwin could have ever envisioned. He secretly wished Gilly and Dakota were both here to see it.

Outside, Christopher climbed down from the ladder after hanging the shop's sign.

"Hey, can everyone step outside for a minute? I need you to tell me whether or not this looks straight," said Christopher.

Irwin, Olivia, Harper, and Cornelia followed Christopher out to the front of the store.

"How are we supposed to know if it's straight if you have the damn sign covered with a sheet?"

complained Cornelia, rolling her eyes. While her clarity of thought over the past few weeks had succumbed, ebbed and flowed, when Cornelia was on her game, she was unstoppable.

"Can I get down?" asked Christopher.

"Not yet," said Irwin.

"For goodness sakes, Irwin, it's time to let the boy take that silly thing off already," complained Cornelia.

Irwin pulled open the shop door to let Darren, still using the boot and not at all happy about it, hobble outside.

"Now that everyone's here, I'd like to say a few words before the big unveiling," announced Irwin.

"Rut Ro. He's going to make us listen to a speech," Harper teased.

"Just a short one," promised Irwin.

"Great," grumbled Cornelia. "Maybe somebody can grab me and hop along Darwin a chair before the old windbag gets on his soapbox?"

"My name's Darren," corrected Darren, clunking behind her.

"That's what I said," said Cornelia, miffed.

Olivia and Harper rushed back inside and dragged two old metal folding chairs behind them.

"Ah, that's better," confirmed Darren, already seated.

A moment later, Roger, Regan, and Janice appeared from around the corner, each carrying bags of books.

"Oh! You put up the sign!" exclaimed Regan. "How super cool is that?"

"It would be a whole lot *super cooler* if we could

actually know what it says," complained Cornelia. "But no. First, we have to listen to Irwin Churchill's speech before the unveiling."

Irwin cleared his throat. "I'll make this quick. If that, of course, works for you, Madam President?" he asked Cornelia. Truth be told, Irwin didn't give a single fig how ornery and obstinate Cornelia became, just as long as she stayed safe. And while admittedly, their long talks had begun to shorten and dwindle, he cherished her company and infrequent moments of clarity.

"You may proceed," said Cornelia.

"Thank you." Irwin nodded and began again. "A few months ago, we were all practically strangers, each living their own lives the best they knew how."

"Oh, *Gawd*," mumbled Cornelia. "It's like the Academy Awards. Next thing you know, he'll drag his third-grade teacher out from behind the door."

Harper chuckled. Olivia plucked her on the arm to stop giggling.

"*And*," bellowed Irwin, "that would have been fine, except we all know that in this vast world of uncertainties and challenges, it wasn't. On our own, we were individually suffering. Some of us consumed by loneliness." Irwin glanced at Cornelia. "Others heartbreak." He eyed Olivia and Darren. "And of course, indecision." Irwin glanced at Christopher and Harper. "By ourselves, we struggled, but together, we have a better chance to succeed and lift one another up."

"Oh, for heaven's sake, get on with it already," grumbled Cornelia.

Irwin shot Cornelia a thumb's up. "We are no

longer just friends, but family, and as such—"

"Irwin! If you don't hurry up, this unveiling of yours will turn into a funeral, and I don't mean mine," grumbled Cornelia.

Everyone clapped.

"Fine, fine, fine." Irwin held back a retort. "So, without further delay…"

Cornelia sat upright and rubbed her hands together. "Now we're talkin'."

"Ladies and gentlemen, I'd like to introduce…" Irwin gave Christopher a quick nod of the head. When Christopher released the sheet, a collective gasp filled the air.

ABERNATHY & CRANE

"Well, I'll be damned!" Cornelia clasped her hands with joy. "That's brilliant! Isn't that brilliant?" she asked Darren, slapping him on his thigh.

Regan, Janice, and Roger joined the excitement, applauding and whistling, while Olivia and Darren shared a mutual confused glance or two.

Harper froze. Her mouth agape. Unsure of what just happened and what it all meant. "I don't understand."

"What's not to understand? We've got ourselves a family business," announced Cornelia. "Right, Irwin?"

Irwin bequeathed upon Cornelia a small nod.

Still confused, Harper searched her parents' faces for answers but realized they were equally as stunned.

Irwin waved Christopher off the ladder then stood next to Harper.

"I don't get it," she said to him, her attention glued to the larger than life sign. "Why's my dad's last name on there?"

"Not your dad's…yours." Irwin glanced down at his feet.

"Mine?" gasped Harper.

Irwin nodded. "Yours, if you agree, of course."

"But how? Why?"

From the side, Olivia and Darren listened while Cornelia chatted up Roger, Regan, and Janice.

"The *how* is easy to answer," explained Irwin. "Even before I met you and your mother, I had been in the process of purchasing this building. I intended to open a bookstore for some time. But after Gilly passed away, I decided to forget it."

"Until you met me?"

"Until I met you—and your mother. I figured that having the shop would be the answer to all our pressing issues. Apartments upstairs for you and your mom. One for Christopher. It made perfect sense."

Christopher, already in the know, grinned at Harper.

"And with me losing my marbles and wandering into traffic, Irwin figured that this would be the best way to keep an eye on me. Did I get that right?" Cornelia asked from her chair.

"Yes, as a matter of fact," replied Irwin. "Quite an astute observation, Cornelia."

I should have known she'd see through my plan.

Harper shimmied up closer to Irwin and

playfully elbowed him in the ribs. "You love me."

"Ow. Stop that," he moaned, swatting at her while trying to inch away. "I tolerate you. Nothing more."

"No. You love me," Harper teased, yanking on Irwin's sleeve.

"Go away."

"Not before you explain the *why*."

Christopher struggled with the closed ladder, dragging it to the front door of the store and using his sneaker to push it open.

Without missing a beat, Irwin took off after him, shouting, "Not like that, you simpleton!"

Cornelia watched from her chair before calling Harper over. "Take it from me," she said. "Irwin shows his affection by taking care of those he loves. With everything that's been going on, he felt that the bookstore would be the best way to anchor everyone together while taking away the issues preventing them from reaching their goals. And despite his irritable nature and obvious lack of social grace—"

Crash!

The ladder clipped the side of the building.

Irwin practically lost his mind. "Watch where you're going with that thing!" he shouted at Christopher. "And don't you dare hit my walls!"

"Like I was saying," said Cornelia, "despite Irwin's obvious lack of social grace, you and your family have become enormously important to him. He sees you as a granddaughter. He's always wanted a bookstore, but by opening up this one, he can make sure that you never have to worry again about stuff you have no control over, especially money and a place to live."

Harper's eyes glistened with happy tears. She glanced at her parents standing off to the side and ran into her mother's open arms, sobbing.

"It's okay, sweetheart," said Olivia, soothingly, rubbing her daughter's damp back.

"Did you know too?" asked Harper, probing her mother's face for the truth.

"I didn't, but nothing our Irwin does surprises me." Olivia held her daughter at arm's length by the shoulders.

"Our Irwin." Harper sniffled. "He is, isn't he?"

"No doubt about it. Forever and ever."

Darren gimped forward. Olivia held out her hand and drew him in closer.

"How will I ever pay him back for everything he's done for us, Cornelia?" asked Harper, extricating herself from her parents to sit next to her.

All eyes turned to Irwin, currently sweeping the curb. The quartet could still hear him grumbling under his breath—something about the idiocy of humans and their senseless propensity to pollute.

Cornelia gently embraced Harper's hand. "You already have, my sweetheart," she soothed. "More than you will ever know."

EPILOGUE

Irwin

Irwin removed his gloves and brushed off a few stray leaves from the top of Gilly's headstone. Any day now, snow and ice would blanket the earth again as the temperatures dipped and the ground hardened and froze. People would once again retreat to the confines and warmth of their homes, many holed up under the light of cherished books. For the millions of bibliophiles, winter gave them the excuse they needed to hibernate and indulge without guilt.

The bookshop's opening had been well received by the community. Years back, many big-box bookstores had closed, leaving behind a void. *Abernathy & Crane* filled that emptiness.

"Harper came up with a great idea the other day. She said anybody can sell a book but that we needed to do more than that. Claims we have to be involved with the community and that being a bookstore wasn't enough. I asked her how much this was going to cost me, and do you know that girl had the nerve to stick her tongue out at me?" As the chill in the air whipped past him, Irwin put his gloves back on. "Despite her impertinence, she had a good point. Without prior approval, she started inviting local authors, traditionally published as well as Indie, to shelve their books with us. She's also encouraged the authors to pick a month to do a book talk for free. Besides the posters, it's been a relatively inexpensive project, unlike the talking human bookmarker she had parading up and down Main Street handing out holiday coupons—another one of her bright ideas, I might add." Irwin laughed. "Did I tell you? Harper made honor roll for the second time this year and has applied to a few colleges. Olivia and I are trying to encourage her to stay local, but who knows? Maybe that supermarket boyfriend of hers, the one with the roach legs growing under his nose, will convince her to commute." Irwin shuffled his foot and glanced over his shoulder.

"Christopher's visiting his mother today. He's been feeling guilty for not coming sooner, but he's been burning the midnight oil with his studies lately." Irwin vigorously rubbed his cold, gloved hands together. "Only one more semester before the boy graduates, then off to law school. Smart as a whip but no common sense. Going to be a big-shot lawyer. Hey, do me a favor. I'm not sure if this is even possible, but if there's some way you and his mother can communicate where you are in that otherworldly plane, I'd appreciate it if you let her know from me that her son is a wonderful young man. She did a fine job raising him, although his taste in music leaves a lot to be desired." Irwin shook his head. "I'll tell you, Gilly, it's one constant battle between him and Harper about what music gets played in the shop. Harper's music tastes are worse than his. But that didn't stop Cornelia from joining in the fray. Pissed off both of them when she turned the radio to classical. Almost caused a mutiny. Thank goodness for Olivia. She finally stepped in and made them declare a truce. We're currently being inundated with elevator music from the sixties and seventies, but at least I can understand what the hell those singers are saying."

Christopher waved from a distance. Irwin waved back less enthusiastically.

"Anyway, not everything has been as smooth or easy to fix. For a while, I would have sworn that Darren had a spot waiting for him right next to you if Olivia or Harper had anything to say about it. Surprisingly, I will admit, he's doing a pretty good job of looking out for Cornelia when I'm not around. Drives her to her doctor appointments while I'm at the library. She seems to enjoy his company. And I could be wrong, but between you and me, I think he's given up the fight about being renamed Darwin." Irwin shrugged. "For some ungodly reason, Cornelia refuses to call him anything else. Nobody knows why, including me."

The temperature dipped another few degrees, causing Irwin to shiver. "Cornelia misses you, Gilly. I'm afraid she'll be leaving us soon enough. More bad days than good recently. The doctors tell me that she's got other health issues that she never told me about. A bad ticker for one. I try to make sure she eats right. We all do. But she tells me to mind my own business and keep my nose out of her mouth. I know, disgusting, but that's what she says. She feeds that damn hairy cat better than she feeds herself," he grumbled. A lone tear slipped down his face. "If anything happens, I'm going to depend on you more than ever to keep an eye out for her. You know, introduce her around. Sort of like a guardian angel." Irwin cleared his throat.

"On the upside, turns out Darren's a good handyman. He built some wood shelves for the storeroom that could rival any professional." Irwin lowered his voice. "Between you and me, I think this ex-con of ours is slowly but surely working his way back into Olivia and Harper's good graces. However, Harper informed me on the sly that Olivia isn't quite ready to forgive and forget. Rumor has it she still has him camped out on the couch." Irwin found that amusing.

"Irwin! Are you almost ready to go?" called Harper, sitting on a bench nearby. "Mom just texted and said dinner's at six tonight. She's making her honey-glazed baked chicken and smashed garlic mashed potatoes. Oh, and she said to bring home dessert. Apple or pumpkin pie, whichever you want. She doesn't care which."

"Fine. Did you visit your grandmother?"

"I did."

Irwin waited for more, but when nothing followed, he shouted, "Are you okay?"

Harper smiled. "Yeah. I'm good. I told Grandma that Mom will be by to see her tomorrow."

Irwin winked. "Good. Listen, give me five more minutes."

Harper gave Irwin the thumbs up but remained seated on the bench, taking the extra time alone to process it all.

A cool breeze blew past, causing Irwin to fasten his coat's top button. "Cornelia and Olivia are pestering me to throw Christopher and Harper a graduation party at the shop," he whispered. "You know how I despise parties, but do you think those two meddlesome women care? The both of them, constantly forcing me to do stuff I don't like, and well, it's not *totally awful*."

Irwin replaced the dead flowers with a fresh winter wreath. "Harper picked this out. She said you must be sick to death of the same flowers all the time." Irwin cringed. "Sorry. Poor choice of words." After placing the circlet by the headstone, Irwin bent and placed a kiss on his fingers and rubbed Gilly's name. "I miss you. I wish you   "

"Sorry to interrupt. Hey, Gilly. It's me, Harper." Harper tugged on Irwin's sleeve. "We gotta go. Mom said Cornelia's talking to herself again, which wouldn't be so bad, but she's losing the argument and getting all worked up. Even called a customer a twit when he asked if we carried post-apostolic books. Ordered him to leave the shop, and I quote, 'take your vacuous, malodorous ass with you.'"

Irwin threw his head back. "Why?!"

"Who knows," Harper shrugged, "but Mom said to hurry up."

Irwin pulled the keys for the car out of his pocket and handed them to Harper. "Go warm up the car.

I'll be right with you."

"Can I drive?"

"No."

"Aw, come on. I need seventy more hours behind the wheel before I can take my road test."

"No."

"But why not?" whined Harper.

"Because I feel like living another day."

"You're not being fair."

"Fair has nothing to do with it," countered Irwin.

"I can drive."

"Who told you that lie?"

"Come on, Irwin, *please*?"

Irwin turned. "Do you see what I have to deal with, Gilly? This one's a regular, first-class hemorrhoid."

Harper pinched Irwin on the arm.

"Stop that!"

"Christopher said he would teach me," implored Harper.

"What did I say I would do?" said Christopher upon hearing his name being bantered about. He draped his long, lean arm over Harper's shoulder. "What alternative facts are you telling now?"

Harper rolled her eyes. "Jerk."

"Enough. Christopher, please take our juvenile delinquent back to the car with me. I'm almost done."

"Okay."

"Oh, and whatever you do, don't let her convince you she can drive."

Christopher laughed. "You got it, boss. You heard him. Let's go, grasshopper," he told a pouting

Harper.

"Traitor," Harper snapped, trailing closely behind Christopher, at times skipping to keep up with his long strides.

Irwin watched as the two walked away. He couldn't help but smile. "All in all, having Harper in my life has been…" He searched for the right words. "…incredible. A pain in the royal behind, but honestly incredible." He placed a last, soft kiss on Gilly's headstone. "I love you."

Despite Harper's dire warning, Irwin took his time getting back to the car. He didn't feel much like rushing, comfortable to remain still. All too aware how life had given him trials, some he never thought he'd get through. Others he never wanted to face again. But today, for this moment in time, Irwin allowed his blessings to reign.

In the quietude of the cemetery's lifeless air, Irwin thought about all the things he'd forgotten or chosen not to say to those who meant the most to him. He remembered all too clearly the many occasions when it had felt safer to remain silent…stoic in the face of real and valued involvement. Happy to stay hidden behind his emotions rather than putting them on full display. Irwin contemplated how moving forward, he'd do things differently. But where and who to begin with?

As Irwin approached the car, he could hear laughter. The two of them were so loud that they didn't even realize he was there. Irwin bent over and wrapped his knuckles on the car window, startling the squabbling duo. "The door's locked," he said.

Christopher popped the lock, and Irwin slid into the front passenger seat.

"Ready?" asked Christopher.

Irwin nodded. It had been a long day, and he was starving. "Drive!" he commanded in jest. "Honey-baked chicken awaits us," he said, stealing a quick glance into the rearview mirror.

"Don't forget Mom's garlic smashed potatoes," answered Harper from the backseat, snapping her seatbelt closed. "We still need to stop and get an apple or pumpkin pie, although if anyone had asked me, I'd have said sweet potato, but who am I, right?" Harper checked her phone. "Hold up. Cornelia must have called. She left me a message." Harper pressed her ear to the phone. "Um, Irwin? She said to tell you also to pick up a pint of shrimp lo mein."

"I thought you said we were having baked chicken?" He turned fully around.

"We are. The lo mein is for Bones."

Irwin grumbled. "That mangy, entitled furball."

For a split second, the car went silent until Harper, unable to contain herself any longer, started to giggle with Christopher joining in. The more Irwin grumbled, the harder the two laughed until finally, Irwin broke through the noise.

"I don't know what's so funny," he said, miffed.

More hilarity ensued.

Irwin shook his head. "That damn cat. Cornelia treats him like royalty. I ask you, what royalty do you know who uses a shit box?"

Rip-roaring laughter.

"Fine, fine. You two yuck it up all you want," said Irwin, "but know that I willed that two-pint feline dictator to the two of you when I kick the bucket."

Harper stopped laughing. "You wouldn't dare!"

"Well, not yet maybe, but I will." Irwin shifted in his seat and raised his chin indignantly. "Mark my words!"

Harper slunk down in the back seat, fanning herself, taking in large gulps of air, and she tried to breathe through her mouth to stop the giggles. "I bet you will."

Irwin gazed out the window, blocking out Christopher and Harper as they prattled on with their inane, ridiculous banter as to whether chickens could breastfeed.

From the passenger seat, Irwin stared straight ahead. Unbeknown to either of his two young companions, the tiniest of smiles appeared on Irwin's content face. The face of a man who had finally found his place in the world and a life filled with good people—people he now called friends *and family*.

THE END.
...or maybe not.

Acknowledgments

I am grateful to all who helped make writing *Unlikely Friends* such an incredible experience:

I wish to thank Limitless Publishing for taking me on, believing in my book, and for giving *Unlikely Friends* a welcoming home. Christina Kaye, my talented editor: thank you for your kindness and encouragement. Lydia Harbaugh, Marketing Director, who always made the time to answer my questions and concerns no matter how redundant.

To the Lady Writers—Susan Moore Jordan, Catherine Schratt, Kelly Jensen, Belinda Nevill Gordon: thank you for your excellent editorial suggestions and insightful manuscript comments. Love you ladies!

My early readers—Harriet Van Houten, Diane Bukoski, Anne Quirindongo, and Jen Bradley: thank you for your wisdom, encouragement, and especially your eagle eyes. This typo queen couldn't have done it without you.

To my family near and far. You are my heart. My reason for writing. I am grateful to you all for your continued love and support. xo

About the Author

Sahar Abdulaziz has authored seven books: *But You LOOK Just Fine* [Health/non-fiction], *As One Door Closes* [Contemporary Fiction], *The Broken Half* [Contemporary Fiction], *Secrets That Find Us* [Fiction/Thriller/Suspense], *Tight Rope* [Thriller/Political Fiction], *Expendable* [Psychological suspense] and her children's book, *The Dino Flu*. Abdulaziz's work covers a wide range of hard-hitting topics: mood disorders [depression, anxiety, PTSD, OCD, PPD], domestic violence and sexual assault, marital and family dysfunction, racism, sexism, and prejudice, but most of all–survivorship. Her multidimensional characters have been described as having "substance and soul."

Originally from New York, Sahar moved to Pennsylvania in 1993 with her growing family. She holds a Bachelor's degree in psychology and a Master of Science degree in Health and Wellness Promotion and Administration, as well as a certification in Community Health Administration. In 1995, she received a Certificate in Sexual Assault and Domestic Violence Crisis Intervention Counseling, and shortly after, as a Domestic Violence/Sexual Assault Counselor/Advocate. She volunteered for many years as a hotline worker and counselor/advocate. In 2016, Abdulaziz received an award for Community Written Expression at the Second Annual Monroe County Image Awards and in 2018, nominated for the Rabata, 'We Are Aisha' Award in the category Writer/Author. Most recently, she has guest co-hosted for Sistah Chat

Radio, WESS 90.3 FM, Gynesis Radio, and is a member of the Pocono Liar's Writer's Club. Rep'd by Djarabi Kitabs Publishing and Limitless Publishing, LLC.

Facebook:
https://www.facebook.com/AuthorSaharAbdulaziz

Twitter:
https://twitter.com/Sahar_Author

Website:
https://www.saharraziz.com/

Instagram:
https://www.instagram.com/saharraziz/

Join our Reader Group on Facebook and don't miss out on meeting our authors and entering epic giveaways!

Limitless Reading

Where reading a book
is your first step to becoming
limitless...

LIMITLESS PUBLISHING *Reader Group*

Join today! *"Where reading a book is your first step to becoming limitless..."*

https://www.facebook.com/groups/Limitless Reading/